THE
HUNTER'S
SON

OTHER BOOKS AND AUDIOBOOKS
BY GREGG LUKE:

Altered State

Do No Harm

The Survivors

Blink of an Eye

Bloodborne

Deadly Undertakings

"The Death House" in *Twisted Fate*

The Healer

Infected

THE

HUNTER'S

SON

a novel

GREGG LUKE

Covenant Communications, Inc.

Printed in the United States of America
First Printing: November 2017

23 22 21 20 19 18 17   10 9 8 7 6 5 4 3 2 1

ISBN 978-1-52440-252-5

*To my son-in-law, Tom Ballard: a man who likes
a good adventure as much as I do.*

ACKNOWLEDGMENTS

I'M ALWAYS A BIT NERVOUS about writing acknowledgments in a novel because I invariably—and quite unintentionally—leave someone out. This story was a long time in the making—almost ten years! I can't remember everyone I asked to critique it throughout that decade, but I do know I had initial help from Julie Luke, David Dickson, Kirk Luke, and Rebekah Smith. Later, as I resurrected it, author Jeff Savage gave it a read to evaluate my voicing. Then, to make it more accurate to the period, historical fiction guru Heather Moore gave me an amazing (and humbling) critique. The finishing touches were provided by my amazing editor, Kami Hancock, who always does her best to make me sound good.

My sincere and heartfelt thanks goes out to all (named and forgotten) who contributed their time to bringing this story to life.

And there were some who died with fevers,
which at some seasons of the year were very frequent in the land—
but not so much so with fevers,
because of the excellent qualities of the many plants and roots
which God had prepared to remove the cause of diseases,
to which men were subject by the nature of the climate.
Alma 46:40

CHAPTER ONE

YOU WILL NOT BE SCARED, I told myself with little success. Only a few minutes had passed since I had entered the cave, but already I was fighting an overwhelming urge to turn and run. My heart thumped against my chest and pounded in my ears. Sweat dripped from my body as if I'd been working in the fields for hours. A hollow knot tightened in my belly as I edged forward, straining to see into the darkness.

A low voice moaned from deep within the cave, "Jarem, son of Anatoth, the hunter."

My breath caught. Footprints outside the cave indicated that perhaps a dozen young men waited somewhere in the darkness ahead. I could hear faint whispers, and the smell of sweat and freshly disturbed dust hung in the dank air. I cursed my eyes for not adjusting to the darkness faster. *Think clearly now*, I told myself. *The light is to your back, so they can see you before you can see them.*

"Jarem of Oranihah!" the voice called again. It was deep and resonant and yet still somewhat youthful. I swallowed forcefully to clear the tightness in my throat.

"I am here," I said with all the manliness I could muster.

"Come closer," the voice commanded.

My father had taught me that it's easier to see things in the dark if you do not look directly at them but, rather, just to one side. I tried this and detected a bend in the cave straight ahead. Easing my way forward, I entered a chamber just beyond the bend. It was pitch-black inside. I paused to listen.

Something stirred to my left: the whisper of cloth against skin. I held my breath and focused, listening between heartbeats. Soft, breathy sounds came from five or so vague shapes in front of me. Standing in silence, I slowly turned my head from side to side to pinpoint the positions of those with me.

I knew the identity of most of the young men in the cave. They were roughly the same age as I was and full of mischief and adventure, so I was prepared for just about anything.

I let out a chuff, trying to sound bored. "Now what?"

"Silence, dog!" the voice snapped. A muffled snicker issued from a dark shape on my right. "You are here only because we want you here. You are alive only because we want you alive. And you will speak only when we want you to speak."

The young man was trying to sound frightening, but I really had no reason to be so scared. This whole ordeal was an initiation into the Brotherhood of the Leopard, a secret group to which my friend Samuel belonged. I thought it sounded adventurous.

"It is our understanding you wish to join our brotherhood," the resonant voice continued.

"Yes. I have heard—"

"That was not a question, worm!" Something hissed through the air, whipping against my shins. I winced at the sting but made no sound. I was determined not to show any weakness.

"The Brotherhood of the Leopard does not allow just any simpleminded fool to enter its secret order."

Only handpicked *simpleminded fools, then?* I didn't say.

"You must first prove yourself worthy. No matter what we ask, you must do accordingly." Another snicker sounded to my left. "Are you brave enough to accept the challenge? If you fail, you will never be allowed to try again."

I drew a deep breath and puffed out my chest. "Yes."

"Fellow leopards, do you accept this dog's petition?"

A chorus of young voices growled like jungle cats in approval. As my eyes adjusted, the dark shapes slowly became less obscure, though I still could not see any of them clearly.

"Very well," the lead voice continued. "Jarem of Oranihah, answer this question: To whom do you swear total loyalty?"

"To you—I mean, to the Brotherhood of the Leopard." *Think clearly now,* I again scolded myself. *Try not to sound foolish . . . or afraid.*

"Will you swear beyond your loyalty to your parents, to the Nephite people and their judges, and to . . . your betrothed?" This time, instead of a chorus of growls, a riot of laughter erupted around me.

I knew my friendship with Ishbel, the tanner's daughter, would come up eventually. My father was a hunter; her father was a tanner. We were constantly in each other's company. But although we had become best friends, I didn't feel any passion toward Ishbel. Our relationship was more like that of a brother and sister. We'd play games together, talk of our fathers' businesses, go on errands together. But she wasn't my *betrothed*. I considered explaining this to the others in the cave, then decided against it. It would only give them enticement to tease me further.

"Yes," I stated boldly. "The Brotherhood of the Leopard comes before all."

"Well spoken," the leader said. "We will give you one chance. Repeat after me: I am a leopard. I will hunt like a leopard, I will fight like a leopard, and I will kill like a leopard. I will always live by the law of the leopard."

I did as instructed.

The resonant voice grew louder as it proclaimed, "Let all who are not leopards beware! A new leopard is born this day!"

Those present let out a fierce roar. The combined voices reverberating throughout the alcove were quite impressive.

"Now prove yourself by sealing your oath." A furry object bounced off my feet. I picked it up and explored it with my fingers. It was the forepaw of a large jungle cat—probably a leopard. Samuel had warned me about this part of the initiation. I wasn't afraid. It just seemed like a foolish thing to do.

"Make the mark!" the lead voice roared.

I'd come this far; I might as well see it through. Tensing my stomach muscles, I pressed the claws against my flesh. The idea was to draw blood without showing fear or pain. I clenched my teeth and quickly drew the paw across, leaving four bleeding gashes in its path. I grimaced, gritting my teeth against the searing sting, but made no sound.

The cave was silent. I assumed the others were waiting for an outcry, but I made none. I slowly exhaled and tossed the paw in front of me. Again, there were roars, and I couldn't help but swell with pride.

"Enough," the leader said to silence the others. "Well done, new leopard. Now you must survive the ordeal. Are you willing to complete this task?"

"Yes."

"Good. This is what you must do: You will dwell the rest of this day and this night in this cave. You must not leave for any reason whatsoever—not for food or water or to run from anything that may enter this cave. Only when tomorrow's light appears may you come out, but no sooner. Do you accept this ordeal?"

That sounded easy enough. I had spent countless days and nights hunting with my father in the jungle and quite a few by myself. A day and a night in this cave would be child's play. I now felt foolish for being so frightened earlier.

"Yes," I responded confidently.

Standing motionless, I watched the dark shapes leave, their breathing sounds and body odors going with them. I wasn't afraid to be alone in the cave, but the sudden absence of background sounds was strangely disturbing.

I half expected one of the group to jump around the corner in an attempt to startle me. But after a few minutes of silence, I figured they weren't coming back.

I was alone.

I tried to relax but couldn't. Any noise I made echoed harshly off the walls of the small alcove. My breathing sounded coarse and tense. Something wasn't right about the situation. I slowly turned from side to side, concentrating, but could not determine what was wrong. It wasn't simply the absence of noise; something didn't *feel* right. Standing alone in the darkness, I tried to remember everything my father had taught me about evaluating things I could not see. *Use all your senses*, he'd said. I took in every sound, every smell, the weight of the air against my skin, the feelings in my soul. My intuition told me I was in danger.

"Run for your lives!" a woman shouted outside the cave.

"This way, quickly," another called.

"Head for the jungle!" a man joined in.

I started toward the cave's entrance—then stopped. I wondered if maybe the young men had enlisted the help of some adults to trick me into coming out of the cave. I smiled at first, but the cries continued to increase in both volume and intensity. The villagers sounded truly alarmed.

"Lamanites! Run! Run!"

"Lamanites?" I gasped as my muscles tensed.

I'd grown up hearing that Lamanite warriors were ruthless savages who loved to kill simply for the sport of killing. I'd never met a Lamanite *warrior*, but I had met several Lamanite hunters and merchants while conducting business with my father. Most were average men and women doing what they could to feed their families. But *warriors* were altogether different. And I'd listened to enough gruesome battle stories that the mere mention of them sent chills down my back.

Recently, a number of reports had surfaced of Lamanite warriors amassing armies just across the border in the wilderness. But they proved to be mostly hearsay. In fact, I'd gone hunting with my father just the previous week, and we saw no signs to confirm such reports. Besides, the Lamanites had not attacked the Nephite people for years.

"There can't be Lamanites here," I whispered to myself. "They wouldn't dare cross the border." Yet the more I tried to convince myself, the less I believed. And for the second time since entering the cave, I was very scared.

As the cries and shouts grew more fervent, I knew I *had* to look.

I peered around the alcove corner toward the entrance of the cave. There I saw a strange spear standing upright just beyond some large stones. It hadn't been there when I'd entered. Slowly edging my way forward, I struggled to make sense of the chaos outside. I was sure the Brotherhood of the Leopard would not create such an elaborate ruse simply for my initiation. But if this *was* real, why hadn't they come to warn me?

As I neared the cave's entrance, a man's voice shouted, "Wait. I need to get my spear."

I froze.

Not twenty paces in front of me, a large, stocky man entered the cave. Bright yellow and red pigments painted his face and chest; a thick band of black framed his eyes. Oily, dark hair hung to his broad shoulders from under a snakeskin headband. I estimated he weighed half again what an average man would. He wore a bloodstained animal skin tied around his waist and sandals on his feet. I had no idea who this warrior was, but I knew he wasn't a Nephite.

The man yanked the spear up with such ferocity that I flinched and in doing so scraped my sandal against the stony floor. The warrior instantly crouched into an attack stance, his spear pointed directly at me. I remained as motionless as possible but felt myself trembling. Sweat again began to bead all over my body. The warrior didn't move for the longest time. He stared directly at me but wasn't advancing.

He can't see me, I reasoned. *His eyes are still used to the daylight.* I pleaded with God to help me remain motionless and silent.

Suddenly the man stepped forward two paces, staring hard into the cave, sniffing the air. His gaze swept past me several times but never locked on my position. He spoke in a forceful tone, "If you value your life, come out now."

I didn't move. He may have sensed something, but he couldn't tell I stood only a few cubits away. I knew if I even twitched an eyebrow I would betray my position. I was invisible as long as I remained motionless.

Finally the man grunted and turned on his heel as if to leave then paused, cocking his ear over his shoulder. I felt my legs losing their strength. They began to quiver uncontrollably. Could he hear them shaking? I closed my eyes and concentrated on remaining completely still. Sweat now dripped from my frame. The warrior grunted again and marched out of the cave.

Silently letting out my pent-up chestful of stale air, I lowered to my knees and slowly crawled to the pile of large stones at the mouth of the cave. Oranihah was barely within sight through the thick jungle, but I didn't need to see the whole of it to know what had happened. Flames and smoke rose from several places in the village. With sickening realization, I knew this was not a ruse. My stomach soured, and bile rose in my throat. I got up to run for the jungle then instantly sank back to my knees. My friend Samuel lay directly on the other side of the rocks. A deep hole pocked the center of his chest where the warrior's spear had struck. His eyes stared lifelessly toward the sky; his mouth hung open as if calling for help. In his belly was an arrow of unmistakable make. It was Lamanite.

Foolishly, I quickly rose again and struck my head on an outcropping of rock. A flash of white pain was immediately followed by darkness clouding my eyes. I remember falling, but I don't recall hitting the ground.

CHAPTER TWO

JUDGING BY THE SUN'S POSITION, I knew I'd been unconscious for about two hours. I exited the cave and immediately saw that Oranihah was lost. Unbelieving, I gawked at the horrific scene from the vantage point of a grassy knoll. Many buildings and homes burned unchecked, dead bodies were piled in a careless heap on the roadside, and Lamanite warriors strolled around like ordinary citizens.

A small group of Nephites stripped of almost all their clothing, hands bound tightly behind their backs, knelt helplessly in the middle of a field. Two Lamanites stood over them, taunting them mercilessly. Focusing on the captives, I couldn't see my parents or my sister among them. A sinking feeling told me I would never see them again. I tried to ignore that feeling then tried to deny it, but to no avail. I knew my father would have jumped to the forefront of the village's defense. Judging by the extent of the damage and the small number of Nephite captives, it was easy to conclude that my father was dead. The mere thought of never seeing him again made the back of my eyes sting with tears. But I tried not to give up hope. I couldn't lose faith.

Deciding the best chance to save my people was to head for Zarahemla, the Nephite capital, I began to crawl backward—then suddenly felt that I was not alone. A presence loomed over me. I turned and looked straight into the eyes of the Lamanite warrior who had entered the cave earlier. He was leaning casually on his spear, grinning at me.

"So. Where do you think you're going?"

A thousand responses flashed through my mind. Then one stuck, and before I could consider its consequences, I found myself standing and walking briskly toward the warrior. The impulse was a lesson my father had taught me: *When confronted by something fierce, act fiercer.*

I stopped directly in front of the man, planted my feet, scowled, spat, and pointed my finger at his broad chest. "You've got two choices, Lamanite. You can turn now and walk away unharmed, or you can die where you stand."

My mind instantly cried, *Jarem, have you lost your mind? Run!*

The warrior scowled, but I saw confusion in his eyes. He stared, perplexed at my young frame, seemingly unable to bring words to his mouth. He glanced around but, of course, saw no one near. I was almost his height, but he outweighed me threefold—and very little of that was fat.

Pressing my momentary advantage, I said, "To be fair, I'll give you a few moments to make up your mind—but only a few." I turned and began walking toward the jungle. "I'll wait over here," I said over my shoulder.

I'd made it a good ten paces before the warrior came out of his stupor and called after me. "Wait, you Nephite dog! Get back here."

I sprinted for the jungle, but the warrior, in a surprising burst of speed, caught up and grabbed my shoulder. I spun to break free, but his grip was viselike. His fingers pressed deep into my shoulder as he dropped his spear and clenched my throat, choking me. Following a second flash of inspiration, I stopped struggling, let my eyes roll back, and went totally limp. The Lamanite paused then released his hold. Instead of falling down, I kicked him hard in the groin, turned sharply, and bolted up the hillside.

I'd made it about twenty paces before I saw him gather enough composure to launch his spear at me. Twisting reflexively to avoid the spear, I stepped sideways on an exposed tree root. My leg buckled. I heard a loud snap and felt a shocking jolt of pain shoot up into my gut. Crumpling to the ground, I cried out in agony.

Before I could catch my breath, the Lamanite was on me, angrily tying my hands behind my back.Flushed red with anger and breathing hard, the warrior growled, "I'm going to kill you—very slowly—for that. No Nephite whelp is going to get the best of me."

He yanked me up, but I instantly fell back down. My right leg was throbbing, rendering it completely useless. Glancing down, I saw my shin bent at a sickening angle where no joint naturally occurred. It was all I could do not to cry out again.

"You think you're in pain now?" the warrior hissed. "By the time I'm through, you'll have a new understanding of the word *pain*. And I'm going to enjoy teaching it to you." He smiled maliciously. "Let's start with your good leg."

Placing the point of his spear on my left thigh, he made to push it through when another man's voice called out, stopping him.

"Stop! You there! Soldier!"

When the warrior looked up, his face displayed pure astonishment. He backed away, bowing. "Master Healer," he said with deep respect.

The man he called "Master Healer" sat atop a grand horse. He looked like a mighty warrior himself, yet he wore no battle clothes or face paint. Still, he carried himself with unmistakable authority. He slid from his horse and casually dropped the reins. Standing next to the warrior, he looked to be two handbreadths taller and was equally muscled.

With a furrowed brow, the healer stepped past the warrior and looked down at my leg. He pursed his lips and gave a low whistle. "I believe you have clearly won this battle, my friend," he said to the warrior. "Excellent work. Now go report back to your commander."

"Yes, sir. Right after I kill him," the warrior replied.

The healer's tone hardened. "No. You will do as I instruct without delay."

"But—but I'll be quick. He's just a worthless Nephite boy," the warrior stammered. "Let me send him to the grave."

"You are correct in saying he is insignificant," the healer said, gliding his hand over my break but without actually touching it. "As for sending him to the grave, you've already succeeded. His leg is severely fractured. That's what you wanted, wasn't it? A slow, painful death?"

"He'll not die from that," the warrior said, pointing with his spear. "I've seen worse breaks, and this pup is just stubborn enough to live through that one."

The healer slowly stood. "You may be a great warrior, my friend, but do you profess to be a better healer than I?"

"No. No, Master Healer. I only meant—"

"I know, I know," the healer said, holding up his hand in a calming gesture. "I understand. So this is what we'll do: You will go help your brothers with the other captives in the village while I do a thorough examination here. If this boy's break cannot be mended, I will kill him in your behalf."

I grimaced, dreading death from either man.

The warrior stiffened. "Master Healer, this is *my* fight, and I demand the satisfaction of finishing it."

"You demand?" The healer slowly turned to the warrior. He took a step forward and planted his fists on his hips. "You *demand*? You demand nothing of me, is that clear?"

Anger darkened the warrior's face. He stood firm but did not meet the healer's eyes. Thick tension electrified the air. If it came to blows, I wasn't sure which man would win.

"Do not challenge me on this, my friend," the healer said steadily. "You will not like the outcome. Besides, how will you explain to your captain that while your warrior brothers destroyed a village, you spent your skills on a boy who cannot be more than nineteen years of age?"

After a moment or two, the warrior turned and marched off toward the village, cursing nonstop. I saw the healer's shoulders relax before he knelt beside me again. "This may hurt at first, but my intent is not to cause you suffering."

His words made no sense, but I wouldn't believe him even if they did. His people had just butchered most of my village—including my family. He'd already caused me a lifetime of suffering.

"You're a liar," I snapped.

"Actually, I value honesty above all else," was his calm reply.

As he poked at the swollen flesh around the break, jolts of pain flashed with renewed vengeance. It was all I could do not to scream. Continuing on, even though I was clearly suffering, his face held a look of curiosity mixed with delight. I believed he truly *did* enjoy torturing me.

I bit my lower lip and tried to keep my travail to a low whimper.

"I'm impressed with how well you hold your tongue, young man, but I assure you it is not necessary with me. If it hurts, let me know. I will not think ill of you."

I said nothing. I was not going to show weakness of any kind in front of this strange Lamanite.

Pausing his torture, he stood to retrieve something in a satchel hanging from his horse. Was this the end? Was he selecting a knife with which to slit my throat? Or a club with which to crush my skull? The man seemed to be intentionally taking his time with whatever he was doing, clearly prolonging my misery. The warrior had called him a healer, yet I doubted he was planning to heal me. I was a Nephite. I was his sworn enemy.

Intense pain mixed with growing frustration made me lose all sense of reason. Not knowing what else to say, I harshly corrected him. "I'm only sixteen, you filthy Lamanite."

The healer sized me up with one eyebrow raised. "You're quite tall for sixteen. And I perceive you are as honest as you are brave." Curiously, his tone was friendly; it didn't register any offense at my insult. Quite the contrary, he seemed almost amused.

"You see, I can sense that about most people," he continued. "It's a skill I've developed in my profession. The people you can trust—it shows through their eyes."

He knelt beside me again, holding a squat bamboo container topped with a skin and a smaller clay flask. "Now, let's fix this leg."

"Don't touch me," I growled. Jerking my leg away, I instantly realized my mistake as another searing jolt of pain surged from my wound. I drew in short, gasping breaths and prayed for the throbbing to subside. Tears leaked from the corners of my eyes. The healer remained on one knee, smiling gently. Was his happiness a result of my pain? Probably. But his dark eyes seemed to hold a large measure of caring, too.

Even so, he was a Lamanite—an enemy to my people, a killer, a liar, and a thief. It was his people who had just murdered my family and my friends. Could I really trust him to help me? At the moment, I had no choice.

"Are you—really a healer?" I asked between rhythmic pulses of pain.

"Yes, I am. And a good one, too." He paused to remove a stopper from the flask. "For a filthy Lamanite," he added with a smile.

In spite of my pain and my distrust, I managed a small grin at his comment. The man certainly *acted* friendly, but my mind still cried out, *Enemy!*

Tipping the flask, he allowed a tiny glob of purplish paste to settle on a small green leaf. "Here. Place this on your tongue," he said, handing me the leaf, "but do not swallow all of it at once. Let it sit and dissolve in your mouth."

I balked. "What is it—poison?"

"It is medicine. Although any medicine can be a poison if taken incorrectly," he said with surety. "This quantity, however, will not kill you. It will temporarily hide your pain so I can set your break. The wound feels relatively even, but to mend correctly, it needs to be set back in place, and that *is* going to hurt."

"This paste *hides* the pain?" I'd never heard of such a thing. Sure, there were soothing poultices and such that my mother applied to wounds I occasionally got, but she never gave me anything like this. Some men used wine to *drown* their pains, but that was simply getting drunk. "What do you mean it *hides* the pain?"

He shrugged. "For want of a better word. It causes your mind not to register the harshness of the pain."

This paste sounded too good to be true. My curiosity trumped my distrust. I wanted to know how such a substance worked. I had always had an inquisitive nature. My father explained that there doesn't always have to be an answer to everything. Not to have a complete knowledge of things was how we developed faith. But my mind was an ever-probing one—always wanting to learn, always seeking to know and understand.

"How does it do that?" I asked.

He cocked his head to one side. "For most it would simply be enough to have the pain gone. But since you ask . . ." He paused and gently pushed my hand holding the leaf toward my mouth. I complied and placed the paste on my tongue. It tasted slightly bitter at first; then I tasted nothing at all. The

Lamanite healer continued. "The paste is made from a resin found inside the pod of a flower that grows in our foothills. The local people call the flower *poppy*. It has astounding effects on all forms of pain, but it is also used by some as a means of merriment—a sort of dream creator. That is when it becomes dangerous. The amount I gave you is safe. The pure resin would kill you—and that is not my intent. When used wisely, this medicine can work miracles."

I found it odd that a Lamanite would speak of miracles. I'd learned that Lamanites were a pagan people who followed soothsayers, astrologers, and sorcerers. Miracles indicated the presence of an all-powerful God. At least that's what my parents always said.

Within a minute, my vision began to swim and my head felt strangely thick. Even stranger, I was suddenly happy. Very happy. I knew I should still be angry and hateful, but I wasn't. The healer looked closely at my eyes and listened to my breathing. Nodding, he next applied a thick, spicy-smelling liniment generously over my wound. To my great astonishment, the pain didn't seem to matter anymore.

"What is that you're using?" I asked, trying to concentrate.

The healer seemed amused again, as if no one ever asked him about his secret concoctions. "It is made from balsam bark; but it also has extracts of arnica, lignum, willow, and tobacco. It will reduce the swelling and somehow prevents infection."

"You mean you don't know how it works?"

"There are many things I do not know. Only a fool thinks he knows everything. Now close your eyes and count aloud to ten for me, please."

It seemed a strange request, but I complied. "One, two, three—"

I heard a muffled, gritty *pop,* and a pulse of light flashed behind my eyes. When my head cleared, I looked down and saw that my leg was now straight. It throbbed but without incapacitating pain. The healer next went about splinting my leg with stout branches and strips of cloth. Then, with seemingly little effort, he picked me up and placed me on his horse.

"My name is Chemish," he said. "As I'm sure you have gathered, I am a master healer in the land of Nephi. And what do they call you who are as curious as a jungle cat?"

I couldn't help but smile. "I am Jarem, son of the hunter, Anatoth of Oranihah. And I belong to the Brotherhood of the Leopard." Even as I said it, the fact that I was a member of that secret alliance seemed childish.

But Chemish didn't act as if he thought so. He drew his fingers lightly across the fresh cuts on my belly, pursed his lips, and gave another low whistle.

"Very impressive," he said, looking up at me. "But despite what you *used to* be, I'm afraid you now belong to the Lamanite people."

His pronouncement emphasized the grimness of my predicament. I knew I shouldn't have trusted him! I was a prisoner, the captive of a savage people. Anything could happen to me at this point, and I was powerless to stop it.

As if he could read my thoughts, Chemish patted me on my left thigh. "Do not concern yourself just yet, young leopard. We are not all blood-thirsty savages," he said then added, almost to himself, "Some of us abhor wanton killing."

The master healer led his horse down the knoll toward Oranihah. My head still felt thick and tingly from the purple paste, but I forced my mind to think of ways to escape. *If only I could move about while my leg mended . . .*

I cleared my throat. "When will I be able to walk again?"

"Not right away, but soon. As I said, the break was a clean one."

Hoping to gain some advantage, I said, "Well, I thank you for my leg. And for saving my life."

Chemish glanced over his shoulder. "I am a healer. It is what I do."

Perhaps, but I felt indebted to this man. Although a Lamanite by birth, he was certainly not one by nature. At least not from what I had seen. Even though he rode with warriors, perhaps my initial measure of him had been too harsh.

"Still, I owe you a life, and that I will repay. I swear it."

Chemish stopped and faced me. For a long time, he said nothing. He scratched his jaw and smiled. "Curious. Such valor from a boy your age is rare and refreshing. I thought such characteristics were all but lost. Tell me, where does one so young learn such honor?"

"From my father," I said proudly. "He is a great hunter and warrior. I shall be glad to introduce you to him."

As soon as I finished speaking, the healer's expression changed to one of sadness. His eyes lowered, and he busied himself adjusting the bridle on the horse. "I would like that," he said softly, "but I fear you must prepare yourself for the worst."

I wondered if that meant he already knew about my parents. I wanted to ask, but my head suddenly felt unbearably heavy. I could hardly focus on anything except maintaining my balance. I leaned forward and hugged the horse's neck.

I remember entering the village. Someone pulled me from the horse and placed me next to some baskets. The village was awhirl with activity and yet felt burdened with overwhelming sorrow. The unending commotion clouded my senses. Soon it became too hard to concentrate on anything.

I closed my eyes and had little desire to open them again.

CHAPTER THREE

A GENTLE, RHYTHMIC BOUNCING MOTION awoke me. The familiar sound of hooves treading the ground told me I was still on horseback. I opened my eyes and grimaced. The harshness of the sun burned my eyes—even when I squinted. I moved to rub them and realized that I was not alone on the horse.

"The medicine I gave you causes the black portion of your eyes to widen, much like they do during the night." It was the healer's voice. "It makes all light seem more intense."

Not only had the medicine affected my eyes, but my head still swam and my mouth felt dry and pasty. Worse, my throat was on fire. It hurt to swallow.

"So how does our leopard feel?" the healer asked.

"Fine," I croaked.

The master healer chuckled as he produced a leather flask and unstopped it. "Take a sip of water. Don't gulp it down. Just sip."

I did as he said and felt the cool liquid trickle down. It was painful and soothing at the same time.

Before long, my mind cleared, and my eyes adjusted to my surroundings. The jungle around us was an area I didn't recognize—not at first anyway—but there was something vaguely familiar about it.

"Where are we?" I asked.

"I believe your people call this 'the wilderness,'" he answered.

Hearing the sound of horses behind us, I twisted to look and instantly received a stab of pain in my leg. I winced and drew a quick breath but didn't cry out. I was determined not to show weakness. There were six or so Lamanites on horseback and a few young Nephites walking behind them. The captives were tethered with rope. I couldn't see the larger part of the war party and assumed it had gone elsewhere.

My first impulse was to jump and run, but that would get me nowhere. I removed the healer's arm from around me and leaned forward. My mind was awhirl with frustration and worry. I had to focus. What had happened to my family? What was going to happen to me? I felt so helpless. I wanted to weep but refused to do so in front of this Lamanite. I had to be strong. Strength, endurance, and bravery were skills vital to a hunter. I liked to think I possessed a goodly amount of each. But my current situation called for something more. At this moment, information was my best ally. The more I knew about my situation, the better off I'd be. I tried identifying our surroundings, but my mind was still fuzzy from the medicine.

It wasn't long before the sun disappeared and the moon began to rise on my right, which meant we were headed north. I sat up to get a better reckoning of our whereabouts.

Again looking behind, I asked, "Where is everyone else?"

"Who? Your people?"

"No, I mean the other warriors; the rest of the Lamanite army."

"Well, I know their main objective was Ammonihah. I suppose they went there or into the land of Manti."

I was amazed at this man's honesty. He'd just confided his army's battle plans to me—his sworn enemy. *But then*, I thought, *why not?* In my present condition, I wasn't much of a threat. It also occurred to me that Ammonihah was south of Oranihah, and we were traveling north—*opposite* the direction the warriors were headed. That didn't make sense.

"Why aren't you going with the Lamanite army?" I asked, confusion filling my tone.

My captor chuckled. "Do you always ask so many questions? I'd think you'd be happy to be away from the battlefront."

"You're their healer, right? I'd think you'd be with them to treat their wounds and help them fight."

He said nothing for a time, and I wondered if I had provoked him with my reasoning. After another moment he said, "Yes, I see how that would make sense."

Thankfully, there was no anger in his voice. I waited for more information, but none came. I held a shrug. "So?"

He chuckled again. I'd never heard of a Lamanite warrior who laughed so easily. The stories I'd heard always painted them as being perpetually furious and bloodthirsty.

"Well?" I persisted.

When he responded, there was disappointment in his voice. "I, um . . . I was surprised to see so much bloodshed."

What a ridiculous answer, I thought. "It's a war party, isn't it?" I said, unable to hide the bitterness in my tone. "All they seek is bloodshed."

"True. But I was told this venture was to obtain horses, cattle, and such. I had no idea the plan was to wipe out as many Nephites as possible. I came along as a favor. If I'd known Shem was in command, I wouldn't have come."

"Who's Shem?"

The healer grunted in disgust. "He's a cruel, arrogant monster who thinks nothing of slaughtering innocent people. He didn't join the raid until after we reached your city. I refuse to be associated with anything he's involved in, because it always leads to the same end. So I quit."

"But . . . isn't quitting the army considered desertion?"

"Yes, but I'm not a soldier. I came to get a better look at your people and perhaps to gather some materials. I normally don't do this kind of work. And your people have always fascinated me. I simply wanted to see more for myself."

"But you're a healer—a *master healer*. You'd be needed in battle." I glanced over my shoulder, waiting for his response and wanting to see his expression.

"A healer of natural ailments and accidents. Believe it or not," he said thumbing his chest, "this Lamanite does not like killing."

At first I didn't believe him, but he sounded very sincere. I faced forward again. "And this Shem warrior does," I stated.

Chemish chortled bitterly. I felt his body tense behind me. "Shem has always had an evil streak. Once, in his youth, he cut off a dog's leg simply to see if it could walk on three. The poor creature laid there yelping in pain. Shem kept whipping it, telling it to get up and walk, but it only yelped louder. Its pitiful howling went on for hours. When Shem couldn't stand it any longer, he threw it down a deep ravine."

"What happened to it?"

The healer's voice hardened. "I climbed down and put it out of its misery."

"So Shem has no concept of kindness?"

"None," he said through clenched teeth. "Everything he does is with the intent to cause pain and suffering."

The healer clearly fought to control his anger. He said he didn't like killing. Shem obviously loved it. No wonder he was the leader of the Lamanite army. It made sense he'd be cruel—even murderous. Still, I couldn't understand why Chemish had worked himself into a rage simply talking about it. I decided to drop the subject, but the healer continued—almost as if speaking to himself. There was a strange sorrow in his voice.

"I should have tried to stop him," he said softly.

"Stop him from killing the dog?"

"Stop him from slaughtering your city. It's said that he never takes prisoners. He kills everyone who opposes him. That's just the way he is."

I was speechless. I couldn't believe he'd kill *everyone*.

"What about us? We were allowed to leave."

"I don't think he knows about you. I don't think he even knew I was there."

That made no sense. How could the leader of the army not know a master healer was with them? And why would he kill everyone? Certainly, he'd spare the women and children, or at least take a number of slaves to sell. A complete slaughter was unthinkable.

I felt sick to my stomach. "Are you sure?"

"I am," he said with remorse. "You don't know Shem. Once he gets the bloodlust in his heart, no one can stop him. Killing gives him a sense of power. He feeds off it. He rarely takes prisoners because guarding them wastes manpower. So he lines the captives up and murders them. He makes sport of it—and I refuse to have any part of that."

Unwelcomed tears stung my eyes. I fought to keep from trembling but failed. I clenched my jaw to keep cries from escaping. A pain-filled emptiness welled within me. I couldn't breathe. Shem and his army had murdered everyone—including my family—for sport? It couldn't be true.

"Everyone?" I whispered.

His hand rested gently on my shoulder. "Yes, Jarem. Everyone."

My soul coiled into a knot of hatred. With devastating clarity, I realized just how many things would never be the same. My mind focused on all the things I should and shouldn't have said and done. When was the last time I told my father that I loved him? What was the last thing I said to my mother? Did my sister know how much I really cared for her?

Scalding tears ran down my cheeks. I no longer tried to stop them. I wondered why such things had happened. It wasn't fair. I felt numb. I tried to recall the last thing my father said to me: Was it honest praise or necessary reprimand? I tried to remember the last look I had seen on my mother's face: Was it pride or disapproval? How could they be dead? I choked and started to sob.

The hand on my shoulder gave a comforting squeeze. But it was an enemy's hand. *His* people had destroyed my city. *His* people had killed my family. Even as friendly as Chemish had been, I hated him now because he was a Lamanite. I jerked my shoulder free and slumped forward on the horse.

I made a vow at that instant. I swore by my name and the name of my father I would have vengeance. I would do all I could to learn of my family's fate. If they were dead, I would find Shem and exact justice. I knew seeking vengeance went against my upbringing, against the teachings of my parents and of the Church. But I didn't care. I would learn all I could and use that information to my advantage.

"When will your army return?" I asked, hoping I might meet Shem and fulfill my vow.

"I have no idea. Depending on how many survive, it may be weeks or months before they return."

"Oh," I said. *So much for immediate retribution.*

My mind searched for anything that might ease my loss. It hurt more than I could have ever imagined. I was overwhelmed by a sharp emptiness, a piercing wound that bled my soul of all hope.

We rode in silence for some time. I caught a muffled word or two behind me, accented by a laugh or a curse. I found it impossible to concentrate on anything in particular. The realization that I was alone struck me as nothing ever had before. True, there were other captives—I recognized some of them from the city, although I didn't know any of their names. I was truly by myself.

Then, like a still, small voice from the darkness, unexpected words came to my mind. They were my father's words—a glimmer of hope I could latch on to: *A man's fate is controlled by no one but himself.*

I was a prisoner, true, but I was alive. I *could* do something about my life, but only if I kept my wits and my faith.

Pushing vengeance from my mind, I resolved to conquer my sorrow and better my situation. I didn't know when or how, but I knew I could. I knew I had to, to survive. I vowed not only to survive but, even more, to thrive.

My first priority was to escape. It might take a week, it might take a month; perhaps it would be years before I could get away. But that didn't matter. I would escape. I would make it home.

CHAPTER FOUR

THE SKY WAS FILLED WITH stars by the time we stopped to make camp. Chemish helped me over to a fallen tree next to a wide river. He made me another small plant leaf with a daub of the purple paste on it.

"Take this. It will help the pain. If you need more later on, let me know. Try to get some sleep. Rest will help your leg heal more than anything else."

He patted my shoulder and walked away. I watched the activity around me, thinking only of escape. I wasn't sure, but I guessed the river beside us was Sidon—the river that separated the Nephite and Lamanite territories. I was an excellent swimmer, but it was too dark to judge the distance to the other side. And with my leg still useless, that route seemed too risky.

A warrior sat the other Nephite captives next to me: four boys and two girls. They looked as ragged as I felt, but I was glad for their company. One boy was completely limp and unresponsive. The warrior bound our hands behind our backs and left.

I whispered, "I am Jarem."

"I am David," a boy about my age said. "This is my brother, Ramhah." The other boy was around seven years old. His face was tearstained; his eyes, hollow and vacant, stared at the ground as if he were in a trance.

A stocky boy with closely shorn hair and a round face rolled onto his knees. "I am Amlon. I say we wait until these heathens are asleep, then we slit their filthy throats." His voice was loud and boastful. I worried one of the warriors might overhear his threats.

"Don't be a fool," the older of the two girls whispered. "If they hear you, we're all dead."

"I'd rather die than be a slave to a Lamanite," he grumbled.

"Keep talking like that and you'll get your wish."

I admired the older girl's wisdom. I'd never seen her before—I would remember if I had. She was beautiful. She was about sixteen, with a lean figure, shimmering black hair, and striking pale-blue eyes.

Amlon looked her over with a leer. "If I were *you*, I'd be more than a little worried about what they were going to do with *me*."

She frowned at him. "Well, I'm grateful you're not me—and even more grateful that I'm not you." She turned to me. "My name is Zanesh, and this is my new friend, Sarai."

The younger girl remained silent. She had a thin frame and appeared to be no more than eight or nine. Leaning forward, she rested her ashen face on her knees, refusing to look up. The fourth boy lay quietly to the side of our group, saying nothing. I nodded toward him. "Is he asleep? He hasn't moved since they set him there."

"I think he's dead," Amlon said. "He's been bleeding pretty badly most of the way here. Their sorcerer put a covering on his wound, but it's all soaked through. I think his bowels were punctured."

"Their sorcerer?" I asked.

"Yes, the big man you were riding with. At first I thought you were dead too, because you just lay on his horse as limp as a banana peel."

"He's their healer," I explained.

"I saw you talking with him, Jarem," Zanesh said. "Do you know what will become of us?"

"No. But I think Amlon is right: we'll probably be sold as slaves."

"Then we must escape," David said. "As soon as possible."

"I agree, but I can't try until my leg is healed. It's broken, you see."

"I'm leaving tonight," Amlon said. "If we wait until we're in their heathen cities we'll never escape. You can wait if you want. I'm going find a way to break these bands and leave tonight."

"Where to?" David asked. "Oranihah was destroyed."

Amlon didn't answer right away. It was a good question. Oranihah was gone, and any other nearby city or village was more than likely destroyed too. Zarahemla seemed to be the only choice, but that was many days' journey from here.

"I don't care," Amlon hissed, glancing at the Lamanites behind us. "I'm still going." He stood up.

"Then I pray God goes with you," Zanesh whispered.

"If God were with us, we wouldn't be captives right now!" he spat.

Drawing a sharp breath, Zanesh's eyes narrowed. "If God were *not* with us, we'd be dead right now."

I couldn't argue with her insight. She was right, and I felt that we all knew it. Even Amlon. He sat back down with a huff.

We remained quiet for a time, each lost in our own thoughts. David finally broke the silence by recounting his capture. "I was fishing just north of the city. I heard a noise, and suddenly there were three Lamanites holding spears to my neck."

Then Amlon described his story and proudly displayed an angry wound across his shoulder. "It was a great fight, and I nearly gutted the heathen. But another Lamanite grabbed me from behind."

Zanesh spoke next and broke into tears several times as she described the capture of her family and how she was separated from them. I then related my experiences, trying not to embellish my fight with the warrior. Amlon rolled his eyes when I mentioned the part Chemish had played in rescuing me.

"It's true," I said. "I really think he saved my life, though I don't know why. He says he doesn't like killing. That's why he left with these other men."

"He's still a Lamanite," David said.

"And one Lamanite is as rotten as the next," Amlon added. "You can't trust them as far as you can spit."

They were probably right.

When the moon crested overhead, Amlon scooted next to David, and the two began trying to untie each other's restraints. Zanesh softly attempted to console Sarai. I simply sat there trying desperately not to think of my family.

A light rain chilled the air and made the night long and miserable.

CHAPTER FIVE

I AWOKE WITH A START. A large jewel beetle crawled across a dew-covered leaf in front of me. The morning sun hit the beetle's back, reflecting an iridescent wash of green, gold, and purple, much like the colors on a hummingbird's breast. The more the insect moved, the more the colors shimmered and transformed. For such a simple creature, it was strangely beautiful.

Just then, a sandaled foot stepped on the beetle, abruptly ending its life.

"You, boy. Where's the other one?" the sandal-wearer asked.

I looked up at a truly hideous face. The Lamanite warrior boasted several streaks of red paint that ran from his brow, over his shaven head, and—as far as I could tell—to the back of his neck. His eyes were outlined in black. He bore a hideous scar down one cheek that distorted his mouth and caused his speech to slur. His sudden appearance caught me off guard.

"The other what?" Certainly he didn't mean another beetle.

"Don't play the fool with me," he hissed. "The other *boy*; the fat one," he said, jabbing a finger at a patch of flattened grass.

The volume with which he spoke woke the others. Zanesh sat up, instantly on guard. "What fat boy?" she asked.

"The large one with the cut on his shoulder and the big mouth," the Lamanite snapped. "You know. *Him*." He again pointed to the empty spot.

It was then I noticed that Amlon was gone. The others looked around as if they hadn't seen him for days. I gave an *aha* expression and nodded to the spot in question. "You mean him?"

The warrior was an older man, perhaps in his fortieth year, and had clearly lost any measure of patience long ago. He rammed his spear into the center of the flattened grass. "Yes, him!" he bellowed.

"I don't know." It was the truth.

The warrior stood with his legs spread and his hand on the hilt of a dagger, as if ready to draw it. He clenched his teeth and pointed a gnarled finger at me.

"Don't play games with me, you little whelp, or I'll break your other leg with my bare hands. Now tell me where he is!"

"We don't know," Zanesh said defensively. "He was here last night when we went to sleep."

"He must have slipped away during the night," David added.

"That was the last time any of us saw him, Captain. That's the truth." I didn't know if he was a captain or not, but I thought some manners and straightforward talk might calm him a little.

I was wrong. His face flushed; his eyebrows contorted into a huge knot. He quickly unsheathed the dagger and, with a growl, turned to the girls.

"Did you see him?" he asked Sarai, using the dagger as a pointer. With her hands still bound behind her back, the little girl cowered next to Zanesh. Her eyes were wide with terror; her chin quivered so fiercely I doubted she could have spoken even if she wanted to.

"Well?" he yelled.

Sarai's mouth opened but nothing came out. Instead, she shook her head then buried her face in Zanesh's shoulder.

The warrior lifted Zanesh's face with the tip of his dagger. "And you claim to have no idea either." It was not so much a question as a confirmation. "You realize, with a twist of my wrist I can make your face as pretty as mine?" He smiled as if he were proud of his disfigurement.

Zanesh didn't flinch. Coolly, she said, "We woke up and he was gone. That's all we know."

The warrior grunted and went to the fourth boy, who was still unconscious or worse. He nudged him. "What about you?"

When there was no answer, his face turned red again. "Wake up, Nephite," he said before delivering a vicious kick to the boy's side. When there was still no movement, he knelt and touched the boy's neck, then placed his hand over the boy's heart.

"I should have guessed," he said to himself as he stood. "The good-for-nothing whelp is dead." He delivered a final kick to the lifeless boy, then returned to me and raised his dagger. "I guess I'll have to carve the information out of you. Is that what you want, Nephite?"

Just then, someone from camp hailed the warrior. He waved, then sheathed his dagger, yanked his spear from the ground, and scowled at me. "Someone is going to suffer for the fat one escaping. And if I have my say, it'll be you."

Exactly what I had done to incur his wrath, I didn't know. As he marched back to camp, I could sense everyone's eyes fixed on me. I squirmed uneasily as the pain in my leg began to pulse with renewed intensity. Zanesh was saying something to me, but I couldn't hear it. I was in a fog of self-pity, too busy trying to convince myself that I was not scared. It felt as if the warrior was looking for an excuse to kill me—and Amlon's disappearance had provided the perfect reason.

"How is your leg?" The master healer's voice broke through my fog.

"What?" I still could not concentrate.

Chemish knelt beside me and freed my hands. I gratefully rubbed my wrists as he examined my leg. He unwrapped the covering and gently prodded the swollen area. It hurt, but not as badly as I thought it would.

"Yes, this looks about right. I'll put on a fresh poultice. But first . . ." He reached into his satchel and pulled out two smaller pouches. From one he withdrew a pale-green leaf. Folding it in half, he tapped out a thin line of white powder from the second pouch into the fold. "Gently chew on this to work it into a juice then swallow it quickly."

I opened my mouth to speak, but he quickly held up his hand. "I know, I know: 'What is it?' It's a stevia leaf, and the powder is willow bark. The willow is very bitter, so I hide it in stevia because it's naturally very sweet. The powder will help with your pain and should reduce the swelling of your wound." He stood. "You'll be walking soon, but you won't be able to run for some time. Oh, and don't worry about Korum," he added.

"Who?"

"The painted man who was howling like a monkey. He has a very short temper, and he's angry for having to return with us instead of continuing on with the other warriors."

"Why didn't he go with them?"

"It doesn't matter. Now take your medicine so we can get moving. I'll make sure nothing happens to you."

I began chewing on the leaf-and-powder combination. It was bitter and sweet at the same time, just as he'd said.

Zanesh stood. "Healer, why are you doing this?"

Chemish smiled at her then moved to remove her restraints and those of the others. "I thought you would like to hear some good news for a change."

"Is it good news knowing we're going to be slaves?" David asked harshly.

The smile never left the healer's face as he worked. "It *is* good news to know you're going to live." He looked back and forth at David and Ramhah. "Or would you prefer I leave you in Korum's care?"

Neither boy gave him an answer.

Finished, Chemish rubbed the back of his neck and sighed. "I'm sorry. That wasn't meant as a threat. I'm simply saying that, given your current circumstances, you might want to make the best of things."

"Thank you," Zanesh said.

Chemish nodded. He then nodded at the lifeless boy. "Is he dead?"

"I think so," I replied after swallowing the pulpy mash in my mouth.

"Good. He was beat up pretty badly. He had some severe injuries to his organs. There wasn't anything I could do—at least not here in the wilderness. So I gave him some pain medicine and hoped he would pass during the night." He nodded again and turned back to David. "Will you help me bury him? I will not leave a boy's body to the ravages of scavenging animals."

David complied.

As the company of warriors prepared to leave, two of them were dispatched to search for Amlon. David, Ramhah, Zanesh, and Sarai were herded together. Their hands were tied again, but the master healer insisted they not be tethered to a common rope. He said the trail was too rough for such restricted movement and he didn't want to treat any more broken legs. Korum was not happy about the order.

Chemish applied more liniment and braced my leg extra firmly. "Is that too tight?" he asked, lifting me onto his horse.

"It's fine," I responded flatly.

We followed the river until we came to a bridge that could support our horses. Stepping onto the planks, my heart sank even further. Crossing the Sidon meant we were now in enemy territory.

CHAPTER SIX

"I'm sorry your friends have to walk," Chemish said when we began moving up a steep incline.

I didn't respond, but his comment gave me second thoughts about the master healer. The man seemed to truly care about helping me, and I wondered if perhaps I'd misjudged him. He may be an enemy, but he certainly wasn't acting like one.

My father had taught me to judge each man by his deeds. Because his hunting excursions took him into many different lands, he had friends from several lineages—Nephite, Lamanite, Mulekite, Amalekite, and more. He said people were built from the inside out; that there were good and bad people everywhere—I just had to know how to see it. Perhaps this Lamanite healer *was* a good man after all.

"Jarem, I believe you to be an honest individual," Chemish said, surprising me that his line of thought was similar to mine, "so I feel comfortable asking if you really *do* know where Amlon went."

"South would be my guess," I said with a shrug. "If he had no difficulties, he could be close to the border between our lands by now. *How* he got away I haven't a clue."

"Why didn't the others go with him?"

"I don't know. Perhaps he felt the others would slow him down."

Chemish grunted as if that made perfect sense but said no more. A few minutes later, Korum rode up beside us. Before he could open his mouth, the healer said, "He knows nothing, Korum."

"I'll be the judge of that," the man barked. "Tell me what you know, boy."

"Why would Amlon confide anything in me?" I asked. "I can't go anywhere with my broken leg. Besides, the more secret he kept his plans, the less chance he had of being caught."

The hatred on Korum's face intensified, causing him to redden again. It frightened me to look at him.

"Liar!" he yelled. "You're nothing but a snake-tongued Nephite liar. I bet your father was a liar too, wasn't he?"

I bit my lip and said nothing. It wouldn't do any good to rise to Korum's insults, and it'd be even worse to counter it with one of my own. He glared at me in challenge, gripping his dagger tightly.

"What's the matter, Nephite? No more insolent remarks?" he sneered. "Or are you too cowardly to speak?"

I didn't think I was being insolent or cowardly, but apparently he did. "I'm telling the truth. I don't know where Amlon is," I said evenly. "I'm not being insolent."

"So, you *are* a coward, then. No doubt your father was a spineless coward just like you. Wasn't he, boy?"

I held my breath—and my tongue—and simply shook my head. Korum unleashed a string of offensive comments before he turned his horse and rode back to the others.

"You hold your temper well," Chemish said after a moment's pause. "Most Lamanite boys I know would have filled his ears with curses."

"Don't think I didn't want to," I said quietly.

"Curious. Tell me, Jarem, why didn't you?"

I chewed on my lower lip, thinking of a way to explain my feelings. It was true that Korum frightened me, especially because my injured leg prevented me from defending myself. But that wasn't why I chose to ignore his insults. The real answer came from a lesson my father had taught me long ago. I started to speak, but my voice caught.

Again, as if reading my mind, Chemish asked, "Was it something your father said?"

I nodded. My eyes began to burn, even though I had resolved not to cry. Thankfully, Chemish didn't push for an answer. We rode quietly for almost an hour before I conquered my emotions enough to speak.

"My father rarely lost his temper," I explained softly. "He never used God's name in vain or swore in anger or frustration."

"Is that so unusual for a religious person?"

"Perhaps not. But there's a reason he didn't. He told me that he used to have the temper of a wild boar with a toothache. And he said that when he got really angry, he'd lose track of everything around him. 'Blind anger,' he used to call it."

"I know many individuals like that," Chemish agreed.

"Father said he once got into a fight with some man where we used to live. It was over something so minor he couldn't even remember what it was. He said one shout led to another; one push led to another. My father got so mad all he remembered was leaping at the man with both fists swinging. The next thing he knew, a bunch of men were pulling him off the other man. There was blood everywhere."

"Did the man die?"

"Yes, but that wasn't the worst of it. At least, that wasn't the part that changed Father. As his eyes focused on things other than the dead man, he saw a little girl, pale with shock, kneeling next to the man. She was the man's daughter. Father said he never felt sicker in his whole life . . . something about the terrified look on her face. Anyway, he hated himself for a long time because he had caused so much heartbreak when he could have simply walked away. That was when he became a hunter—so he could stay out of the village and away from people for long periods of time."

A lump caught in my throat, so I paused to steady my voice.

"He always took me hunting with him," I said softly. "He taught me many things."

"So this lesson was, 'don't lose your temper'?" Chemish asked.

"More than that. He said anger begets anger. It's like a fire that feeds on itself. He said, 'Never let your emotions control your actions.'"

"Curious. I have often felt that way but have never known exactly how to put it into words," Chemish mused. "I would have enjoyed meeting your father. I'm sure I would have liked him."

The words "would have" struck me like a fist to my stomach. The simple fact was that my father's death had resulted from the bloodlust of Chemish's people. I didn't feel sorry in the least for the healer's missed opportunity—he didn't deserve the honor of meeting my father.

The memories of my father were bittersweet, but the realization that more memories would never form weighed heavily on my heart. Chemish's words echoed in my head: *I would have. I would have.*

It would have *been nice if none of this had ever happened*, I thought. This healthy, trouble-free Lamanite still enjoyed life to its fullest—something my family would never do again. And although he acted differently than the warriors, the healer was still a Lamanite. At that moment, I hated all Lamanites.

"I want to be with the others now," I said harshly.

If he sensed my bitterness, it didn't show. "Certainly."

We stopped to let the others catch up. A young Lamanite warrior was riding beside Zanesh and Sarai, trying to initiate a conversation. Zanesh was steadfastly ignoring him. When the girls saw me waiting, their faces lit up. The Lamanite scowled. I instantly felt better seeing their reaction. They were my people and my friends.

Before they got to us, to my surprise, Chemish slid off the horse and handed me the reins. Zanesh seized the opportunity by stepping to my side.

"Jarem, may I ride with you?" she asked.

"And what is wrong with my horse?" the young warrior asked, openly annoyed at her request. "I've been offering you a ride all morning—and now you beg of *him?*"

"If Sarai doesn't mind, I'd be happy to," I said, ignoring the Lamanite's outburst.

Chemish held out his hand. "I'll walk with the young lady, if she'll let me."

Sarai clung to Zanesh's arm and flashed me a frightened, questioning look.

I smiled. "It's all right, Sarai. He's very nice . . . for a Lamanite. And you can walk in front of us so we can keep an eye on you, in case you need help."

Even as I said it, the words sounded weak. We were prisoners; I had a broken leg, and yet here I was offering her protection? It was nonsense.

Zanesh stroked the little girl's hair. "If Jarem says it'll be all right, then it will. I trust him."

Hesitantly, Sarai took the healer's proffered hand. Chemish led off, talking to the girl in light tones, pointing out interesting plants and animals.

I helped Zanesh onto the horse. She seemed as light as a feather—which meant I was already getting my strength back. Sitting in front of me, she leaned back as I reached around to gain control of the reins.

"It feels good to have *strong* arms around me," she cooed while glancing at the young warrior.

I knew the comment was meant to irritate the young warrior. My arms were amply muscled, but not to the extent Zanesh's tone suggested. The young Lamanite cursed under his breath, gave me a hateful glare, and spun his horse in the opposite direction.

Zanesh chuckled softly.

"You really shouldn't bait him like that," I cautioned. "I fear what Amlon said about you is true. Your remarkable beauty may be a curse and a blessing."

Did I really just tell her she's remarkably beautiful? I felt my face flush.

"I know," she said with a hint of despair. "I appreciate your concern, Jarem. And your compliment."

While I loved hearing her say my name, I knew her tone indicated that she recognized the true weight of our predicament.

"I am just sorry I can't do more to protect you and Sarai."

"I know," she said again, leaning against me. "I could tell from the start you're a good man. And I have a pretty good idea about what the future holds for each of us. That's why I try not to think about it."

"I'm sorry I mentioned it, then. It's just . . . well, the way that young warrior was looking at you made me angry."

"He's an immense fool," she huffed. "His name is Limni. He's been bothering me ever since we left Oranihah. He acts a lot tougher than he really is. And from what I've seen, he has practically no authority—other than being a Lamanite."

"Maybe not, but we're a small group. Things might be different when we reach their cities. He may have connections to officers with more power."

"Yes . . . perhaps you're right," she admitted. "But for now, he's gone. It's much nicer being with you."

Her remark made my heart flutter uncomfortably. I'd never really taken the time to bother with girls before. I was always too busy hunting with my father or working the fields. A few young men my age had already married, but I wasn't too eager to rush into that commitment.

I took a deep breath. "I like being with you too," I said, trying desperately to hide my awkwardness.

As we rode, we talked about our lives as they were in Oranihah. It felt comforting to bring good memories to mind. Zanesh said her family was new to Oranihah, and although we had never met, she had heard of my family. But talking about her family made her cry. I struggled not to do so myself.

When she began trembling, I gathered my resolve and whispered, "It'll be all right. You'll see. Everything will work out if we have faith."

She shook her head. "No, Jarem, it won't. Don't you understand? They killed my parents—I saw it happen. My future holds nothing but misery now."

"Perhaps, but you really don't know that," I argued. "Who knows what tomorrow holds? Yesterday was filled with heartache and sorrow. Today isn't much better. But the next day—even the next hour—hasn't been determined yet. It could be worse; it could be better. We just need to do all we can to make sure it's better."

"How can you be so optimistic?" she replied sharply. "We're heading deeper into Lamanite territory with every step. We'll probably be killed or sacrificed to one of their gods, or . . . or worse. I'm sorry, Jarem, but the future doesn't look very delightsome to me right now."

I knew precisely how she felt, but I also knew that dwelling on the negative only brought more negativity. She was despondent at the moment, as was I; nevertheless, I was determined to cheer her up, because in doing so, I knew I'd feel better myself.

"What about Amlon?" I whispered.

She wiped her eyes. "Do you think he made it? Is he safe?"

"I can't say for sure, but he's got a good chance."

She turned slightly and gave me a questioning look. "How do you know?"

I smiled at her. It was easy to do. "The warriors went looking for him in the wrong direction."

She waited for more news, but I offered none. I was toying with her—partly to get her mind off her sorrows.

"Jarem, if you're going to keep things from me, you'll be sorry," she said in a light tone.

I had to laugh. "Fair enough. The warriors doubled back along the trail on which we came. Amlon followed the riverbank."

"Did he try to swim across?"

"I don't know. He probably went as far as he could along the bank before swimming. Anyway, I don't think any of the Lamanites saw his tracks."

"But you did?"

"Yes. Remember, I am a hunter. These Lamanites are warriors. They kill for sport; I kill to eat. When filling your belly depends on being able to follow a trail, you notice things in greater detail. These men are definitely not hunters."

"I see," she said with an edge of nervousness. "Do you think we'll be killed for sport?"

"No. I really don't think so."

We didn't speak again for some time, each lost in our own thoughts. I kept an ear to the jungle and tried to memorize the lay of the land. Parts of the terrain looked vaguely familiar, though I knew I had never traveled this way before. We were approaching a very mountainous area, and the trail narrowed, slowing our progress.

Zanesh put her hand on my knee and asked, "Has the Lamanite healer said anything about keeping you?"

I blinked. "What? No. He hasn't." That possibility had never even entered my mind, though I could see the logic in it. Chemish had spent most of his time with me. Still . . .

"Why would he need me? He's the best healer in their land—so he says. I'm sure he has plenty of help from apprentices or other healers. Plus, he seems to have a lot of authority because the other Lamanites show him so much respect."

Zanesh nodded but said nothing more.

We soon crested the rim of a mountain and looked down into a wide valley. Immediately my senses told me many things about this place, and my mind began matching up stories with what I was now seeing. As we descended into the valley, I heard the rumbling of a waterfall in the distance. It was one of the landmarks indicating the boundaries of Nephi, the land of the Lamanites.

"Did the healer know anything about your family?" Zanesh asked, bringing my thoughts back. "You said you weren't together when the attack came."

"No. But if I know my father—" My voice choked off. I swallowed several times to stop the sob threatening to rise from my chest.

As if sensing my remorse, Zanesh quickly added, "Oh, Jarem, I'm sorry. I shouldn't have—"

"It's all right," I quickly interrupted, shaking my head forcefully. Taking a deep breath, I continued. "I've got to accept the truth. In fact, my father would have been the first to say, 'Let your mourning be respectful, but let it be brief. Life will go on with or without you.' He didn't believe in wasting time on things you cannot change."

"I like that," she said, again leaning back against me. I liked the feel of that. It made me feel stronger, more like a man. We were surrounded by the enemy, but being with her made that seem almost tolerable. She had a need for me . . . and I for her. And our mutual reliance somehow made our sorrows more bearable.

That was important. I knew that if we were to survive, we could not do it alone. The others—David, Ramhah, and Sarai—were also crucial to our existence, and I determined to talk to them the first chance I got. The more we knew about each other, the more confident we'd be about the future— whatever that future might be. I knew my knowledge of the jungle could help. Closing my eyes, I silently prayed for help to do all I could to save our small group—for in doing so, they would save me.

CHAPTER SEVEN

CHEMISH ALLOWED ME TO STAY on his horse until well past noon. Sarai and Zanesh took turns riding with me while the other walked with the healer. Cresting a second rise, we had a commanding view of the scene below. Zanesh drew a deep breath filled with awe.

The valley was thick with vegetation, highlighted with an occasional stream or a patchwork of cultivated fields. We seemed to be avoiding most of the larger settlements along the way, although I didn't know why.

"How long before we reach their capital?" Zanesh asked me in a stilted whisper.

"I'm not sure. But I fear it's close, maybe two or three days."

She hugged herself. "Jarem, I'm afraid."

I whispered in her ear, "Don't give up. I have an idea. We may have a chance to escape tonight. This group rotates guard duty in a set pattern, and they've become rather lazy now that we're deep in their territory." I paused and glanced around. No one was close enough to hear. "It has to be tonight, though. And I'll need your help, but . . . well, it won't be very pleasant."

"I'll do whatever you ask. But what about your leg?"

"My leg's feeling much better, and if I can get the healer to tighten this brace, I should be able to make pretty good time. You'll just have to trust me. Say nothing to Sarai."

She took my arm and wrapped it around her frame. "I do trust you. Tell me what to do."

I heard a horse move up behind us, so I quickly whispered, "I'll explain later. Right now, go and walk with Sarai, and try to talk of something cheerful. Get her spirits up, because the happier she is, the more energy she'll have."

Limni rode past us and took lead of the group. He flashed another hateful scowl at me as he passed, and tried to catch Zanesh's eye. She looked the other way.

"Can't I stay with you?" she pleaded.

Her request warmed me, but it was probably just the terrible situation we were in that drew her to me. Without thinking, I gently kissed the top of her head.

"Go to Sarai. I need to do a few things first. It'll be all right."

I hugged her tightly before she slid off the horse and caught up with Sarai.

Riding up to Chemish, I brought the horse to a stop and teased, "You seem to like walking more than riding."

"I suppose I do. I like running, too."

"You mean like in a race?"

"That too. But sometimes I run just to run."

I was confused. Nobody ran because they *liked* to. "I've always heard that too much exertion weakens the body, which makes it easier to get sick."

"Not so, my young friend. Think about what happens when you work hard: You breathe harder, your heart beats faster, your muscles swell, you sweat. All this causes immediate fatigue." He raised a finger, emphasizing his point. "At first that may seem to validate your belief, but you must ask: Why does your body respond that way?"

"Because it doesn't like it?"

He shook his head. "Just the opposite. Our bodies respond to what we demand of them. You probably couldn't draw a bow the first time you tried. But the more you tried, the stronger you got, until at last you could nock an arrow, draw the bow, and hit a target. What changed from the first time you tried to the time you succeeded?"

"I got stronger."

"Exactly. Your muscles got stronger because you demanded it of them. Think of how you feel after you've worked hard and then rested. Do you not feel invigorated? Is not your mind clearer, sharper? And the more you do it, the better you feel. Why is that?"

"Because I demand it of myself?"

"And in doing so, your body builds an ability to resist illness. At least that's been my observation. I can't tell you the number of illnesses I've encountered that stem directly from slothfulness."

"I never knew that," I admitted.

He shrugged. "Curious, isn't it?"

Thankfully, our brief conversation had led perfectly into my plan. "I wish I could do some walking . . ." I said, leading the conversation.

Chemish looked at me and then at my leg. "Tell me if this hurts," he said, placing his palm on my heel and pushing up. I felt a dull throb but no real pain.

"It's not bad."

"Good." He then placed an ear against the wound and slowly turned my leg. Again, I felt mild discomfort, but none of the deep sharpness from before.

"That's not so bad, either," I said. "I'm very impressed with your skills."

He looked at me with one eyebrow raised in question.

"Well, not bad for a Lamanite," I added, casually looking away.

He laughed and patted my leg. "At the next camp I'll make a walking-splint and a staff that should allow some movement."

"Thank you."

We started moving again and in a short time, we reached a mass of huge stones. As we approached, I spied two persons hiding in a cleft. There were irregularities in the shadows cast by the stones, and I saw a sandaled foot where a boulder rounded at the base. I glanced around and was certain no one else had seen them. Knowing bandits were present along common roads, regardless of nationality, I thought it best to warn the others.

Korum was directly in front of us. I called to him. "Captain, there are a couple of men ahead, behind those large stones."

He turned and glared at me. "You're seeing things, Nephite."

"No, I'm quite sure. Look there, in the cleft between the stone on this side of the trail," I said, pointing.

He stood in his saddle and squinted. "There's no one there," he said in a tone that suggested the conversation was over.

I didn't want to make him angry, but at the same time I knew I was right. When we were about thirty paces away, I called out to the strangers, "Hail—you behind the rocks!"

As the men shifted, their shadows again belied their position. But they didn't leave their hiding place. Everyone in our group followed my line of sight to see who I was calling to.

"Yes, I mean you behind the large rocks. You can come out now."

Why I hailed them, I couldn't say. I guess more than anything I wanted to prove I was right. Chemish mounted his horse behind me and stood in the saddle. "You certainly have a keen sense of vision, young man." He sat back down.

Knowing they were caught, the two men begrudgingly left their hiding place and stood in the middle of the trail. Korum growled through his teeth and raced ahead to meet them. We could hear his colorful curses well before we reached the strangers.

The men moved to one side of the trail when we reached them. They turned out to be lookouts set to guard the entrance to this land. As we passed, they scowled at me with looks of pure hatred.

"Better luck next time," I said with a shrug.

"Shut your mouth, Nephite," one of them snapped.

I heard sporadic wisps of air escape from Chemish's pursed lips and felt his body jiggling. He was trying to suppress laughter. Finally, he couldn't hold it any longer and let out a resounding guffaw. I glanced behind me and saw him wobbling back and forth, holding his ribs as if they hurt, and at one point nearly falling off the horse—which made him laugh even more.

"Jarem, you are an extraordinary young man."

I bowed in mock humility. "Thank you, Master Healer."

The short-lived event had formed a bond of admiration between Chemish and me, though to what extent I couldn't tell. It didn't matter. Whatever the bond, I knew I would have need of it later. For now, I was glad to be developing even a tentative friendship with this enemy.

CHAPTER EIGHT

SOON THE VALLEY SPREAD BEFORE us in multiple hues of green. Many portions were evenly sectioned into cultivated fields and pastures. Streams meandered throughout. It was beautiful; not at all like the untamed wilderness we had just exited.

"Welcome to the land of Nephi," Chemish said formally.

"It's breathtaking," I said, letting my astonishment show.

"Does this surprise you?"

"Quite honestly, yes. I've always heard Lamanites are savages that live in the wilderness and are about as civilized as monkeys."

"Whoa. Hold your tongue," Chemish balked. "Your honesty is refreshing, but it lacks tact. It's true we do not have cities as great as yours, but . . . 'as civilized as monkeys'?"

I smiled. "Sorry, but it's what I was taught. Don't Lamanite parents tell their children exaggerated stories about my people?"

Chemish shouted, "Exactly! That's part of the reason I wanted to come on this excursion—to see for myself what your people are like. I've learned that secondhand information is only a *possibility* of the truth. I'm a man of learning. I seek out proof of everything."

Again, the healer's comment brought a question to my mind. "What about faith?"

Chemish harrumphed loudly. "A religious concept invented to keep people from searching for the truth."

I frowned. I'd always thought of it as a religious concept that led people *to* the truth. But I didn't feel it was an appropriate time to argue the point. I was not in a position to press my opinions, and I wanted to do all I could to remain in his favor. Still, I hoped that one day I'd have the chance to explain the truth about faith to him.

We reached the base of the valley just before sundown and began to prepare for camp.

"How long before we reach our destination?" I asked as casually as I could.

"At least another day's travel," Chemish said. "There's really no rush."

The healer constructed a new splint that began below my knee and extended a little past my foot. It was firm enough for me to put most of my weight on without causing debilitating pain. He also fashioned a walking staff from a length of ironwood. The warriors led us to a clearing near a thick patch of jungle and sat us next to a fallen tree. They gave us small portions of dried sloth, dried taro, and a gourd of papaya juice. It was the first real meal we'd eaten in days.

"Are you sure this is safe to eat?" Sarai asked Zanesh. She turned to me and raised her eyebrows.

"I think so," I said. "If we're to be made slaves, it'd be foolish to poison us."

"Yeah," David said bitterly. "But they give us just enough to survive. I say we don't eat a thing."

"But you'll get sick and weak," Zanesh argued.

"Exactly," he said. "No one wants to buy a sick slave."

"And then what would they do with you?" Zanesh countered. "Kill you?"

"I think I'd rather be dead than a slave," he grumbled.

The girls ignored his remarks and ate their meal. I did too. My empty belly welcomed the food and drink. It did wonders for my spirit, and I noticed it had a similar effect on the girls.

After eating, I whispered my plan to Zanesh. She agreed to help, even though her part would prove most unpleasant. But if we became slaves, unpleasant experiences would dominate our lives. We needed to escape. Our lives depended on it.

As the camp settled in for the night, I knew Limni would be posted as guard for the second watch. He always was. The warriors never changed their routine, and I was grateful for their predictability. Before retiring, Korum bound our wrists together then tied us in pairs: David to Ramhah, Zanesh to Sarai.

As Korum bent toward me, I asked, "Could I speak to the healer, please?"

"What for?"

"He said I could get some medicine to keep my leg from hurting through the night."

Korum hesitated a moment, then jerked his head toward camp. "Be quick, Nephite."

I nodded and hobbled to Chemish's tent. He was writing in a vellum book and barely noticed my approach. When I asked for some pain medicine, he tossed me the pouch he kept his supplies in.

"You know what it looks like," he said. "Take only a small amount. You're healing very well and shouldn't need much more." And with that, he resumed his writing.

I placed a large glob into a rolled leaf and returned to my place with the Nephites.

Korum waited impatiently, his face set in its meanest scowl. "What took you so long?" he snapped.

"My leg is broken, remember?" I said, sitting next to Zanesh.

"I should just kill you and be done with it," he growled, storming off—and forgetting to bind my wrists to anything.

Before long, chirping and croaking sounds signaled the awakening of night creatures. Some of the warriors snored. Pretending to be asleep, I waited until the first guard was replaced by Limni. Then, whispering gently, I awoke Zanesh. She roused immediately.

"Are you ready?" I whispered.

She swallowed hard and nodded.

Sitting up, she yawned loudly, winning Limni's attention. She stared wistfully at the young warrior. It took only a second for him to respond. He came over and knelt beside her. Being only a few cubits away, I continued my ruse of sleep while watching through squinted eyes.

She whispered hoarsely, "I am very thirsty. Could I have something to drink?"

Limni offered her a goatskin wine flask. "I can't hold it without waking her," she whispered, nodding at the binding that joined her to Sarai. Limni set the flask down and removed a knife from his belt. Zanesh struggled to her knees, angling in such a way that turned Limni's back to me. As the young warrior began cutting, I quietly unstopped the flask and completed my part of our plan. Zanesh provided an irresistible distraction.

"Can we talk?" she whispered, reaching for the flask.

Limni scowled. "I've been trying to talk to you for two days, and only now you agree? Why?"

"I couldn't talk to you in front of the other Nephites, now could I?" she softly teased, placing a hand on his knee.

Limni hesitated. I could only imagine the confused expression on his face. Visibly torn between caution and Zanesh's intoxicating advances, he finally nodded.

"Over here," he said, standing. She gave him the wine flask and stood.

As he headed toward camp, Zanesh stopped short. "No, over here," she said, still keeping her voice hushed. Taking his hand, she led him to the end of the fallen tree, just within earshot. Limni followed willingly.

"How long have you been a warrior?" she asked, patting the space beside her, coaxing him to sit.

"More than a year. This is my third assignment," he said, clearly unsure what to make of her forwardness.

"You must be very brave and strong to be a warrior."

He puffed up noticeably. "I can beat any man twice my age."

Zanesh's tunic was draped loosely around her shoulders. An evening breeze played hypnotically with her hair. She hugged herself. "I'm getting cold. Could I have that drink now?"

Limni put an arm around her waist. "I've got better than drink to keep you warm," he oozed.

"That will only warm the outside," she said, squirming from his embrace. "I need something to warm me on the inside first."

The young warrior handed her the flask. She held it to her lips and paused before handing it back. "First, show me how a *real* warrior drinks."

Limni grinned and drained half of the wine flask in several loud swallows. He then gave her the flask, but she set it aside without drinking. Without pause, he slid his hands around her waist. She played with the necklace he wore, trying to avoid any closeness. Her methods of avoidance were very smooth, as if she'd been through this before. That didn't surprise me. When he tried to kiss her, she turned her face.

"Shouldn't we wait until everyone is asleep?" she asked coyly.

"Why? I am a Lamanite warrior!" he said loudly.

Zanesh placed her fingers to his lips. "Shhh. Just to be sure no one is watching, that's all," she whispered.

Limni grunted, humored by her request. "As a warrior, I—" He stopped and shook his head as if clearing a sudden fog. "I can have any woman I choo—" He rubbed his eyes and shook his head again. "Any I choose." He began massaging the sides of his head. "I—I feel . . . strange."

He tried standing and ended up on his knees. He reached for Zanesh, but she backed just out of reach. Still reaching, he fell forward—flat on his face. There, he remained completely still.

Zanesh looked toward camp then nodded at me. All was quiet. Together, we propped Limni into a sitting position against the fallen trunk. He was fast asleep. The camp remained unaware of our exploits.

"He fell asleep, just like you said he would," Zanesh whispered. "What did you put in that wine flask?"

"It's a gift from their healer."

"What?"

"I'll explain later."

I crawled over to David and Ramhah while Zanesh gently woke Sarai. Freeing the boys, I quickly explained what had happened. David nodded. He and Ramhah decided to go in one direction while the girls and I went in the other. Our chances for escape were better that way. We shook hands and wished each other luck. The brothers quietly headed down toward a river.

I turned to my companions. "We'd better move quickly," I whispered. "Step exactly where I step and make no noise. No talking from now on until I say so. Understood?"

Sarai nodded, and Zanesh kissed my cheek. "We trust you," she said in my ear. I felt my face heat up but turned before she could notice. I was excited and terrified. They trusted their lives to me, and I suddenly felt woefully incompetent.

Walking single file, we slipped silently into the darkness of the jungle.

CHAPTER NINE

WE'D TRAVELED A GREAT DISTANCE before pausing to catch our breath. Almost instantly, I sensed something was wrong. We were not alone. I motioned for Zanesh and Sarai to hold perfectly still as I strained to listen.

We were on an animal trail—one rarely used by people. The only movement I detected was a slight breeze nudging the trees above us. A small stream trickled nearby. There was nothing else. Then—

"Get down slowly," I whispered to the girls. They dropped soundlessly to their hands and knees. I put my finger in front of my lips, silencing them.

I heard a low, guttural noise—the rhythmic drawing and releasing of deep, throaty breaths. It was the sound of a large jungle cat, probably a jaguar on the prowl.

My muscles reflexively tensed. I moved noiselessly to one side, away from the girls, behind a stand of palms. Zanesh held Sarai close and covered her eyes. The breathing was closer now, very easy to hear. My skin prickled. A dry pastiness coated my mouth, making it difficult to swallow. The girls were pale and shaking. The deep breathing suddenly got louder, more rapid—right behind a curtain of broadleaf plants to my right—as if something had excited the cat. It had caught our scent.

"What is that?" Sarai whimpered.

The breathing stopped.

Zanesh covered Sarai's mouth and whispered in her ear. My heart pounded so loudly I was sure the cat could hear it. I gripped my staff, holding it in front of me like a weapon.

The sound of vegetation slowly giving way was unmistakable as the cat crept toward the girls. Sarai let out a panicked cry in spite of Zanesh's muffling.

Then I saw it: a huge, spotted jaguar crouching behind a stand of tall ferns not two paces away. Its shoulders bobbed, readying itself for a lunge. My instincts took over.

"Psst," I hissed sharply. The cat flinched, jerking its large head toward me, its ears flattened back. When our eyes met, I lunged forward, jabbing the pointed end of my staff squarely on its nose. The jaguar recoiled, its green eyes wide with pain and shock. It hissed ferociously, displaying its enormous fangs. I leapt to my feet, yelling as loud as I could and lunging again. The jaguar swiped at the staff, but I lifted it just in time, and its claws caught nothing but air. I advanced rapidly, screaming like a wild man, and struck the jaguar's head twice. The cat hissed and spat then turned tail and dashed into the jungle.

I stood staring for a moment at the spot where the predator had been. I was aware of a terrible throbbing in my leg and an overall trembling in my body. I felt sick to my stomach and unsure of my surroundings.

Then everything went blurry, and I collapsed.

* * *

"Jarem? Jarem, please," a soft voice entered the darkness in my head. I felt a cool mist settling on my skin and the soft caresses of someone stroking my hair.

I opened my eyes and saw Zanesh's tearstained face directly over mine. She offered a wide smile. It was the most beautiful thing I'd ever seen. I smiled back. She leaned down and hugged me. The hug was the most wonderful thing I'd ever felt. Then I realized two persons were hugging me. The other had to be Sarai.

"Oh, Jarem," Zanesh wept. "You saved our lives *again*."

I couldn't recall saving their lives the *first* time, but I wasn't about to argue. I sat up slowly, still feeling quite disoriented.

"What happened?"

Zanesh wiped her eyes. "You don't remember? The jaguar was about to attack us, and you drove it off."

It all came back to me—including the painful throbbing in my leg.

"I—I'm sorry I screamed," Sarai said ashamedly.

My heartfelt for the little girl. I couldn't blame her for being afraid. I pulled her into a tender embrace. "No need to apologize. I felt like screaming too."

The night sky had turned brassy, heralding a new day. I placed the smallest daub of Chemish's purple paste in a stevia leaf and stuffed it in my cheek. We took a moment to drink from a rapidly flowing stream, and then I looked around to get my bearings. A faint pathway paralleled the stream up the mountainside. I was certain the pathway was far from the trail we'd followed through the jungle. With any luck, we'd crest the mountain away from the main trail and soon be out of the land Nephi.

I set a steady pace up the mountainside. Before long we were dripping with perspiration. The path was steep and ill-defined, and I had to rest often because of my leg. But the frequent stops also helped Sarai, who was doing her best to keep up without complaint. She was being very brave for such a young child. I was as proud of her as any parent would be. We paused at midday to eat some fruit we'd picked and to sleep for an hour then continued on. By the time we reached the summit, the day was almost over. A thick cloud enveloped the mountaintop, limiting our visibility. We rested in a clearing amongst a dense grove of mountain ferns that grew as tall as a man.

"Aren't we going to go back on the same road we came here on?" Sarai asked, rubbing her feet.

"I know it would be easier," I said, "but we can't. We're still in Lamanite territory, and it'd be too risky. We'll have to find our own way out."

She seemed to ponder what I said, then nodded.

"How is your leg?" Zanesh asked.

"I need to tighten this brace," I said, tugging at it. "The more it moves, the more my leg hurts. But having this staff helps. How are you faring?"

She smiled weakly. "I can't remember the last time I had this much enjoyment."

We all grinned but couldn't bring ourselves to laugh. We were simply too tired. After a pause, Zanesh got to her feet. "I'm going to find some food."

"Be careful out there. Take some bearings so you remember how to get back—"

"I've gathered food before," Zanesh said, cutting me off harshly.

I couldn't tell if she was angry or just extra tired. "Excellent. Sarai and I will build a shelter. This mist will turn to rain before nightfall."

We tended to our tasks and within two hours were enjoying a meal of plantains, tubers, and papaya under a lean-to of bamboo and broad taro leaves. We no sooner had huddled under the shelter than a heavy rain began.

The mountains' heights were known for their abundant rainfall—the kind of rain that came down in constant sheets rather than just drops. This was one of those storms. It lasted all night. And while our lean-to kept off most of the water, the sheer volume of rain made complete dryness impossible. The night was miserably long and wet.

CHAPTER TEN

THE SUN WAS UP BEFORE I was—which was quite unusual. I normally awoke well before the dawn. But my body craved sleep, and knew I would get precious little of it over the next few nights. This day promised to be a beautiful one. The clouds had broken up, and much of the night's rain had already found its way down the mountainside. The girls were still asleep, snuggled close to each other at the back of our lean-to.

I got up quietly and did some exploring. From the vantage point of some large rocks that rose above the vegetation, I could see a great distance in every direction. To the south, the mountain's ridgeline looked somewhat familiar. I pictured what it might look like from the other side and concluded that not far beyond lay the wilderness. To the north lay the land of Nephi dotted with numerous Lamanite villages. And somewhere between us and those villages was a group of angry warriors led by Korum, who, no doubt, was actively pursuing us. I smiled at the thought of his frustration, but my joy didn't last. We were far from being safe. In fact, the very thought of Korum gave me a renewed desire to continue south as soon as possible.

I returned to our lean-to and found Zanesh awake and trying to start a fire. The morning was brisk, and the thought of a warm blaze was nearly irresistible. But the smoke would signal our position, so I stopped her.

"As soon as we get moving, we'll warm up," I said with as much enthusiasm as I could muster.

She nodded and encouraged Sarai to start moving. We hiked to the rocks and the crest, where I pointed out our most likely route of escape.

"Can't we use a road now?" Sarai asked.

"I think we'd better not until we get closer to the border. But I'll do my best to keep us on animal trails so it'll be easier."

We ate some leftover plantains and proceeded south. As long as we stuck to the crest of the mountain, the trees were less dense, making the trails easier to follow. We moved cautiously, pausing often to listen for warning noises or anything out of the ordinary. After a few hours, my caution increased, and I led us on a trail down the mountain. We were safer surrounded by dense jungle. With the help of my walking staff, we actually covered a great distance before midday.

We stopped by a clear pool to soak our feet. Some silvery minnows swam around our feet and nibbled at our toes. Sarai giggled delightedly. Zanesh found some breadfruit nearby and quickly went to work preparing a kind of mush. She sweetened it with berries and let it sit in the sun for an hour. It was tough but delicious.

Just before sunset, I found a narrow footpath in the underbrush. The path was manmade, but it looked as if it hadn't been used for some time. We walked until it was dark then stopped at a small clearing on one side of the path. The clearing wasn't very big, but it was carpeted with soft, spongy green moss and sheltered by tall banana trees. We collapsed on the moss with heartfelt groans. Hopefully this footpath was one the Lamanites had forgotten about.

My leg throbbed relentlessly, but the sharp pain was no longer there. I was convinced the bone was mending. Above the banana fronds, thick clouds obscured the stars. It was going to rain again. I quickly fashioned a simple roof using vines and broadleaves. We ate some bananas and prayed that the rain would miss us.

"What I want most is a good meal," Zanesh said with a wan smile.

I shrugged. "We've been eating pretty well so far, thanks to you."

"Yes, but you should see me in a real cooking room," Zanesh said. "I could do wonders with just about anything you brought home."

Her comment fostered very pleasant possibilities, and the knowing smile on her face suggested she had similar thoughts. And *that* thought made me feel very good indeed.

Luckily, the rain never fell, making the night much more pleasant. Our course had taken us down from the higher elevations, which accounted for the warmer conditions. Things were finally looking up.

I drifted off quickly but slept fitfully. I knew I wouldn't sleep well until we were back in our own lands.

* * *

Just before sunrise, I was awakened by a man's surprised voice. "My, my. What do we have here?"

I quickly knuckled the sleep from my eyes. Above me stood one of the most evil-looking men I'd ever seen. He stood almost as tall as a horse's head and had muscles I never knew existed. His eyes showed menacingly through a wide strip of black paint running temple to temple. His black hair was pulled tight and adorned with feathers in the back. Several earrings hung from his multi-pierced lobes. He looked like the perfect warrior—strong, confident, merciless.

"The night is over, children. Time to get up," the stranger commanded. His tender smile contrasted eerily with the rest of his appearance.

"What are three Nephite children doing so far from the border?" a second man's voice joined in.

I sat up and felt for my walking staff. Two shorter warriors stood behind the tall one. They looked fierce but not as dangerous as their leader. They were all Lamanite.

"Did you have a nice sleep?" the leader asked in a condescending tone. I couldn't help but feel that, in spite of his war paint, there was something familiar about him. Perhaps I'd seen him in the attack on Oranihah.

I glanced at the girls. They were both awake and frozen with fear. I was speechless, knowing only that I had to get to my feet if I were to have any advantage fighting these Lamanites. As I rolled to my knees, the large one reached me in one stride and shoved me back to the ground. He then grabbed Zanesh's arm and yanked her effortlessly to her feet.

"My, my, my!" he exclaimed, whistling a long, low note. "You are a feast for hungry eyes."

I grabbed my staff and jumped to my feet. "Let go of her," I demanded. "Let go, or you'll be sorry."

The large one stared at me with one eyebrow raised but said nothing. He then threw Zanesh forcefully to the ground and squared up to me. He was easily a head taller than I was. His eyes bore into mine with pure hatred.

Not breaking eye contact, he spoke to his brethren. "It appears these wayward Nephites have some fight in them." He then carelessly turned his back to me and continued. "Do you think this spirited one will have the nerve to attack me from behind?"

Before his men could answer, I raised my staff high above my head, knowing this was a fight I'd surely lose. Not only was the warrior much taller than I was, he looked to have the strength of two normal-sized men. Still, I had to do *something*. Before I saw a muscle twitch, the warrior whipped around and slammed the back of his fist against my face. I spun to the ground, landing heavily on my back. He placed a foot on my chest and leaned over to glare at me. I gasped, straining for breath under his weight. He was crushing me.

"The next time you attack me, you'd better see it through, because if you don't, I will kill you," he said sympathetically, as if explaining an important concept to a child. "Do you understand?"

I tried to speak but couldn't. I nodded several times. He smiled and removed his foot from my chest. Zanesh helped me sit up as the leader stepped back to confer with his companions. My head spun violently, and the urge to vomit came several times, but I held it back.

Sarai was crying, so Zanesh moved to comfort her. Just as my head cleared, I realized the large warrior was in front of me again.

"The gods of fortune have smiled on you," he said ceremoniously. "If it were up to me, we'd make sport with you right here and now then skin you alive and leave your flesh to the wild beasts. As you may have perceived, I do not care much for Nephites. My men, however, feel it would be more profitable to take you with us to Bashan and sell you to the slave trader. The girls will bring a very nice price indeed," he added with an evil glare.

The man then slowly squatted to face me directly. "But I can change my mind at any moment. If I'm provoked into doing so, I will not hesitate to enforce my will. Does the brave little Nephite understand?"

It was infuriating to have him talk down to me as if I were a small child, but I could do nothing about it. I nodded again and stared at the ground in an effort to control my anger.

He stood and turned to his men. "Bind them together, and make it secure. We still have a long way to go."

Sarai shrieked, "No, no, no!"

Before anyone could reach her, she bolted through a narrow gap in the banana trunks and into the jungle. The warriors moved to give chase, but the leader stopped them. An unnerving grin spread across his face. He stood motionless, listening to Sarai crash through the foliage. As the noise of her flight faded into the distance, he drew a long, bloodstained sword from its scabbard and examined it appreciatively.

"This ought to be enjoyable," he said to no one in particular. "Her fair-haired scalp will make a nice prize."

Zanesh jumped to her feet. "No, please. She's just a little girl. Please don't hurt her."

The large warrior glared at Zanesh as if offended by her plea. "Bind these two," he hissed. He continued to stare at her a moment longer, saying nothing.

"Please," Zanesh repeated.

He smirked. "And gag them too."

* * *

It was near dusk before the leader returned. Sarai was not with him. Zanesh broke into tears and buried her face in my shoulder. The Lamanite regarded us with a quick scowl then sat next to the other warriors. I couldn't hear much of what was said, but the fierce one was obviously angry. I then noticed he had no scalp with him. Had Sarai escaped? I prayed she had.

"No scalp," I softly mumbled through my gag.

Zanesh indicated with her eyes that she hoped the same thing. Neither of us wanted to accept that the little girl was murdered. I figured the fierce one would have flaunted Sarai's death in front of us, delighting in our sorrow. The fact that he hadn't *must* mean she'd escaped.

The warriors made quick preparations for the night, and Zanesh and I made ourselves as comfortable as possible. Thankfully, they removed our gags before falling asleep. The clouds broke after a brief rain, and I caught glimpses of the moon and stars as they drifted toward the western mountains.

Emotions welled within me as I remembered such nights with my father. My eyes burned with tears. Why did this have to happen? What evil had we committed to bring this misery upon us? None of it made any sense, and I was beginning to feel very alone again—almost as if God himself had turned his back on me.

Then Zanesh's hand rested gently on my shoulder. She said nothing, but the look in her eyes told me she understood my anguish. She gently wiped away a tear that traced its way down my cheek and brought her mouth close to my ear.

"We'll make it somehow," she whispered.

Then she kissed me lightly on the cheek and rested her head on my shoulder. Her words and her touch did wonders for my soul, but I wondered how much truth they really contained.

CHAPTER ELEVEN

THE TREK TO THE CITY of Bashan began miserably. The warriors had broken my staff in two and tossed it in their fire. It made walking over rough terrain very challenging. Zanesh helped out a bit, but the Lamanites didn't like us touching. Fortunately, my brace held up well, and each day my leg grew stronger and steadier.

Zanesh had it much worse than I did. She had to put up with incessant lewd comments and harassment from our captors. There was little I could do to help her. She seemed resilient enough, but I could tell her endurance was wearing thin.

I took note that our journey headed much farther to the northwest than the direction Korum's party was heading. The thought of never seeing Korum again was refreshing, but this new group of warriors seemed much worse, and exceedingly more dangerous.

On our second night, I overheard a heated conversation between the warriors. What they said answered many questions.

"I'd still like to know how the Nephite soldiers knew exactly where to wait for us," one warrior complained. He wore a bright turquoise earring that whipped frantically about as he spoke. "We were sorely beaten."

"I knew it was a mistake to attack smaller cities along the way," the leader growled. "Ammonihah was our main objective. We should have stuck to it. We could have been there a day sooner and avoided their army had we not delayed."

"Of course, Commander. But how did their army know we were *there*? We weren't close enough to Zarahemla for word to reach that quickly—even for a swift rider in good weather."

The commander pounded a fist on the ground. "Any fool could see that the direction we marched would lead us to Ammonihah and into Manti. Because of our attacks on the other villages, someone was bound to send a warning.

Zarahemla probably got word and knew they could corner us at the river Sidon. If we'd turned around immediately after sacking Ammonihah, we'd all be rich men. Now we have no gold, no cattle, no slaves, nothing!"

The second warrior pointed at Zanesh and me. "What about them?"

The leader snarled with frustration and walked away. I leaned close to Zanesh and whispered, "Did you hear that? These men attacked Ammonihah."

"They were probably the ones who destroyed our village, too," she whispered back.

I frowned. She was right. For all I knew, one of them could have murdered my family. If I'd hated these Lamanites before, it was nothing compared to how I felt now.

The second warrior spat into the fire and grumbled, "He thinks he's so wise."

"Be careful, my friend," the smaller warrior cautioned. "You know the commander's temper is short."

"What of it? When we get back and everyone finds out how miserably we were defeated, he'll be demoted to foot soldier, which is just wha—"

Suddenly there was a flash of steel and a slicing hiss through the air. The Lamanites were instantly on their feet, their swords drawn. The leader stood to one side, his sword dripping with fresh blood. The flickering, dim firelight gave him a look of pure malevolence. His eyes glowed fiercely from the band of black across his face. On the ground between the warriors lay a severed ear with a turquoise earring still attached.

Only then did the smitten warrior realize what had happened. He grabbed the side of his head and screamed.

"Until anyone *does* find out," the leader snarled, "I'm still in command here. Do you understand?" It was more a statement than a question, but the others responded anyway.

"Yes, Commander," the smaller warrior said, smacking his fist to his chest.

"Yes, Commander," the wounded Lamanite said through clenched teeth.

The leader sheathed his sword. "If either of you question that again, you'll lose more than an ear."

The wounded warrior sat as the smaller one treated his injury. The leader angrily stared into the flames and slowly shook his head. "Out of the entire Lamanite army, why was I chosen to lead such a band of incompetent fools?" he asked himself.

My mind was racing with what I had just heard. This large one, their leader, commanded the Lamanite army . . . he led the attack . . . and he was obviously a bloodthirsty man. What was it Chemish had said? That he left the group when he found out the army was being led by this man? Yes, that was it. The healer said he was a ruthless warrior named—

"Shem," I said aloud.

The commander slowly turned and stared at me. His eyebrows furrowed into a scowl as vicious as any I'd ever seen. "How do you know my name?"

I hadn't meant to say his name aloud. My mind was frenzied with the stories Chemish had told me about this brutal man. The healer's descriptions of the monster fit him perfectly. I was terrified, unable to utter a word.

Shem stepped around the fire. "I asked how you know me, boy."

I tried to respond, but my voice failed me. I quickly shook my head.

Before I could blink, Shem's sword was drawn and shoved under my chin. I could feel the wetness of the blood from the other warrior's ear on my skin. I heard Zanesh draw a fearful gasp. Shem raised the blade, forcing my head back until it would bend no more.

"I do not repeat myself often, Nephite. Answer me now or die."

"I—I just guessed," I croaked.

He raised an eyebrow and waited for more.

"I heard it from another Lamanite—when my village was attacked," I said. "But I had no idea it was you."

He lowered his blade slightly so I could breathe again. I swallowed hard and tried to gather my wits.

"Which village? Certainly not Ammonihah."

"N—no, sir. It was Oranihah, a village in the valley northeast of Ammonihah."

Shem regarded me for a moment then slid his sword into its scabbard. To the other men he said, "As I said, we should have left the smaller cities alone and concentrated on our main objective."

The smaller warrior stepped forward. "Commander. Korum's division went that way. They split off to attack Oranihah. You accomplished your mission and stripped the life from Ammonihah. *Your* attack was a complete success."

Shem laughed sarcastically. "You mindless fool. If had been successful, we'd have slaves and gold and would be singing songs of conquest. We were beaten."

"Yes, sir," the warrior said, bowing his head.

Then Shem's scowl deepened. "Wait. You're telling me that Korum wasn't with us at Ammonihah?"

"No, sir, he never rejoined us."

"Why not?"

The wounded warrior answered that. "He was ordered back, Commander."

"By whom?"

"By the master healer. He insisted on it."

Pure hatred spread across Shem's face. "Chemish?"

"Yes, Commander," both warriors said in unison.

Shem turned back to me. "Did that cowardly swine tell you about me?"

"Only that you were in command," I lied.

He grabbed the sides of his head and yelled ferociously. The sound echoed through the jungle like an evil spirit. His subordinates bowed low and held still.

"Can't anyone obey simple orders?" Shem screamed at the night sky. "Why am I surrounded by such incompetence?" He stomped off into the dark jungle, growling like a wild beast.

"You know who he is?" Zanesh whispered.

I nodded my head slowly. "From what Chemish told me, he's the worst of the worst—a warrior without conscience. It would be best if we spoke as little as possible when he's around . . . and don't ask for anything."

I didn't tell Zanesh what I really knew about Shem. I was certain it would break her spirit. Shem was even more horrifying than I had imagined. He was powerful and ruthless. He thought nothing of killing and seemed to delight in the sport of it. He was nothing short of evil, and we were in mortal danger every second we were with him.

CHAPTER TWELVE

THE FOLLOWING DAY DAWNED WITH torrential rain, forcing us to find alternate routes over treacherous rivers and around mudslides. Zanesh and I subsisted on what we could scavenge from the trail, most of which was nearly inedible. The warriors had pouches of salted meat and dried fruit, but they didn't share any with us. Being physically and emotionally drained, Zanesh and I both felt grateful when the city of Bashan appeared out of the evening mists—even though it meant the beginning of our slavery.

Bashan lay nestled in a swale between two generously forested hills. From what I could see in the hazy light, the city looked orderly and well kept. Shem led us directly to a small stone structure with barred windows. The warriors removed the lashings from our wrists and thrust us into the dark room. It was dank and smelly inside, but it got us out of the elements. Before closing the door, Shem leaned in.

"You two will enjoy your stay here," he sneered. "Good food, comfortable rooms, lively entertainment. Oh, and do not try to escape. Bashan is a small city, but it is ruled by *my* law. There's only one punishment for attempted escape."

He slammed the door and bolted it.

I immediately sensed we were not alone. The sounds of breathing came from all around the room, but it was too dark to see anyone. I pulled Zanesh close and held her tight. Her breathing tightened—I could tell she was afraid. I gently stroked her hair and shushed her.

"I am Jarem," I said softly, hoping those with us would prove friendly.

No one responded.

"This is my friend, Zanesh. We're from Oranihah."

"I've been there before," a gentle, older woman's voice commented from one corner. "Such a lovely village."

"It was. The Lamanites attacked and destroyed it about a week ago. We were captured while trying to escape."

Trembling, Zanesh held me tighter. The way she leaned against me revealed how exhausted she was.

"You must be very tired," the old woman's voice lamented.

"You are among friends here, Jarem," a male voice added.

I asked, "Are you all Nephite?"

"Mostly. Eliazar and Aminidab are Mulekite."

A weak shaft of light filtered through a barred opening in one wall, but it was still too dark to see our cellmates. At least they sounded friendly.

A bent old woman stepped into the vague light. "You look just awful. Come. Are you hungry?"

"Yes, yes," another voice joined in. "Sit and eat. We haven't got much, but we're willing to share. Please, do not be frightened."

I whispered to Zanesh, "Well?"

She shook her head.

"Thank you, but no," I said. "We're mostly just tired and would like to rest. Is there a dry spot in here?"

They all chuckled lightly. The happy sound seemed foreign in these bleak surroundings.

"Complete dryness is rare this time of year, but you're in luck," an old man said. "Some new straw was laid just this morning; you're welcome to the best of it."

The old woman led us to a small pile of straw into which Zanesh gratefully collapsed. Shaking with fatigue, she curled into a ball and closed her eyes.

"How many are you?" I asked.

"Seven in all. I'm Hannah." She then listed each as if I could see them. "This is Elsha. There's Lam, Boaz, Aminidab, and Sam. Eliazar is out on a task. We're all elderly persons who have lost most of our strength. Why they keep us as slaves I'll never understand."

"How long have you been here?"

"Some more than eight years or so. We're really not sure," a man stated from the darkness. "Why keep track of time when you have no hope?"

My heart ached for them. "I am sorry for you."

"Not as sorry as we are for you," the man said with a bitter chuckle.

I nodded. "Forgive us now, but we are very tired. I bid you a restful night."

"Of course," old Hannah said.

I gave a slight bow then snuggled next to Zanesh and wrapped my arm around her. She was still trembling.

"We're safe for now," I whispered. "I'm here with you, and I won't leave. Try to get some sleep."

Someone gently spread a tattered cloth over us.

"Thank you," I said softly.

After a few minutes of silence, Zanesh muttered, "Tell me again that we're going to be safe."

I held her tighter. "That would be a lie. But we're all right for now. That's all that matters. We can rest until tomorrow."

"And then?"

"I don't know. But I promise I'll do all I can to protect you, Zanesh."

She sighed deeply and soon stopped shaking.

The room was quiet and warm. The light rain continued to fall, pattering against the roof. My mind churned through one idea after another, desperately seeking a means of escape. But none came.

CHAPTER THIRTEEN

THE NEXT MORNING THE PRISON master took me and Zanesh to an area used for washing clothes and bathing. The man's name was Gad. He looked like he'd been weaned on hard work. And even though he was now weathered and gray, when he grabbed my wrist, I felt a good measure of strength left in his muscles.

After having me bathe, Gad painted a thin blue stripe across my forehead. "This marks you as a slave. All slaves wear them, regardless of their nationality. Don't try to wash it off. To be found without the stripe means immediate death."

"What if I sweat it off?"

He nodded. "I'll watch for that. But most slaves watch out for each other. If you see someone's stripe fading much, let them know. Or let me know, and I'll reapply the mark."

"Are you master over many slaves?"

"It depends. The slave market is usually a profitable one," he explained. "But there's been a lull in obtaining new slaves recently, which increases the price. That's good for me because young, healthy slaves like you and the girl will command a king's ransom."

I hated being referred to as merchandise, but I chose not to let it show. "Do we belong to you, then?" I asked.

"No, no. Most slaves in Bashan belong to Shem. I merely oversee them. But I get a cut of what they bring in, so the more work I get out of you, the better my pay."

Again, openly referring to me as a beast of burden gnawed at me. But Gad's stark frankness was refreshing. The man was completely without guile.

"Will Shem come back for us?"

"I wouldn't count on it," he said with a chuckle. "He numbers all of his slaves and has a keen mind for how much profit they should bring. Keep in mind, he hates Nephites more than any other. He's happy owning them, but only if he doesn't have to see them."

Because Gad was being so open, I decided to see if I could do likewise without reprimand. "*Shem* and *happy* are not words I would use together," I said with a snort.

Gad laughed heartily. "Quite so. But he trusts me, and that's all that matters."

"Trusts you how?"

"As I said, I oversee his slaves—their health, work skills, productivity. I also have leave to negotiate rates and punishments should a slave commit any crime against a Lamanite."

"And if a slave refuses to be a slave?" Zanesh broke in. I wasn't aware she'd been listening so closely.

His expression went flat. "I have authority to dispose of them."

"Dispose?" she asked.

He looked away and said, "I can sell them or have them killed."

"How about freeing them?" I ventured.

His head snapped back, and he gave me a hard look. "You belong to Shem. When you become unprofitable, you have no value to him. To him, the only good Nephite is a dead one. Always remember that and you may live to my age." Then, seeing the hatred in Zanesh's eyes, he added, "And do not even think about escape. By Shem's edict, the moment a slave is missing, one of those left behind is punished."

I hated the idea of causing any of my new friends any pain—especially Zanesh. If I did find a way to escape, I would have to take everyone with me. Currently, that seemed impossible.

*   *   *

Slavery became a routine of drudgery. I hated it. It didn't matter if the weather was good or bad; we were called out when a need arose. When we weren't working, Zanesh and I learned what we could from the others.

Lamanites from all around hired out Bashan slaves to perform various tasks: the men for heavy outdoor work; the women for household chores, especially among the wealthy class. We soon found out that slaves in general were not treated well. They were beasts of burden. To beat a slave was considered corrective action; to abuse one was personal entertainment; to kill one was forbidden but not necessarily a crime. All the killer had to do was pay the owner the slave's current value.

"Because we belong to Shem, no one dares kill us," old Boaz explained. "But since Shem hates all Nephites, he doesn't mind if we're beaten on a regular basis."

"That doesn't make sense," I argued. "If we're injured because of a beating, then we can't work, and that makes us unprofitable."

"Gad watches out for us, for the most part," he said with an undertone of sadness, "but there's only so much he can do. It's been worse lately because of the conversions."

"Conversions?"

He nodded. "Rumor has it that many Nephite slaves now live as freemen due to the success of missionaries in some areas. I met one slave passing through Bashan who said a very large Lamanite city to the west had all but converted to the Christian religion."

"That's wonderful news!" I exclaimed.

He shrugged. "I am Nephite, but I am not a Christian. I wonder if I would be freed if I didn't convert. Perhaps being a slave is my best option."

My gorge rose with bitterness. "Being free *has* to be better than being a slave."

He stood up and moved to the small window to gaze out at the nighttime drizzle. "I don't know. Perhaps. Here, I have a roof over my head and food to eat. Who's to say I would fare any better as a freeman in a foreign country? I could try to make it back to Nephite lands, but once a freed slave is outside the protection of a city, what's to stop a Lamanite from another city from forcing them back into slavery? There are no nationwide rules on slavery, Jarem. You may be free in one city but not in the next."

"But rules change. You said Lamanites are being converted, correct?"

He turned and favored me with a look of surrender. "You are a Nephite in Lamanite lands. That is something you can never change."

His defeatist attitude greatly depressed me. Boaz had all but given up. Perhaps he hadn't started that way. Perhaps he'd simply been a slave so long he'd lost all hope. I vowed not to let that happen to me.

When I shared those feelings with Zanesh, she agreed. "We must always keep our sights on eternal principles. Faith can get us through anything."

That was true. But what would happen if our faith dwindled?

*   *   *

Work came sporadically—mostly because of the weather. When we did work, it was without forewarning and could come at any time, day or night. Much to my surprise, we were rarely fettered. Security was lax because of Shem's unconditional threat over us. I had the opportunity to escape on several occasions. But the thought of being responsible for the suffering of one of the others—and of leaving Zanesh—always kept me from running.

Remarkably, none of the slaves complained much. It was as if they'd resolved to make the best of their hopeless circumstance. I found it inspiring. If anyone had a right to complain, they did. Zanesh and I committed to do the same—at least until an undeniable opportunity to change our circumstances presented itself.

Despite her resolve, Zanesh fought severe despair those first few weeks. I wasn't much better off, but I kept my mind busy by learning, my muscles strong by working hard, and my emotions in check by concentrating on helping my friends. Like the others, I learned to tolerate an intolerable situation.

Our jail was little more than a converted stable. We were to sweep out all the old straw and were given fresh straw every full moon. Our waste was kept in a covered bucket that was emptied twice daily.

"The Lamanites keep their livestock in better conditions than those in which they keep us," Elsha said with a bitter chuckle. "And their horses live in palaces."

Fortunately, Gad allowed us to bathe weekly. When someone had finished a particularly filthy task, they were allowed to wash off immediately. Unfortunately, not everyone took advantage of that allowance.

Our food was allotted according to our workload. When times were slow, we got scraps that most dogs would turn away from. There was always a serving of maize and taro, but fresh fruit and meat were a rarity.

Because of my strength, the physically demanding tasks became mine. Ditch digging seemed a constant need because of the frequent rains in the area. Felling trees, moving rocks, and tending herds were tasks I was often hired for. But road construction was perhaps my most frequent task. The Lamanites laid out meandering highways made of crushed rock over channeled beds of sand. The design was simple and effective but was prone to washing out after heavy rain storms. The Nephite style of roadbuilding was much better, but I rarely made suggestions for improvement. It was not my place, nor did I want to help them improve.

Zanesh was frequently given household tasks like cleaning, washing, food preparation, and serving. Even child-rearing. Because of her caring nature, many high-ranking Lamanite mothers trusted her to tend their children while they attended parties and other events. It was not unusual for the same master to request either of us several times in the same month.

I did my best to work hard and without complaint, and I tried never to be a threat. I figured the more the Lamanites trusted me, the more tolerant they'd be. Zanesh followed my example and quickly proved to be of exceptional value. We never knew how long we'd be at any particular assignment; that was determined by whoever purchased our labor. But each time we left, we would say goodbye, share a brief hug, and swear to return as soon as possible—as if we had any control over that promise. It was one way of dealing with the anxiety of separation in this foreign, hostile land.

The others in the prison hired out occasionally, but only for short periods of time, and usually for menial and filthy tasks. Poor old Eliazar was repeatedly hired to clean the tapir corrals—a particularly unpleasant and smelly task. The small man was never able to completely wash the stench from his skin or clothing. It became sort of a game to see who could first smell Eliazar approaching before he came through the prison door.

For the most part, I enjoyed the heavy labor. My leg had healed nicely. The harder I labored, the better food I was given, and I grew strong with the work. Within a few months, my shoulders broadened and my arms thickened. I grew as powerful as any man, though I still thought of myself as quite young. One day as I rinsed off, I noticed Zanesh's eyes lingering on my chest and thought perhaps I'd missed a spot.

"What are you staring at?" I asked, brushing at my chest and stomach.

"Oh—um—nothing," she said as if I'd caught her doing something wrong.

"Do I have something on my chest?"

"No. Well, yes. But it's nothing you need to worry about." Her eyes crinkled with a mischievous delight before she returned to her mending.

* * *

Returning from a weeklong road project, Gad promised me a few days of rest. The sight of our prison was almost gratifying—mostly because I knew Zanesh was there. But all was not well. As soon as I entered the converted stable, the others told me a wealthy family had hired Zanesh as a housekeeper. I curled into my corner, not knowing when, or even if, she would return.

Early the next morning, the prison door opened and Gad called my name. The morning sunlight was harsh, and I had to squint because of it as I exited the dark prison.

"He'll do," I heard a gravelly voice say.

Without further comment or instruction, I found I was a part of a small group of Lamanites and one other Nephite heading into the jungle. With us came several packhorses and bags stuffed with supplies.

"Where are we headed?" I asked the Lamanite next to me.

"To work," was his gruff reply.

Because of the abundance of supplies, I guessed we'd be involved in a fairly complex project—one that would take a number of days to complete.

It ended up being longer. Much longer.

CHAPTER FOURTEEN

OUR DESTINATION WAS A DEEP gorge nestled in the mountains some five days' journey from Bashan. During the trek, I had a lot of time to think about my family again. Oh, how my heart ached for them! And how my hatred rose toward my captors. I also thought a lot about Zanesh. I already missed her and wondered if she missed me. As a slave, there was little I could offer her beyond consolation when things became unbearable. I prayed she would be watched over and comforted in my absence—however long that proved to be.

When we reached the gorge, two Lamanite work parties were already there organizing materials—one on each side of the gorge. Several Nephite slaves were present, but we weren't allowed to speak much. My group made camp on the south side of the gorge before we joined the work party. Apparently we were going to build a bridge.

The distance to the other side was roughly two hundred cubits. A powerfully built Lamanite stepped to the edge of the gorge, nocked an arrow in his bow, and let it fly with a loud *thwang*. The arrow had a thin line attached, which fed from a generous coil at his feet. The arrow flew well but missed the rim and stuck in the gorge wall just out of reach. The jeering from the north side was rude and belittling, but the man took it good-naturedly. He reeled in the arrow and nocked it a second time. Angling it higher, he let it fly. This one flew perfectly and nearly missed hitting a man on the far side.

We attached a thicker line to the thinner one for the north group to haul across the chasm. Now it was the north group's turn. A stout Lamanite stepped to the edge of the gorge and let fly his arrow—but his barely made three-quarters of the distance. Not surprisingly, a chorus of taunts and insults erupted from our Lamanites. It was all in good humor, but the construction foreman wasn't smiling. He never did. He was an extremely heavyset man who did very little work and who complained constantly. His name was Joath. He liked to strut around talking as if he could not only build the bridge singlehandedly but do so with better skill and in less time. The only thing I saw foreman Joath excel at was eating double rations at mealtime and drinking enough wine to float a barge.

It took the north group three tries to make the distance with an arrow. Soon we had two braids of rope spanning the gorge, each about the thickness of a man's thigh. The rope was made from fibrous hemp in an interlacing weave that was flexible as well as strong. These main lines were secured atop four massive tree trunks, which stood nearly ten cubits tall. They'd been anchored deep a few paces from each rim of the gorge—two on either side. The crews had done that work some time before our arrival. The trailing ends of the main ropes threading over the trunk tops were angled down and secured to large boulders behind each trunk. By the time these tasks were finished, the sun was low on the horizon. We stopped work and prepared for the night.

The next two days, a third and fourth main rope were suspended at ground level below the first two. These base ropes were a size thicker than the top ropes, and for good reason. The idea was to place planks across the lower ropes to create a walkway. To add stability and strength, numerous balustrades of thinner rope would eventually attach the bottom ropes to the top ones. In their present state, however, the base ropes bobbed and swayed with every little breeze, and the gorge had a constant wind blowing down it.

After the four main ropes were in place, both parties spent several days collecting additional materials to construct the walkway planks and balustrade ropes. A few of the slaves seemed very adept at braiding rope from hemp and vines. I couldn't seem to get the hang of it, so instead, I was put to cutting and shaping planks for the walkway. It involved using a hammer and wedge to split logs into workable lengths. We'd then shave these down using an adz and various rasps to fashion the ideal width and thickness of each plank. Lastly, holes were bored at each end to allow for ties to lash them to the base ropes. It was exceedingly tedious work, but as long as I worked as hard as the others, I was left alone.

One drawback to such routine labor was that my mind wandered a lot. I tried to focus on learning the lay of the land, on good times with my family, on the teachings I'd received from church leaders. But invariably my thoughts always drifted back to Zanesh. Was she safe? Was she happy? Each time I asked myself those questions, I scoffed. How could any slave ever be happy? I certainly wasn't.

One day I awoke in a particularly foul mood. I went about my business, hating everyone and everything. Then I overheard one of the Nephites comment, "This is bad, but it could be worse," and I remembered my father saying that happiness was a state of mind.

"You should never allow your situation to determine your happiness," he had counseled. "It's how you *respond* to your situation that determines your joy or sorrow. You see, my son, happiness is a choice, not a result."

The more I pondered his words, the more sense they made. If I *chose* to find joy in my work, to feel a sense of satisfaction in accomplishment, then I could be happy. But no matter how hard I tried, my emotions always fell short. I was a slave—a beast of burden for mean and relentless taskmasters. I couldn't run away because it would cause others to suffer. I was stuck in a situation that offered zero happiness. Even so, I prayed that somehow Zanesh could be happy. And if not happy, at least safe.

It would take a full month to complete all the planks and ropes we'd need. For the most part, I remained content in my work. But the pace was never fast enough for our foreman. He ridiculed us continually and occasionally whipped us for no reason. Joath was an exceptionally cruel and short-tempered man who delighted in the misery of others.

The following day, I would learn just how cruel he could be.

CHAPTER FIFTEEN

WITH ENOUGH MATERIALS READY, WE prepared to secure the planks between each of the base ropes to create the walkway. The task was extremely dangerous because of the instability caused by the constant wind whipping down the gorge. I assumed one of the Nephite slaves would be chosen to begin the assembly, but I was wrong.

Ever since we'd arrived, I'd witnessed foreman Joath repeatedly harass a young Lamanite who was small of frame and slow of speech. I didn't know how old the young man was, but I guessed he was somewhere in his thirteenth year. His name was Abinikek, but Joath called him "Monkey Boy," probably because his arms were long and spindly like a monkey's. Abinikek didn't wear the blue stripe of a slave, but he was certainly treated like one.

That morning Joath had everyone gather at the rim of the gorge. He ranted for an hour about how long it'd taken to do such a simple project.

"We're several days behind!" he roared. "It's a disgrace. Every one of you needs to double his efforts, or there will be serious consequences to be paid." He then pointed to the young Lamanite. "You. Monkey Boy. Take the first plank out to the center of the span and secure it."

I frowned in confusion. Young Abinikek blanched white with fear. Sound reasoning decreed that we should start attaching planks at the rim, where it was more stable, then slowly work out to the center. A murmur passed through the gathered crowd. I guessed everyone had the same thought. But I also wondered why Joath didn't make one of the Nephite slaves attempt the dangerous task.

"I—I don't think I c-can," Abinikek said in a halting voice.

"I—I don't think I c-can," the foreman echoed in a mocking, high tone. He stepped up to the boy and slapped him hard. "I don't care what you think. I gave you an order. Now do it."

The young man timidly selected a thin, narrow plank of wood. Joath cursed and picked up a thick, heavy plank. "It needs to be strong enough to secure the base ropes, you fool. Use this one."

A few of the Lamanites chuckled at the scene; others were as speechless as I was. Abinikek didn't move. The foreman yanked the small plank from Abinikek's frail hands and tossed it over the edge of the gorge. He then shoved the large plank against the young man's chest. The boy could barely balance it with both hands. There was no way he'd be able to carry it out to the center of the span while hanging on to the swaying ropes. Glancing at the swaying base ropes, Abinikek's knees faltered, and tears brimmed in his eyes. Joath seemed to delight in the fear he caused.

I had never understood why the strong felt it necessary to pick on the weak. Did it make them feel stronger? Or was it a means of hiding some inner weakness they harbored?

"Well, Monkey Boy?" the foreman demanded. "What are you waiting for?"

The young man wiped his eyes, set his jaw, and thrust out his shallow chest. If he was trying to look confident, it didn't work. He looked like a willow bough pretending to be the trunk of a mighty kapok. The Lamanites hooted with delight. A few of them openly made bets on how far he'd get before he fell. Even some of the Nephite slaves laughed at the spindly young Lamanite.

I felt myself growing angry. *Calm down, Jarem*, I warned myself. *This isn't your affair.*

Abinikek cast a desperate glance toward the work party, as if seeking deliverance. All he got was more jeering and laughter. Dragging the plank to the base ropes, he looked down the deep chasm. Wind tousled his hair and pushed against the plank, but he didn't back away. He was certainly trying to be brave. I admired him for that. But I questioned just how far he'd get before losing his grip and plunging to his death. His arms were painfully thin and his ribs showed through his back. It was almost as if muscle didn't know *how* to grow on his bony frame.

He glanced around and spotted a length of rope. He tied one end through the holes at one end of the large plank and then secured it to his back, thus freeing his hands. Straddling one of the base ropes, he eased his way out over the gorge. The top rope was too high for him to reach at the bridgehead, so he was forced to scoot along the base rope in a painfully slow shuffle. Just a few paces out, the base rope became less steady and the young man paused several times to steel his nerves. His entire body trembled mercilessly. To make matters worse, the wind had picked up and pushed against the plank on his back as if it were a sail.

"Stop stalling, Monkey Boy!" Joath yelled. "You're taking too long."

"Someone's got to help him," I hissed through my teeth.

Time seemed to stand still as we watched the boy move at less than a snail's pace. And yet no one moved to help. It was as if they *wanted* him to fall.

Anger boiling over, I took a step toward the bridge—but one of the Nephites grabbed my shoulder, stopping me. He flashed me a look not to interfere. I drew a deep breath and again tried to calm down.

It took nearly an hour for the young Lamanite to reach the center of the span. His trembling was now full-on shaking. He had no stability at all, and he swayed to and fro with every gust of wind. Luckily, at that distance the top ropes arched down to where he could reach them. He grabbed a coil in the top rope and rested.

"Stop stalling!" Joath yelled.

Abinikek nodded and tried to stand twice, but his legs trembled so violently he couldn't find footing. Sitting with his face buried against his shoulder, he made no further effort to stand.

I knew immediately he was in trouble. Easing toward the edge of the gorge, I could see the young man was crying. Still, no one moved to help.

Furious at the delay, Joath hurled venomous curses and threats at him. Others in the crowd joined in. The foreman grabbed a club and began pounding it against the lower rope. "Get moving, you worthless boy!"

But Abinikek didn't move. He couldn't.

Joath stopped yelling just long enough to grab a bow and arrow. "Get moving, or you'll meet your end," he hollered.

The young man remained frozen.

"So be it," Joath growled before launching an arrow. Luckily, he was a terrible shot. The arrow missed Abinikek with room to spare. The foreman nocked another arrow and took aim.

My fists clenched in rage; my breath burned in my throat. "Come on," I hissed, encouraging both the young Lamanite and myself to get moving.

Thwang! The arrow flew directly at Abinikek, but a sudden gust of wind spun him at the last moment, and the arrow lodged in the plank on his back with a solid *thunk.*

Abinikek let out a cry of shock. The look in his eyes revealed utter terror. His expression confirmed that he knew he was about to die. It was only a matter of minutes.

I came to the same conclusion. I also knew one of the Nephite slaves would be commanded to finish the task when the young Lamanite fell. And as I was the youngest and strongest among us, I was sure to be picked . . . so why delay it?

CHAPTER SIXTEEN

I WALKED PAST FOREMAN JOATH without saying a word, grabbed a plank of equal size to the one Abinikek had, strapped the plank to my back, looped a coil of lashing vine over my shoulder, and moved to the bridgehead.

"What do you think you're doing?" Joath snapped at me.

"Building a bridge," I said before stepping onto the base rope opposite the one Abinikek had chosen. Joath didn't try to stop me.

The ropes swung fearfully but, luckily, I could reach the top ropes for stability. Moving forward, hand over hand, foot past foot, I discovered there was actually a rhythm to the swaying. I moved *with* the motions instead of *against* them and made very good progress. I was scared, but I was more afraid for the young man ahead of me.

I reached Abinikek in only a few minutes. The young Lamanite sat with his legs wrapped tightly around the base rope and one arm gripping the upper rope.

"Don't worry, my friend," I said across the gap. "Once we get one plank in place the ropes will steady."

With eyes red from tears and wide from fright, he stared at me in disbelief.

"I'll do most of the work, but I will need your help." I didn't phrase my statement as a question. It was better to simply say what needed to be done and then do it.

I unlashed the plank from my back and held it between my legs. With one hand, I managed to thread some lashing vine through one of the end holes and tie it off. I cut off a generous length of vine using Abinikek's knife then turned the plank over, standing it on end, and tied more vine through the opposite end. Securing an end to the base rope on which I stood proved difficult, but I was able to wrap just enough lashing to prevent it from falling. The far end of the plank rested against the inside of the top rope.

"This is where I'll need your help," I said to Abinikek. "I'm going to lower this plank slowly to your side. When it touches, I'll need you to lash it to the base rope."

Abinikek didn't answer. He continued to stare at me with terror-filled eyes.

I smiled. "My friend, you've already made it to the middle of the bridge. That was the hard part. This next task should prove easy."

He nodded almost imperceptibly.

Feeding the vine out bit by bit, I slowly lowered the plank to Abinikek's side. Unfortunately, the swaying base ropes made it land right behind him. If the ropes swayed any farther before the plank was secured, it would drop and we'd have to start over.

"Now listen. You need to lash your end to the base rope. We can't let it fall."

"I—" He swallowed hard and fought to control his breathing. "I c-can't move."

"Yes, you can. Look, I can't do this alone, and neither can you. But we can if we work together. Now, if you just turn around a bit, you can wrap the vine around the board rope a few times. That'll keep it from falling off, and then I can come over and secure it."

He drew in a sharp, shuddering gasp but didn't move.

"You can do it. I have faith in you."

Slowly, he shifted around and grabbed for the vine dangling on the far side of the base rope. He got it on the second try. Whipping the vine around, he looped it around the board three times.

"Excellent. Now pull it tight. That's good. Thank you. Now hold it tight until I come over. Um," I paused. "You might not want to watch this," I said with another smile.

He immediately closed his eyes.

Timing the bounce and sway of the base ropes, I slid my body across the plank, facedown. With both ends only slightly secured, it was a precarious situation. If the lashing on either of the base ropes loosened, the plank would drop and I'd plummet to my death. Luckily, I made it without incident. Sitting beside Abinikek, I quickly tightened the lashing then began to loosen the vine holding his plank to his back. He whimpered at my tugging.

"It's all right. I almost got it. You just hold on tight."

I removed his plank and laid it across the gap next to mine. I lashed the end at my lap then crawled across my secured plank to lash the far end. Once both planks were in place, the swaying and bobbing diminished considerably.

"You can open your eyes now," I said, crawling back across to him.

The young man was still trembling with fright, but seeing my success, he had a glimmer of salvation in his eyes.

"Here. Let me help you turn around and sit on the planks. It'll feel much safer."

Abinikek moved painfully slowly but eventually let go of the upper rope and fell on the planks. He was breathing like he'd just run from Zarahemla to Manti. I gently patted his back and coaxed him to sit up. It took a few minutes, but he eventually was able to relax and even dangled his legs over the edge of the planks like I did.

"My name is Jarem."

"I'm Abinikek," he said.

"Yes, I've heard your name before, but we've never had a chance to speak. You're a brave man, Abinikek. Braver than that fatted ox back there," I said, nodding toward Joath. It was dangerous to openly insult one Lamanite in front of another, but I felt this young man needed a friend, and I was willing to take the risk to become one.

Abinikek smiled while averting his eyes. "Do you really think so?"

"Oh yes. Joath would never come out here," I said softly. "I doubt this bridge will hold him even when it's finished."

Abinikek laughed then covered his mouth.

"Listen, I'll make a pact with you," I said, patting him on the knee. "Let's secure the top ropes to these planks, then we'll work our way to the north side. Joath won't be able to follow until this bridge is completed, and by then he'll have lost interest in calling you names."

He glanced at the frothy river and jagged rocks a great distance below and shook his head. "I can't do it, Jarem."

"No, you can't; not alone, anyway. But together . . ." I didn't finish the sentence and instead got up and reached for the upper rope. I stood there fighting for balance but smiled at Abinikek.

"You really think I can?" he asked.

"I wouldn't be out here if I didn't. Now let's finish this and get to the other side."

Abinikek smiled an unsure, fearful smile, but his smile also contained enough confidence that I knew he'd go through with it.

We took a few more minutes lashing our remaining vines over the top ropes and around the bottom ones. It was only a temporary stay, but it too added stability to the infant bridge. I tied a final length of vine around Abinikek's waist and then around mine. We worked our way to the far side, making pretty good time. We could hear Joath yelling at us, but the wind made it difficult to understand him. When we reached the north cliff, we collapsed on an embankment of grass.

A few Lamanites patted Abinikek on the shoulder; one offered him a flask. He took a deep swig—then spit it out, hacking and coughing. He handed it to me. I sniffed the open spout and flinched. It was very strong drink—stronger than any wine I'd ever smelled. I shook my head and handed it back. A fierce-looking Lamanite came up, slapped Abinikek on the back, and said, "Well done, skinny boy."

The offensive name didn't seem to bother my new friend. We both believed he'd just done something no one else dared do.

When the excitement waned, we found a barrel of water and drank deeply. Wiping his mouth, Abinikek turned to me with a kind smile. "Thank you, Jarem."

"It's nothing," I said with a shrug. "You probably would have done it after a while. I just helped."

"No. I saw what you did. You risked your life to help me—without being asked to do so. You saved my life. And I swear I will repay you somehow."

CHAPTER SEVENTEEN

THE REST OF THE DAY was spent fastening the foot planks, beginning at each end of the bridge. Again I wondered why they hadn't done that in the first place. I guessed Joath simply wanted to abuse his authority.

When night came, it started raining again. Instead of returning to the south camp, I was put in a tent with four other slaves in the north camp. Once there, they fed us a small ration of tasteless pottage. The other slaves were pensive, choosing to keep to themselves rather than talk. Since I was exhausted, I followed suit.

About midway through the night, Abinikek crept into our tent. The rain was still heavy, and I didn't hear him until he was right next to me. He nudged me awake and motioned for me to be quiet. If the other slaves were aware of his presence, they didn't make it known.

In the dim light, Abinikek handed me a small bag. I went to speak, but he again motioned for me to be silent.

"No. Just listen," he whispered. "There's food in the bag; good food. Eat and refresh your strength so you can escape. I'll show you which direction to go."

The thought of disappearing into the jungle was always on my mind, but I hadn't seriously considered it in a while. I shook my head and began to eat the fresh fruit and dried meat in the bag.

"What about me?" one of the other Nephites whispered urgently.

"Yes," said another. "You must show us where to escape, or we'll all suffer when he leaves."

"They speak the truth," I whispered to Abinikek. "If I go, the others will suffer for it, including my friends in Bashan. I appreciate what you're risking, but I cannot leave."

At first the young Lamanite didn't respond. The darkness masked his face, but I had little doubt it held a look of disbelief. He pointed to the others. "You would remain a slave for them—people you hardly know? Why?"

I shrugged. "I believe everyone is my brother—even you, Abinikek. I'd be miserable knowing that my escape caused my brothers to suffer. I couldn't live with that on my conscience."

Abinikek considered my words, nodded, and quietly left our tent.

After a time, one of the slaves whispered, "You are very brave, Jarem, and very foolish. It is good to think of others, but you are young and have an entire life before you. Do you wish to spend it in slavery forever?"

"Forever is a long time," I replied. "I don't plan on being captive all that time. When the moment is right, I'll escape. For now, I must be patient. We all must be patient. Remember, our forefathers were slaves under the Egyptians for four hundred years before they were delivered."

"May you live that long, young brother," an older Nephite whispered. "You have the wisdom of one thrice your age. I hope you live to share it."

I thanked him and lay back, staring at the top of the tent. I truly did pray I'd find a way to escape and live to a ripe old age. I had to be patient, had to wait for just the right time. But I also had to admit that I was growing restless. I'd already been gone from Bashan several weeks. I had no idea how much longer I'd be kept away. Had conditions there worsened since my absence? Would my friends still be there when I returned? What if I never returned?

I rolled to my knees and prayed for Zanesh's safety and comfort and for the well-being of my friends. I prayed for guidance and understanding. I didn't know why I was suffering the things I was suffering. I couldn't tell if it was a test or perhaps simply unfortunate happenstance. My parents had said that life was like that sometimes—an unpredictable route fashioned by good and bad experiences.

"Remember that whatever you're going through, someone else is going through even worse," my mother had been fond of saying.

True, my slavery was hard and shameful. But I was still alive. What about Zanesh? Was she now experiencing something vile and demeaning? I had no way of knowing. But I did have faith to trust in God. If He had a plan for me, it was up to me to follow it. I just wished I had a better idea of what that plan was.

CHAPTER EIGHTEEN

WORK ON THE BRIDGE WAS drawing to an end. Once all the foot planks were in place and the top ropes were attached to the lower walkway, we set about stabilizing it with anchors on each side of the gorge using large stones hauled from a quarry two days' trek away. When we finished, the bridge was very secure. I felt proud of my part in its construction—even as a slave.

Just as we were packing our tools and remaining materials, Joath received orders to build a second bridge five days' journey from the first bridge. Word was sent back to prison master Gad in Bashan that I would be used for this second project as well. My heart sank. That meant it'd be much longer before I saw Zanesh again.

Steeling my courage, I asked Joath, "May I send word back to my friends that I am well?"

"No," he snapped. Then, in a moment of unusual compassion, he added, "I have purchased your time for this next project. That alone will indicate you're still alive."

I nodded, accepting the small favor, and set my mind to not being depressed. I determined that I would work even harder at the second site, focusing on the task at hand, if only to help the time pass quicker.

* * *

Days became weeks, weeks became months. We spent a large amount of time scouring the jungle for more materials and an equal amount of time preparing those materials for use on the new bridge. Thankfully, the time passed quickly with the hard work and my conversations with Abinikek. We became fast friends. He regularly brought me fresh fruit, bread, and meat, some of which I ate, but most of which I shared with the other Nephites.

"You are very generous," Abinikek said to me one evening. "You could have so much more if you didn't always give it away."

"You are the one being generous," I remarked. "If you didn't supply me with fresh food, I could not give it away."

"Yes. But my people believe a gift is something to treasure for one's self. It is a sign of favor from the gods. The more possessions you have, the better person you are."

I considered that for a moment. "So, if a man has a large grove of bananas, larger than his neighbor's or anyone else's in the village, does that make him a good man?"

"Of course," he said as if I'd asked a foolish question.

"You can judge him to be of good character and merit by what he possesses?"

"Yes."

"I see. Then what if the rains come—like those we've had this past week— and it breaks every tree in his grove? Is he no longer a good man?"

He frowned. "Well . . . it makes him a poorer man."

"True, but is he no longer a *good* man? Does the loss of his grove mean he can no longer help a friend build a fence or give comfort to the sick?"

"Well, no."

"Ah. So, then, judging a man by how much he owns isn't really a good measure of his character, is it?"

He frowned even more. "But it shows how successful he is."

"Am I successful because I receive gifts from you?"

"Yes. It shows you have earned a reward."

"Is that why you give them to me—because I earned them?"

He ducked his head. "No. I give them to you because you are my friend."

"Just as you have proven to be my good friend." I gripped his shoulder warmly. "In that regard I *am* truly successful. And that is why I share all that I have. As a slave, I don't have much; but what I do have, I willingly give to those who have nothing. That way, we're all happier."

"And that makes you a good man," he said with a warm smile. "I hope someday to be as good."

"You already are, my brother."

Abinikek and I continued to have many wonderful conversations during the building of the second bridge—mostly because we were allowed to work side by side. I believe it was due to our shared achievement over the first gorge. Abinikek had proven himself to the other Lamanites. True, I may have helped, but the young Lamanite had completed a task no one else would have. That made him a man. Consequently, Joath never again harassed him; never again called him Monkey Boy. No one did.

As newfound brothers, we shared everything, including stories of our youth. We discovered we had many things in common: boyhood adventures, times of sorrow and happiness, and dreams we still entertained.

"I've always wanted to be a great hunter like my father," I confessed during a break in our labors.

His eyes lit up. "I've always wanted that too. I wish my father had named me Nimrod, after the great hunter of old."

"I remember stories of Nimrod," I said, returning his enthusiasm. "So why did they name you Abinikek?"

"It means 'father's pride.' I've always strived to live up to my name, but because I'm small of frame, I don't think he is very proud."

"Has he said as much?"

He hung his head. "Sometimes you hear words that aren't spoken."

I patted his shoulder. "After what you did on the first bridge, I think every man here has a new measure of respect for you. Word will get back to your father. When it does, I know he'll be very proud."

To change the mood, I told Abinikek of the many explorations I'd made to unknown lands. When he joined in with like adventures of his own, an idea came to me. I don't know why I hadn't thought of it before. I asked him to describe in great detail the roads, rivers, and communities he knew. As he did, I painted detailed mental pictures, memorizing as best I could the terrain of these Lamanite lands. I learned of cities and villages, highways and trails, mountains, and canyons. To me, such information was priceless. From Abinikek's limited experience, I learned of several possible routes of escape without ever having seen them.

While I loved talking of such things, the conversations were difficult for me. The memories of what his people had done to my family and my village still haunted me. But I was determined to live the lesson I'd shared with Abinikek. A man should be judged by his character, not his circumstances or his ancestry. As time passed, the bitterness of my sorrow became easier to swallow.

A few days later, Abinikek revealed his desire to join one of the secret societies of his people. I couldn't help but laugh.

"Are you mocking me?" he asked.

"No—I'm laughing at myself. Just before I was captured, I too had joined a secret society: the Brotherhood of the Leopard."

Abinikek's eyes grew large. "That sounds so fierce."

"It sounds so foolish! And it was. I don't even know why I joined. I guess I just wanted to fit in." I parted my tunic and showed him the scars on my belly. "I had to make these myself using an old leopard's paw." When his eyes widened even more, I continued. "Don't be astonished. Only a fool is proud of his own folly."

"I tried to join an adventurous group of boys not long ago too," he said with averted eyes.

"Tried to?"

He nodded.

"What was it called?"

"Promise not to laugh?"

"Yes."

"Satan's Monkeys."

I broke my promise as I rolled on the ground, laughing uncontrollably. Abinikek tried to look angry, but he ended up laughing with me. "It was even more foolhardy than it sounds," he said. "I had to eat twenty bananas, drink a bottle of new wine, then catch a baby monkey and bring it to the secret cave."

Now tears were pouring from my eyes.

"I ended up spending more time purging my belly in the bushes than chasing monkeys. I was terribly sick. When my bowels finally settled, I was so exhausted that I just spent the night in a tree. I wrapped some vines around myself and fell asleep. The next day I awoke with a small infant monkey curled up against my neck and shoulder. I don't know how it got there."

"If it was a dark night, it may have thought you were another monkey," I ventured.

"Maybe. But it was what I'd been sent to catch, so I grabbed it," he said, shaking his head. "I thought I'd go deaf from its screeching. I thought it was just crying to be released, but it was really calling for help. Even before I got out of the tree, I was surrounded by monkeys screaming and screeching and throwing things. As soon as I got to the ground, the males in the troop jumped on me, scratching and biting and shrieking. I tried to shake them off, but I couldn't, so I ran straight for the village wearing this coat of angry monkeys."

Catching my breath, I managed to say, "Were you harmed?"

"Not much. My village gathered around and just laughed. It finally occurred to me to give the baby monkey back; so I did, and all the monkeys fled back into the jungle. I was bleeding and humiliated—all for a chance to join a group of boys who weren't even my friends in the first place. Anyway, word of my misfortune spread from village to village, and soon everyone was calling me Monkey Boy."

I had to agree the name fit. My Brotherhood of the Leopard experience paled in comparison to his, and for that I was truly grateful.

CHAPTER NINETEEN

IT TOOK ANOTHER THREE MONTHS to complete the second bridge. Fortunately, we'd entered the dry season, so the work was less arduous. Even so, because this was a repeat of the task we'd just completed, the time did not pass as quickly as I'd hoped. The longer I was away from Zanesh, the more I worried about her. I prayed nightly for her protection . . . and for my own.

On the last morning of the project, Abinikek showed up early to our tent. He looked like he hadn't slept well. Sorrow weighed heavily on his face.

"Good morning, my friend—" I began, but he cut me off with a raised hand.

He swallowed several times as tears shimmered in his eyes. "Jarem, you've been a better friend to me than anyone else in my whole life," he said softly. "Each time I offered to help you escape, I secretly hoped you'd refuse, because I didn't want to see you go. Now you are returning to Bashan, and I am moving on to a new task." He held out a small leather pouch. "Take this."

"What is it?"

"A trinket. I owe you so much more, but it is all I have."

"Abinikek, my brother. You owe me nothing."

"I owe you my life. Please do not refuse this time."

I placed a hand on his shoulder and touched my forehead to his. "Then I accept."

He choked back a sob and stepped away. "I hope that this may someday help to buy your freedom. It is the least I can do for the best friend I have ever had. You are the best man I've ever known."

I smiled and took the pouch. I wanted to say something in return, but my voice caught in my throat. He grabbed my shoulders firmly then turned abruptly and walked away. A strange mix of feelings washed through me. I was sad to see him leave, and yet I was very glad to be going home to Bashan. I'd had enough of bridge building.

I reconsidered and scoffed. *Home?* I was going back to prison, not home. Whatever Abinikek's future held, it *had* to be better than slavery. I tucked the pouch inside my tunic and got ready to leave. Then something else caused me to pause. It was something he'd just said. *You are the best man I've ever known.* A man. I still thought of myself as quite young. True, I'd been away from Oranihah for over a year now. But had I truly become a man in that short amount of time? What was the exact point at which a boy crossed into manhood? Was it age? Was it experience? Or was it a combination of the two? What, in Abinikek's eyes, made me a man?

I offered brief farewells to the other Nephites. They were heading to another city. I'd developed friendships with them too, but none to the extent of my friendship with Abinikek. Deep in thought, I mindlessly hitched a large pack on my back and got in line for the trek to Bashan. I had no idea how long the trip would take, but that seemed unimportant just then. My thoughts had turned to Zanesh. Had she changed too? Would she see the change in me? Would she approve?

"You there. Slave Jarem. What are you doing?"

Snapping from my reflections, I looked at the man speaking to me. It was Joath. "Yes, master builder?"

"What do you think you're doing—showing off again?"

I had no clue what he was talking about. His face looked stern—but with a touch of humor.

"We all know you're as strong as a horse. But that doesn't mean you have to carry their packs."

The group of Lamanites around him broke into laughter. It was only then that I noticed I had donned one of the horse's packs. I didn't know how I'd gotten it onto my back, but that didn't matter. It was there, making me look like a fool.

I shrugged off the pack and slung it onto a horse. I then donned one meant for slaves and tightened the straps.

Was that what Abinikek had seen as a sign of manhood? My strength?

* * *

The return to Bashan was long and tiring. My thoughts centered on Zanesh. Was she healthy? Was she happy? Was she even still there? The questions raged inside me until I felt ready to burst.

The first evening of our return trek, we camped in a grassy clearing some distance from the trail. My feet were fettered, but it wasn't necessary. Given the chance, I would have run to the prison in Bashan.

The small pouch Abinikek had given me remained tucked inside my tunic. He had mentioned that it contained something of value; something which could help buy my freedom. Because of that, I felt impressed to keep it hidden from my captors, though I had no idea what it could be. Later that night, I opened the pouch expecting to find a gold or silver coin. What fell into my palm was a bracelet of such elegant design that I simply stared in awe. It was a gentle braid of ziff woven gracefully around five evenly placed gems. The gems were clear-green, almond-shaped stones that seemed to glow with an inner light of their own. It was breathtaking. I had no idea where Abinikek had gotten it, but I was sure it was worth a ransom.

I quickly put the bracelet back in the pouch and hid it beneath my tunic. I knew exactly what to do with it . . . and it had little to do with my freedom.

CHAPTER TWENTY

WE ARRIVED IN BASHAN AT noon several days later. The small prison was still smelly and dank, but it was as sweet as any home because my friends were there.

"Oh, Jarem, it is so good to see you again," old Hannah cried, embracing me.

"Yes, yes," Eliazar joined in. "Many slaves never return from such extended labor. Especially while on such a dangerous task. Why did it take so long?"

"We were commanded to build a second bridge."

"So you are twice as blessed for surviving such labor," Hannah said. "We're so glad you are back with us, Jarem. My, how you have grown!"

"Thank you, my friends. It's good to back." I glanced around, wishing my eyes would adjust to the darkness quicker. "So . . . is *everyone* still here?"

I heard the low laugh of three men along the back wall. "Just us old mules," one of them said. "But not that pretty woman of yours."

I liked the way he'd identified Zanesh: that woman of *mine*.

"Is she still in the city?" I asked.

"Zanesh has been hired out at a nobleman's house," Boaz explained. "She goes there quite a lot lately—sometimes for days on end. I think they are fond of her."

My shoulders slumped in disappointment.

"But she should return this evening," Hannah added quickly, as if sensing my melancholy.

"I see. Thank you all."

I sat, resting against a wall. Many of the others sat around me, prodding me with questions about my experiences. I relayed the exciting moments but left out the miserable times. They expressed awe at the length and height of the two bridges. The men wanted to know every detail about the construction process. Even though I was very tired, I did my best to entertain their questions with enthusiasm.

* * *

Later that evening, Zanesh entered the prison and sighed wearily. As the door shut behind her, she stood motionless, waiting for her eyes to adjust. I felt my heart skip a beat and then begin to pound thunderously in my chest. I glanced around to see if anyone else could hear it. Although disheveled, Zanesh looked absolutely breathtaking. It seemed as if she had matured three years during my absence. Before me stood a beautiful young woman. She no longer possessed the juvenile attributes of a girl. There was a refined quality about her that belied her circumstances.

I felt terribly nervous as I gawked at Zanesh. Would she recognize me as a man now—as Abinikek had indicated—or simply regard me as the boy who was sold into slavery with her?

"Good evening," she said with forced cheeriness.

The sound of her voice filled me with joy. I stood but remained in the shadows. My heart continued to thrum. I had never felt this way about anyone before. It was new and scary and totally exhilarating.

Zanesh turned in my direction and squinted into the darkness. She could see my form but clearly didn't recognize who I was.

"Good evening," she said, taking a step toward me. "Are you new here?"

It was then that I realized how tall I'd grown; I now looked down at her instead of nearly eye to eye. She stepped closer, extended her hand in friendship, and held it there. "My name is Zanesh."

I quickly took the bracelet from the pouch and slid it onto her wrist. She gasped sharply, gazing at the gift. Tipping her head to one side, she peered into the shadows.

"Do I know you?" she asked.

"You mean you've completely forgotten about me already?" I teased.

She put a hand to her mouth as I stepped from the shadows. Tears welled in her eyes, and she literally jumped into my embrace, wrapping her arms around me. For a long time we said nothing. Those around us moved silently to the other side of the room to give us privacy. It felt so wonderful to hold her, so completely right. The embrace instilled in me a sudden surge of energy. When I loosened my hug, she tightened hers. She was trembling; her breaths were almost whimpers. I felt the moisture of tears against my chest. I gently stroked her hair and shushed her.

After too short a time, she stepped back, wiped her eyes, and looked up at me.

"I missed you so much," she said. Then, without warning, she stood on her toes and kissed me.

I nearly melted. I felt the need to say something meaningful but couldn't come up with anything. "I missed you too," was all I said.

She hugged me again. "Jarem, I thought you'd never come back. I thought you had escaped and made it home without me."

"Never," I said softly. "Being away from you made me realize how much you mean to me. I will never leave you. I promise."

I took her hand and directed her to a dark corner to sit. "Are you too tired to talk?" I asked.

"Not anymore," she replied, snuggling against me.

I told her everything I had experienced while being away. She remarked on how much I had grown and how good I looked. Although I was certain she was still in shock, I loved hearing those words.

"You've become a very beautiful woman," I said, hoping she believed me, nervous that I might say something too forward.

"I look like an old witch," she said with a shy smile, tucking an errant strand of hair behind her ear.

"Well, you've certainly enchanted me." *Wait—did I just agree that she is a witch?* "But I still say you're beautiful."

She kissed my cheek then snuggled against me again. Apparently I'd said the right thing.

We spent the rest of the night talking softly. She told me of life in Bashan since I'd left. I sensed she brushed over much of it, as if she was ashamed. I'd seen the unwanted attention she'd experienced when we were first captured. I could easily imagine it being much worse now. So I didn't pry. I figured she'd tell me the details when she was ready. And if she never did, that would be fine too.

I told her about Abinikek and the information he'd shared.

"Does that mean you're planning on escaping soon?" she asked cautiously.

"Yes, as soon as the opportunity presents itself. But we have to be cautious. Everyone will be watching me for a while because I've been away for so long."

"That makes sense. But the sooner we go, the better. The family I'm hired out to is evil. His name is Jothan. I hate going there. Their daughter, Eliza, is always accusing me of everything *she* does wrong. And the mother whips me all the time for no reason."

"Have they threatened you with death?"

"No, they wouldn't dare kill me. They'd have to pay my purchase price and answer to Shem. As long as no serious damage is done, they can do whatever they want to me."

"But to whip you for no reason? You should complain to Gad—"

"What good would it do?" she spat. "He likes the way they treat me because he can charge extra for it. As long as I'm alive he'll keep sending me there." She paused and brought her knees to her chest. "And Jothan . . ." She shivered. "The way he looks at me makes my skin crawl. I don't trust him. He keeps trying to get me alone. I keep finding ways to avoid that, but I'm running out of ideas, and . . . and I'm scared, Jarem. Please, I want to get out of here before something terrible happens. Even if it's risky. I want to go home."

I put my arm around her and drew her to me. "I promise I'll think of something. But we have to be cautious for a little longer."

In reality, I also feared for her. It made me furious to think of any man laying a hand on her—especially a Lamanite. Yet there was so little I could do about it. I knew that soon she would run out of ways to defend herself in that household or any other. She was beautiful—and that was a curse for a slave. The thought of Zanesh suffering abuse sickened me. I could only imagine what it did to Zanesh's spirits. She was right: we had to leave soon.

We knelt together and prayed for God's help. We poured out our hearts, asking for something, some miracle to help Zanesh avoid the evils of that family. We pleaded that I might receive inspiration in arranging our escape. And finally, we asked that, if it was God's will, we would always remain together.

*　*　*

The next morning, Zanesh removed her bracelet before leaving for her assignment. "I don't want to risk breaking it or having it stolen," she explained.

That made sense. From that morning on, whenever Zanesh left, she'd return the bracelet to the pouch and hide it behind a loose stone in the prison wall.

Zanesh always left before sunrise and returned after sundown. I could tell she was exhausted, but she always forced a huge smile for me.

"You don't have to stay up," I told her. "I understand if you're too tired to talk and want to go right to sleep."

"But you don't understand, Jarem," she said, shaking her head. "When I go to that Jothan's house, I have to close myself off. I have to put myself in an emotionless state—one without sorrow or joy—simply to get me through another day. It drains me of everything I have. When I come back here, I am so weary I can barely walk."

"All the more reason you should go right to sleep."

"No, it's not physical weariness. It's emotional weariness. I need to feel your spirit, your enthusiasm and positive nature. It refreshes me. I come alive when I'm around you. Why would I want to sleep through that?"

Her revelation made my heart swell. "I feel the same way when I'm with you, Zanesh. You keep me alive from one day to the next."

I cupped her face in my hands and gently kissed her. She relaxed into me and breathed a deep sigh.

Silence engulfed us for several minutes. Then, softly, she whispered, "Don't ever leave me, Jarem."

"I won't. I promise."

CHAPTER TWENTY-ONE

LIFE QUICKLY SETTLED INTO A routine for both of us. While Zanesh went to do household labor, I reported to the stables on the far side of the city. I had worked there once before. Like that time, I labored harder than other stable hands. It was good, safe work—not at all like building a bridge over a deep gorge. The stable master's name was Gidonhi. He was a firm but fair man, and I didn't mind laboring under his command.

I had a natural affinity with horses; they responded favorably to my voice and touch. Many of the horses grew to trust me with any task. My methods clearly impressed Gidonhi. He hired me out daily—for mundane chores as well as for assignments of significant responsibility. He treated me as an equal with the Lamanite stable hands, which wasn't always a good thing. They hated me and took every opportunity to sabotage my work. They complained that a Nephite shouldn't be given so much liberty and authority. But Gidonhi didn't care what they thought. He was a master of horses and regarded everyone else as either those who loved horses or those who didn't.

One day as I was grooming a magistrate's stallion, Gidonhi came in to look over some tack. I nodded a friendly salutation and continued my work. The day was insufferably hot and sticky. As the stable allowed little air to circulate, the stallion and I were sweating profusely.

"You like him, don't you?" Gidonhi asked.

I patted the horse on the neck. "He's magnificent."

The stable master smiled. "He likes you too. Why don't you take him out and give him some fresh air."

"Yes sir. To the corrals?"

He tossed me a bridle and reins. "No, I mean take him out. For a ride."

I froze, totally speechless. Only the magistrate and Gidonhi were allowed to ride the stallion. A nearby stable hand gawked in our direction—clearly as surprised as I was.

"I am honored, Master Gidonhi, but I cannot," I said, very confused.

"Why?" he persisted. "Don't you know how?"

It was a foolish question. He had seen me ride several of the horses in the corral. I'd even assisted in breaking a few. I shook my head. "No, sir. As you know, it's forbidden for a slave to ride the magistrate's stallion. I could be killed for such an offense."

He took the reins from my hands and commenced to bridle the horse. "Nonsense. I am stable master, am I not?"

"Yes."

"And in that capacity I am at liberty to do—*or order*—anything I deem necessary for the horses." He continued to harness the stallion as he spoke. "This animal is in need of fresh air and fresh water, and I am too busy to perform the task. Do you know the small lake to the north, up Serpent Hollow?"

"I do, yes," I said. I'd been there a few times with Lamanite stable hands to water and bathe the horses. It was a pristine clearing not far from Bashan. But I was leery. Why was he insistent on *me* taking this horse there? Was it a trap? Or was it a test of my loyalty? I didn't know, but my gut feeling was to follow his command. "It is a very beautiful location."

He gave a curt nod. "That it is. And it's exactly what this horse needs. Mount up."

I hesitantly climbed on and took the reins. "What if I am stopped?"

Gidonhi led the stallion out of the stable and handed me a folded slip of vellum. It gave permission to travel without an escort for the day. I slipped it in my tunic and rode out of the corral, down a side path, and out of the city.

I watched for anyone following me, but no one did. The horse responded perfectly to my directions, and I soon felt quite at ease riding along the common trail. More than once I entertained the thought of riding back for Zanesh then heading into the wilderness. With the permission notice, we could make up any story about being without an escort and could cover a substantial bit of ground before worrying about being caught. But if we *were* caught, it would undoubtedly mean our deaths. I shook the thought from my mind and continued up the narrow hollow.

Traveling alone like this brought back a flood of childhood memories—the kind I usually kept hidden because of the pain they carried. Yet somehow they weren't as painful now. More than twenty months had passed since the fall of Oranihah, and time had helped heal the pain. I felt strange comfort in the fact that, even though I was a slave, I was alive and healthy. Plus, there was Zanesh. The mere thought of her always made me smile.

I soon reached the lake—an unspoiled pool of still water surrounded by groves of trees and a skirt of grass. The stallion drank deeply and cropped the new grass near the water's edge. I took a quick dip in the lake, then leaned against a tree and breathed deeply. I let my mind wander from cares and worries and focused on the natural sounds around me—the calls of birds and insects, the breezes stirring the vegetation, the water lapping on the bank. My father had taught me to clear my soul this way. The psalmist said to be still and know God. It always felt good knowing He was near.

* * *

I don't remember falling asleep, but a thundering of hooves jolted me from my slumber. I leapt to my feet. The stallion was standing rigid, his ears perked. I grabbed his reins and watched anxiously as Gidonhi raced into the clearing. His horse hurled clumps of soil into the air as he skidded to a stop in front of me. I thought he was coming to see if I'd tried to escape, but a look of deep worry on his face told me otherwise.

"Jarem, come quickly," he panted. "There's trouble."

Before I could respond, he spun his horse and galloped down the trail. I hopped onto the stallion and sped after him. We were in Bashan in no time and tethered the frothing horses in the corral. He called for a stable hand to look after the animals then led me into the city.

"I know it's none of my affair, but your friend is in serious trouble."

"My friend?" I asked, fearing I already knew the answer.

"The slave girl, Zanesh."

I grabbed his arm, stopping him. "What happened?"

His eyes bore into mine. "She's been accused of stealing. They're going to execute her."

CHAPTER TWENTY-TWO

I RAN TO THE PRISON at full speed. When I got there, Zanesh was kneeling out front, her wrists tied, blood trickling from her mouth. Her tunic was ripped, revealing several raw welts and whip marks. An ornately dressed Lamanite was yelling at Gad, repeatedly pointing an accusing finger at Zanesh.

"What's going on here?" I demanded, marching up to them.

Gad scowled at me. "You forget your place, slave."

I lowered my eyes and took a calming breath. "I am sorry. Is there anything I can do to help here?"

"This Nephite harlot stole a bracelet from my daughter," the man growled.

Zanesh looked up with a sorrow-filled expression. Her chin trembled; tears pooled and fell. She pointed to her empty wrist. I instantly knew what had happened. Somehow she had forgotten to remove her bracelet before going to work.

Gidonhi came up beside me and watched without comment.

"Is the bracelet made of ziff woven around five green stones?" I asked.

Gad frowned. "As a matter of fact, it is. Do you know something we don't?"

I looked at Gidonhi, who nodded, encouraging me to speak. "I gave it to her."

"Lies!" the man barked. He stepped over to Zanesh and, grabbing a clump of her hair, yanked her head back. "She is the slave that has served my household for most of this season. But now I discover she's been helping herself to my wealth. For all I know she's stolen half my property already. I demand repayment—and her death!" He threw her head forward and delivered a vicious kick to her ribs.

I started forward with clenched fists, but Gidonhi's hand stayed me. He stepped up to the angry man and placed a hand on his shoulder, positioning himself in front of Zanesh. "Let's not let tempers cloud our judgment here,

Jothan," he said evenly. He led the man away from Zanesh and over to Gad. "Prison master. May I have your permission to help sort this out?"

Gidonhi was a large man; one few people argued with. I knew Gad wasn't a friend of his, but the two had mutual respect for each other.

Before Gad could answer, the angry man cried, "There is nothing to sort out! This slave stole from me, and she deserves to die!"

Gad nodded. "You are probably right, Jothan. But since this slave is neither your property nor mine, we cannot kill her without just cause."

Gidonhi lifted Zanesh to her feet and motioned for me to help her remain standing. "We simply need to establish the truth; then, if she is guilty, I will assist with her execution myself."

My breath caught. Jothan thought for a moment then nodded, though he was still red with anger.

"Now, your daughter claims this slave girl stole a bracelet from her, correct?" Gidonhi asked the father.

"She swears it," he growled.

"Was the bracelet a gift from you?"

Jothan faltered. "No . . . but Eliza could have purchased it . . . or a friend could have given it to her. Our family has many influential contacts, as I'm sure you are aware."

Gidonhi chortled but hid it in a cough. He turned to Zanesh. "Jarem claims he gave you the bracelet."

"Yes sir, he did," she said without lifting her eyes.

"Did he tell you where he obtained it?"

"Yes. He said—"

"Silence," he abruptly commanded. Turning to Jothan, he said, "If I can prove that the slave girl did not steal the bracelet from your daughter, will you believe me?"

The father grumbled but finally said yes. "But I'll be hung if she'll ever work in my house again," he added vehemently.

"Fair enough," Gidonhi said. "Prison Master Gad, do you have any knowledge of where the bracelet came from?"

"No. This is the first I've heard of it's existence."

"Excellent. Then this will work. I want the slave girl to whisper to you where Jarem claims he obtained the bracelet, but do not reveal it to us. Then I will have Jarem do the same. You can be the judge on whether or not the stories match."

Gad nodded.

We did as the stable master requested, each whispering to the prison master what we knew to be the truth.

Gad nodded again, seemingly unsurprised by each recounting. "The stories match."

"What?" Jothan screeched.

"I trust Gad's judgment," Gidonhi said to him. "Since my arrival, Zanesh has spoken only a few words, none of which revealed the history of the bracelet. Therefore, only she and prison master Gad know what she claims."

A look of worry crossed the rich man's face, but he nodded.

"Jarem, tell us exactly what you told the prison master."

I repeated my story for all to hear—that Abinikek had given me the bracelet as a token of friendship.

Gad nodded a third time. "That is what I was told from both slaves exactly."

"Lies! More Nephite lies," Jothan screamed. "You planned this ahead of time. You're all in it together! I'm going straight to the magistrate. He'll believe a Lamanite's word over a Nephite's. You'll see." He marched away, spitting a string of profanities.

Zanesh began to cry again, resting her face against my chest. I consoled her and gently stroked her hair. The prison master conferred with the stable master, and both began laughing heartily.

Gad removed Zanesh's bindings. "Take her to the washing pool and get her cleaned up," he told me.

"Thank you," I said, bowing slightly.

Zanesh held out her hand to Gad. "Please?"

The prison master shook his head. "The bracelet stays with me until I get word from Shem. Because you belong to him, so does anything you possess."

I looked at Gidonhi with raised eyebrows.

He shrugged. "I'm afraid he's right."

I led Zanesh to the washing pool and tended to her wounds. Few words were shared, though my heart ached for her. We returned to the prison and sat in our corner. I did my best to comfort her, but there was little I could do besides hold her. She eventually fell asleep in my arms.

When night came, she was feeling much better and recounted to me how she had awoken late and had rushed to the house, forgetting to remove the bracelet.

"The instant Eliza saw it, she demanded I give it to her. When I refused, she ran to Jothan and claimed I'd stolen it."

"Well, there is no need to worry anymore. Gidonhi proved the daughter was lying."

"I don't think that matters," she said. "Jothan will want revenge."

"Maybe. But—as strange as this sounds—as long as we're under Shem's rule, we're safe. No one can touch us without his say-so."

I wanted to believe my own words, but inwardly I suspected I was terribly wrong.

* * *

Just after sunrise the following day, the prison doors flew open, jarring us from our sleep. Two Lamanite guards came in and dragged Zanesh from the prison. I ran after them, but Gad stopped me at the door.

"Wait, please. She didn't do it!" I cried. "The stable master proved it."

"She's not going to be killed, Jarem," Gad said. "I swear it."

I settled only slightly. "What's happening, then? Where are they taking her?"

The look in his eyes was one of compassionate censure. "You must understand. The man she worked for *is* very influential in this city, just as he claimed. There was no way I'd ever be able to hire her out again, and she is therefore unprofitable. So . . . to protect her . . . I had to sell her."

My heart seized before a sudden rush of anger surged within me. "No! That isn't fair. She's not guilty!" I yelled.

"I'm afraid that doesn't matter," Gad said with a large measure of tenderness.

I continued to plead as I watched the guards tether Zanesh to a horse. Utterly speechless, she looked at me with horror-stricken eyes. I lunged forward but was pushed back by one of the guards.

Gad unsheathed his long dagger and laid the tip against my chest. It was not meant as an overt threat—more of a harsh hint. "Don't do anything foolish, Jarem," he urged softly. "Step back inside and calm down."

I did as he said, but it took all my willpower to do so. Gad shut the door and locked it. My entire soul screamed in despair.

They're taking Zanesh from me! I'll never see her again.

The thought was more than I could bear. I trembled uncontrollably. Tears coursed down my cheeks. I yelled through the door until my throat was raw. I wanted to throw up and could only suppress the urge by screaming. When would this madness ever end?

I sank to the floor and curled into a ball. I could barely breathe. My chest tightened painfully; my stomach knotted. But that discomfort was nothing compared to the anguish in my heart. The others in the prison tried to comfort me, saying God was still with us. I found their words insulting.

This was *not* part of God's plans. It couldn't be. It wasn't fair. Why would God turn his back on us like this? If *I* had done something wrong, then he should punish *me*. "But not her, God," I sobbed. "Not Zanesh. Please, not her."

CHAPTER TWENTY-THREE

I WAS NOT REQUIRED TO work the following day. The stable master paid for the time but did not require my labor. He must have thought it was a generous gesture. It wasn't. With nothing to focus on, it gave my mind a chance to dwell on the events of the last few days. And my thoughts kept coming back to the same thing: had I not given Zanesh the bracelet, she would not have been sold.

It was careless of me not to anticipate the trouble such a valuable trinket would bring. I gave it to her because I thought it would lift her spirits. But was my generosity really an act of selflessness? Or was I trying to buy her affection? I acknowledged to myself that I also hoped it would make *me* look better in her eyes. I had to admit I swelled with pride every time I saw it on her wrist. I, a slave, had given Zanesh a gift many Lamanites could not afford.

Zanesh had expressed her fears regarding that evil family countless times. But as valid as her worries were, they hadn't ever amounted to any actual trouble. Nevertheless, I should have known that that particular family—or any Lamanite for that matter—would look covetously on a bracelet of such value.

I cursed myself repeatedly for such blind pride. Zanesh was being punished because of *my* vanity, my foolishness. It was my fault. And I hated myself for it.

My heart was crushed. I felt totally worthless. What dangers would now befall Zanesh? What humiliations would she have to endure? She told me that she could tolerate anything so long as we were together. Now we weren't. I had failed her. The more I thought about it, the more it hurt, but I couldn't seem to fill my mind with anything else. I tried to force myself to concentrate on other things, but it never lasted. Those around me sought to comfort me with words of encouragement and tenderness. But it was no good. I was more miserable than I could ever remember being in my entire life. Even the loss of my family didn't pierce my heart as deeply as the realization that Zanesh was alone and suffering because of me.

*   *   *

I didn't eat or sleep for a long time. The stable master called for me almost daily over the next few weeks. He never said a word about the incident; instead, he filled my days with one task after another. I scrubbed the stables, tended to the stock, and performed numberless duties with scant attention to quality. I completed everything I had to, but never with the same diligence as before. Instead of enjoying work, I now loathed it. Every task was miserable, mundane, something to be completed just so I could leave. Gidonhi noticed this from the start—almost as if he were expecting it—and encouraged me to move on. But I didn't care for his patronizing suggestions nor his mock compassion. I'd lost all patience with my situation, and he quickly lost patience with me.

Some weeks later, on an exceptionally hot and sticky day, Gidonhi asked that I curry the magistrate's stallion. I took the brushes in hand and began wiping down the animal. The air inside the stables was stifling, and the biting flies were attacking in force. As I neared the stallion's flank, he flicked his tail, whipping me across the face. Angered, I cursed and swatted his rump. It happened a second time. And a third. Each time, he turned to look at me with his big, innocent eyes. But in those eyes I saw mockery. It may simply have been the flies irritating him, but it seemed as if he was intentionally goading me. I punched him hard in the flank.

"Stop whipping me with your tail, you filthy beast," I growled.

He turned his head back with a snort and whipped his tail again. Then, as I sat on a stool to brush his legs, he stepped just out of reach. I scooted the stool forward and tried brushing him again, but he again stepped out of reach. I was already angry; now I was furious.

"You move again, and I swear by my family's name I'll make you regret it."

As if he could understand my words—or at least my tone of voice—he took a step forward and whipped his tail across my face. Before I could stop myself, I leapt up and punched him hard in the ribs. He gave a high-pitched whinny and stomped, knocking over the stool. As I bent to retrieve it, he turned and butted me with his head, sprawling me on the filthy floor. Blind with rage, I got up and kicked his belly with all my strength. He bellowed in pain and bolted from the stable. I threw the brush after him, kicked the stool into a corner, and yelled like a wild animal. I wanted to curse at everyone and everything. Clenching my head between my fists, I slumped to the floor and fought to keep myself from exploding in anger, bitterness, and hatred.

Moments later, Gidonhi was standing in front me. His coarse breathing and balled fists revealed his anger, but I didn't care—about him, about the stallion, about anything.

"Do you care to explain what happened?" he said through clenched teeth.
"No," I spat.

A flash of movement, and I was knocked flat to one side. His strike was brutal and heavy-handed, and my vision blurred from the blow. I looked up in time to see Gidonhi reaching for me. I batted his hand away, but he countered by clubbing me on the opposite side of my head with his other hand. The man was incredibly fast and strong. I almost blacked out from his punches. He grabbed my tunic and literally dragged me out to the corral. He shoved me against the fence poles that separated one enclosure from its neighbor. I spun around and cocked my fists. To strike a Lamanite meant death, but I didn't care. Not anymore.

And yet Gidonhi didn't come at me. He stood with his fists on his hips, breathing so intensely he sounded like a leopard preparing for a kill.

"Turn around, you fool. Look at his legs."

I blinked hard a few times, not understanding. He pointed behind me. I turned and saw the stallion in the adjacent corral. His head hung low; his front shins were lacerated and bleeding badly. I drew in a sharp hiss—but at the same time, I felt justified. The headstrong animal deserved it. I then noticed that the top pole separating the corrals was broken in two. I knew the stallion had gashed his shins trying to jump over the barrier, trying to flee from me. I also knew this meant trouble for the stable master—which meant trouble for me. The magistrate would be furious, and Gidonhi's reputation as one of the finest stable masters in the land was now tarnished.

"You realize those scars will be permanent," he said flatly. It was not a question. "Now . . . tell me what happened."

I knew the truth would sound childish, and a lie would only compound his wrath. Yet I could think of no way to explain my rash behavior. The number-one rule in the stables was never to take your anger out on the animals. And I had done precisely that—on the magistrate's stallion, no less! My shoulders slumped. My father's lesson on controlling one's anger filled my mind. I used to be so proud of my ability to control my temper. But considering all I'd been through—all the *Lamanites* had put me through—it didn't seem to matter anymore. I stood staring blankly at the horse's legs, saying nothing.

"Silence?" Gidonhi said. "Not even an apology?" I'd never heard such anger in his voice before.

But I still didn't answer—didn't even shrug a shoulder.

"Fine. How about we let the magistrate decide your fate?"

Before I could react, my hands were lashed behind me and I was shoved out of the corral. I tripped and landed face-first on the gravel path, splitting my lip and getting sand in one eye. I inhaled sharply through gritted teeth.

"Anytime you want to tell me what happened, go ahead," Gidonhi said. "The sooner the better."

"I guess I got angry," I mumbled to the dirt.

He yanked me to my feet. "What was that?"

With head hung low, I growled, "I said I guess I just got angry. I kicked him and he ran out."

"You kicked him because you were angry?" Gidonhi seethed. His jaw clenched repeatedly in an effort to control his own temper. "I expected more from you, Jarem."

"I'm happy to disappoint you."

I don't know why I responded with such an offensive comment. But it was out, and there was nothing I could say to take it back.

Gidonhi led me back to the prison in silence. Removing my lashes, he said, "You will never work in my stables again. I thought you were different. I considered you better than many of my stable hands, but you're not. Get out of my sight before I decide to have you put to death for this."

I staggered into the prison and slumped into a dark corner. I knew Gidonhi was a fair master, but I hated him anyway. He was a Lamanite profiting on slave labor. And I was the slave. It didn't matter to me anymore if anyone benefitted from my work. They could beat me all they wanted. I didn't care. I might do a lowly task here and there, but I would no longer put forth my best effort. Not for them; not for anyone. I doubted they would kill me. There weren't enough slaves as it was, and I was a valuable asset—or at least I used to be. Not anymore.

In my mind, there was nothing left to live for. These Lamanite captors were every bit as evil as I had heard as a boy. They had killed my father, my mother, and my sister. They had taken the girl I'd fallen in love with. They had left me with no reason to breathe.

*   *   *

Over the next few months, Gad assigned me the lowest of jobs. A shovel became a regular part of my routine. I cleared ditches, roads, and trails of mud and sewage. No one in town wanted to hire me; my reputation for being slothful and potentially violent kept me from more dignified work—as if a slave's work was ever dignified. I spent most of my time in distant cities or villages where my character was unknown. Quite often, masters would demand their money back because my work was so poor.

Whipped more times than I could remember, starved to the point that my ribs showed through my skin, I grew weak and sick. My strength ebbed as quickly as my will to live. The Nephite slaves I roomed with did their best to buoy me up, but to no avail. They quoted the prophets of old about standing up to adversity and enduring to the end, but I felt I had reached the end and saw no reason to try harder.

At first Gad was frustrated with me, then disappointed, and finally angry. I used to be his most valued slave, the top of his list of strong and willing laborers. I always commanded the highest price. But as time passed, I became of no value whatsoever—which was exactly how I felt.

Within months, the other Nephites began ignoring me. I was rude, bitter, and coarse. I stopped praying. I ceased to be concerned with personal cleanliness. Some mornings I slept till midday, spent the afternoon in a foul mood, and then wallowed in self-pity all night. After a year I was avoided completely.

It was said that time heals all wounds, but I no longer believed it. My sorrow may have lessened, but my guilt never would. Zanesh's removal was my fault. The Lamanites may have dealt the blow, but I had set it in motion.

I began thinking of ways to break the law so grievously they'd be forced to kill me. It seemed the only way to end my misery. That night, I prayed as never before for a complete release from my sorrows. I prayed that I would never wake up again.

CHAPTER TWENTY-FOUR

THE NEXT MORNING, WHILE HEADING to a menial job, I happened to see myself in a highly polished plate of silver—and was shocked at my appearance. I didn't recognize the man staring back at me. A distinct growth of beard now covered my jaw. I was filthy; my hair was long and matted. I was painfully lean to the point of being sinewy. The sunken aspect of my eyes and the concavity of my cheeks were those of a man decades older. But it was more than just my bedraggled exterior that shocked me. There was no life in me. With brutal understanding, I realized that my soulless appearance was a result of the desolation I had allowed to drain my soul. I was an empty man.

It was a defining moment. Death would solve nothing. Courting misery would only compound my situation. I *had* to do something to pull myself from this crippling grief. And yet I hesitated. The negative feelings I'd harbored for so long were familiar companions. I'd come to know them intimately; I could always count on having them near. Sorrow was the only thing I could truly rely on. I'd grown to find comfort in misery. And that realization frightened me.

Just like following evil leaders, I knew that finding solace in sorrow broke the spirit, opening the door to emotional, spiritual, and even physical destruction. Not only had I reached that threshold, I had crossed over.

I returned to the prison and, thankfully, found it empty. In a dark corner, I knelt. It had been a long time since I had opened my soul to God. I still believed in Him; I simply didn't trust Him. I knew that God did not delight in the sorrows of men. But sometimes sorrow was the only thing that could bring us back to Him, because sorrow was the precursor to humility.

So I started to pray. I poured out my heart and soul, holding nothing back. Within moments, I was sobbing. Hot tears ran down my face as I begged for forgiveness and ached for comfort. I exercised all the faith I could muster, pleading with my Maker to calm the anguish in my heart, to soften the memories that grieved me, and to help me enjoy life again. I prayed for Zanesh, beseeching that—if she was still alive—she would not suffer as I had suffered. I prayed for those whose friendship I had shunned. I prayed for deliverance from the crippling sorrow that engulfed me. I prayed until I could no longer think of what to say, then prayed some more. All through the night the impression kept coming to me to find escape. Not merely to run away but to find a new path.

Sometime before dawn, with my strength gone and my tears spent, I felt myself crumple on the floor.

* * *

I awoke to shouting outside the prison door. Gad was arguing about the price of a slave—not for hire but for sale. I slowly got to my feet. I was exhausted; my muscles ached as if I'd put in a week of hard labor. And yet I felt curiously refreshed somehow—as if I'd been cleansed from within.

"I tell you he's worth ten times that sum! Not so long ago he commanded the highest price around. Now *you* offer me a portion of that to *purchase* him? You insult me," Prison Master Gad huffed.

"From everything I have heard of this slave, he is no longer the prize you claim. No one has offered a price for him in months. You would do well to be rid of him," the second man argued.

"Then why do *you* want him?"

"I believe I could turn a small profit by taking him to a city where he is not known. He is obviously sick and may die on such a long journey. But I am willing to take that chance. Now . . . do we have a deal?"

Silence lingered a moment, and then the prison door was yanked opened. I expected Gad to call for one of the feeble, older slaves, but I was wrong.

"Jarem," he called.

My breath caught.

"Jarem, come out now," Gad commanded.

I squinted at the harsh sunlight as I exited the prison. There stood a skinny, middle-aged man with an unkempt beard and a balding head. He appraised me without comment then handed the prison master a small pouch.

"Done," he said.

"Done," Gad said, refusing to look at me.

"What's going on?" I asked.

The bald man stepped up to me and slapped me hard across my face. "Learn your place, slave."

The man shoved me toward his horse and bound my wrists to a tether. Gad turned his back to us and walked away. There were no farewells, no words of encouragement. I wondered if I would ever see Bashan again. Worse, I wondered if anyone there would miss me.

*   *   *

We traveled deep into Lamanite territory, taking a route I wasn't familiar with. I was fed little and remained fettered at all times. My new owner spoke little, which was fine with me. It gave me more opportunity to memorize the roads and trails and the lay of the land. It was three days before I was allowed to bathe in a stream; seven before I was given a change of clothing. The man treated me like a dog, even though I did little to incur his wrath. I think he was trying to break me. Little did he know, that had already happened. With my new resolve, I was determined to escape the first chance I got, but I wouldn't make a move until the timing was perfect. I knew I'd only get one chance.

The days passed slowly, because all we did was travel. I don't know how many miles we trod. We passed several villages and even a large city, but we never stopped for more than a few minutes of rest. Had I been sold a day earlier, I wouldn't have kept track of time. Now, however, I needed a reckoning for my route home.

Even though I was trying to stay focused and positive, I kept wondering why such a drastic change in my situation had occurred. More importantly, why now? I felt confident I could have escaped from Bashan. I knew that land very well. But the minute I had made my resolve to find a new path, I was shackled and taken deeper into Lamanite territory. It confused me deeply. I had felt so assured God was on my side. This sudden change seemed a contradiction to the inner peace I had felt earlier. Was God changing his mind about helping me escape?

Two days later we stopped in a large city called Midian. My owner said this was our destination. I was to remain here until I was sold again. That was welcome news. I was exhausted.

Bordered by cultivated farmland, Midian was a clean city, and the people here seemed to live a peaceful yet active life. But that gave me little comfort. I knew I was brought here to be sold. I expected my seller would take me to a prison to get cleaned and rested so I would bring a better price. It would be a welcome respite. I could take some time to regain my strength and to learn more about the lay of the land and the temperament of the people.

My spirits began to climb as I was led through a web of streets. Shops and tradesmen lined the causeways. There was a palpable excitement in the air. I received several curious glances from passersby. We seemed to be headed toward the city center. The nearer we got, the thicker the crowds became. Something big was about to happen. A flutter of anticipation danced in my chest. Turning a corner, we entered a large central plaza. To one side of the plaza stood an elevated auction stand.

My spirits plummeted. I would get no rest.

CHAPTER TWENTY-FIVE

A CROWD OF HUNDREDS GATHERED in front of the auction stand. Most were Lamanite, but I also saw Amalekites, Zoramites, and others. It was easy to pick out their different accents and attire. Some individuals wore expensive cloth with ribbons of scarlet woven into the fabric. Others wore silk robes that shimmered in the sunlight. Still others wore elaborate headdresses of quetzal and macaw feathers. Then there were the lower classes who wore mostly tunics of homespun cloth. The wealthy and influential class stood at the front of the assembly; common, poor people made up the rest of the crowd.

I was put with a small group of slaves already assembled, raising the total number to nine. Apparently, slaves were still hard to come by. Before stepping onto the platform, we were stripped and washed, the women's hair was combed out, and the men's faces were shaved. We averted our eyes while the washing took place. It was hard for a slave to maintain any semblance of modesty, so we extended it to each other by looking the other way. Being clean did little to better our appearance. Many of us looked malnourished. I was perhaps the healthiest of the lot, though I had lost most of my muscle and vigor. We were given loincloths and simple, coarse tunics. A fresh blue stripe was then painted across each of our foreheads, identifying us as slaves. As if that was hard to tell.

My owner spoke with the auctioneer while we lined up behind a partition separating us from the crowd. The man examined each of us, haggled bitterly with several owners, and then selected five of the healthiest slaves, myself included. The others had their wrists bound and were led down a back alley. The seller then climbed onto the platform and passed through the partition. The slaves with me were timid and without spirit—men and women humbled by the reality of their slavery. And yet the auctioneer spoke about us as if we were in the prime of life, servants fit for a king. The man didn't embellish partial truths; he flat-out lied.

At his signal, the first slave was led onto the platform. She was a thin Nephite woman with fine gray hair and a shallow face. The auctioneer praised her incredible cooking skills—even though I was certain he had no knowledge of such ability.

"I've tasted her food many times," he lied. "She can make the stringiest serpent taste like the choicest young lamb. Now, who will start the bidding?"

When no one spoke, he grabbed her shoulders and forced her to stand straighter. "My friends. Do not let her looks deceive you. She may seem frail, but her mind holds countless recipes. Keep her in the cooking room, and you will be rewarded with many years of meals fit for royalty."

To me, she looked as if she'd do well to live through another season, let alone many years. But some of the crowd believed the auctioneer, and the bidding began. It took a while, but soon a respectable sum was reached. The auctioneer then began his final calls.

"Last chance to counter," he hollered. "No higher bids . . . none offered . . . this slave is . . . sold!" He smiled and bowed low to the purchaser, thanking him abundantly.

Someone from the audience yelled, "A high price for an old hag!"

The crowd erupted in laughter. The auctioneer scowled at the troublemaker, but he didn't reply. The next slave was a short woman with coarse, reddish hair and a stocky build.

"Here we have a Mulekite—and you all know their reputation for hard work. This slave is a tireless housekeeper. No task is too demanding; no household is too large. She has the endurance of a camel and the strength of an ox."

The woman looked sturdy enough, but having just met her, I again wondered how the auctioneer had acquired such knowledge. I had no question as to how she felt being compared to beasts of burden.

The bidding started in earnest. The auctioneer spun one lie after another, referencing the names of noble families under whom she'd worked, though I doubted she'd worked for any of them. But they sounded impressive, and the price quickly rose to what the first woman brought. When the final bid was determined, the auctioneer was grinning from ear to ear.

The three remaining slaves were men, with me being the youngest. The first one was said to have unmatched carpentry skills, the second to be an expert stone mason. Neither looked like they could lift a sack of meal, but by the time the auctioneer finished embellishing their abilities, no one seemed to care. They both went for a price that seemed to satisfy the seller.

There was then a lengthy silence from the platform. I peeked around the partition to watch. The seller was stroking his chin, pacing back and forth while staring at the platform floor, as if deep in thought. He frowned and shook his head a few times. He looked in my direction, paused, and then continued pacing. Finally, he stopped and addressed the crowd.

"My good friends. I have one more slave to offer . . . but I am undecided about selling him." He sighed and shook his head again, as if deeply troubled by his dilemma.

"Why?" a few people called out.

"Is he no good?" another asked.

"Oh, on the contrary; he is quite exceptional." He thought a moment longer then flicked his wrist at the crowd as if they were a bothersome fly. "No. I've changed my mind; I think I'll keep him for myself."

The crowd grumbled with ill will. Several people asked to see me; a few demanded the chance to make an offer. Many held up purses of money for the auctioneer to see. The calls for the seller to continue grew in volume and intensity. The crowd was playing right into the man's hands. He signaled for me to climb the platform.

I wanted to turn and run. I hated the idea of adding to this man's ill-gotten gains. Yet I also knew my best chance of escape would come while in the hands of a private owner, so I climbed onto the stage and stood tall and proud beside the seller.

An audible gasp was followed by an excited murmur from the crowd, and before the auctioneer uttered a word, one man yelled, "I'll pay five senums of silver!"

A second man yelled out a counterbid, followed by a woman offering even more. The auctioneer ignored the bids and had me slowly turn around several times. The bidding quickly soared to levels that surprised me. After several minutes, the contest had narrowed to two men. Both had a small group of well-dressed servants attending them. I was able to glean from the murmuring crowd that one was a builder and the other a visiting nobleman.

The builder wore a hard, cruel expression; the kind that let you know he was a taskmaster who used pain and suffering to bend slaves to his will. I had seen that look before. The thought of servitude under him made me shrink. The nobleman was dressed in very fine cloth and was adorned with jewels and feathers. The way his servants fussed over him made me realize he was one who satisfied his lusts in pleasure palaces. He ogled me with a lascivious gleam in his eyes. The thought of servitude under him made me sick to my stomach.

With sinking affirmation, I believed an easy escape from either man would be next to impossible.

The crowd hung on the moment. Everyone seemed captivated with excitement. The auctioneer looked about ready to faint as the two bidders glared at each other. Each time the nobleman bid, the builder would raise the amount slightly higher. The small increases quickly annoyed the nobleman. With determination in his eyes, he paused to whisper something to a manservant. The servant mounted the platform and approached the auctioneer.

"Sir, my master grows tired of this quibbling. He wishes to increase his bid substantially but first insists on personally examining the slave."

The auctioneer agreed. Two of the nobleman's servants lifted him onto the platform. He wore a heavy perfume that made my nose burn. I felt his breath on my skin as he moved close behind me. I put as much hatred as possible into my glare when he looked at my face, but that only seemed to excite him. After what seemed forever, the nobleman climbed off the stage.

The crowd was deathly silent.

"I will pay double the present offer. In gold!"

The crowd gasped. I felt like vomiting.

Flushed with rage, the builder shook his fist at the nobleman. "You'll regret this," he cursed. "I'll remove all my services from your city and have my associates do likewise. I swear I will."

The nobleman turned up his nose. "Do what you must, but please take your vile manners and do it elsewhere."

The two held their ground momentarily before the builder marched off. My heart sank into my belly. The resolve of a new life that I had clung to vanished like a wisp of smoke. I was right back where I'd started. Devoid of hope, I simply wanted to die. I directed my gaze anywhere but at the nobleman. My eyes searched desperately for the face of someone—*anyone*—who would help me, who *could* help me. Bile churned at the base of my throat, threatening to surge upward. My knees felt like they would buckle at any moment.

Then my eyes locked on someone in the crowd—a tall man who looked vaguely familiar. Was he a former master? Had I worked for him sometime in the past? He stared directly at me as if trying to voice something through his eyes. I *knew* him . . . but from where? I'd worked for so many different people. Yet despite my best efforts, recognition wouldn't come.

"The bid stands at ten ezroms of gold," the auctioneer said in a voice so excited it squeaked.

I continued to plead for help with my eyes.

"Last chance to counter . . . no higher bids . . ."

Did the tall man comprehend the danger I was in? If so, could he do anything about it?

"None offered . . ."

The tall man began making his way to the platform. I kept my stare fixed on him.

"This slave is . . ."

The man held up a hand and yelled, "Sick! That slave is sick."

CHAPTER TWENTY-SIX

I KNEW THAT VOICE! I remembered its depth and tone as if I'd heard it yesterday. It was the master healer. It was Chemish!

Whispers of astonishment rippled through the crowd as the master healer climbed onto the platform. He gave me a subtle but meaningful wink then looked away. I understood instantly. I gazed straight ahead as if I had no idea who he was. The noise of the crowd hushed to an excited buzz as Chemish began to examine portions of my tunic with profound intensity.

"Wh-what do you mean?" the auctioneer barely managed to say through his own shock.

Chemish stared closely at my eyes then stepped back with a grunt of affirmation. "Just as I suspected. This young man is sick and should be put to death immediately."

The crowd gasped—as did I. What was he up to? I said nothing, but I continued to stare at a point in the distance. I had to trust him. There was no one else.

"No!" the auctioneer cried. "Are you certain?"

Chemish held up his hand, indicating that he needed a moment. He then poked me in random places, nodding his head and grunting. He felt my neck, checked under my arms, and prodded my back. He even checked the bottom of my feet, crooking each leg as if he were inspecting a horse's hooves.

"Wh—what's wrong with him?" the auctioneer asked anxiously.

The master healer stepped back and pointed. "Notice the blank stare and the hollow, gaunt look around the eyes. There are empty areas in his belly and signs of infection in his veins. Yes, yes, I've seen this before . . ."

The auctioneer's face blanched. "Are—are you certain?" he repeated.

"Who is this man?" the nobleman demanded.

Chemish ignored the man and continued his examination. The auctioneer answered, "He is Chemish, the master healer."

Chemish took me by the shoulders and pressed his ear to my chest. "Ah. Just as I thought."

The nobleman scoffed. "This young man is perfectly healthy. I see nothing wrong with him. What supposed dread disease does he have, Healer?"

Chemish gave the man a hard look. "To the ignorant, untrained eye the young man would appear as healthy as . . . a leopard."

He remembered that? I fought to suppress a smile and continued to stare blankly ahead. Chemish proceeded much like a teacher instructing a student. "It is a disorder that affects Nephites around this age, in which the air spoils inside his chest, suffocating his vital organs and tissues and causing a buildup of poisons that infect his entire body. Yes . . . yes, it's very plain to see; quite typical, in fact. Note again the blank stare, the tight pale skin, and the overall look of being possessed by a dumb spirit."

I bit the inside of my lip and held my stance.

The nobleman looked me over with a critical eye, but his confused expression belied his ignorance. "I don't believe you," he said through a deep scowl.

"I can prove it," Chemish said confidently. "If you part his tunic, you'll see scars running side to side across his belly. They are confirmation of this kind of illness."

The auctioneer moved in, tore my tunic open, and gawked at the scars on my stomach. He backed away and gestured with an open hand as if displaying the proof for the crowd's approval. "He has the scars," he announced loudly.

A number of people in the plaza began nodding their heads in agreement; many conferred amongst themselves. Chemish next made a great show of tearing a piece of cloth from his robe and carefully wrapping it around his hand.

"The decisive test which will render my conclusion beyond question is the core-cough reaction. Observe, as a violent cough will ensue when I press against these scars on his belly."

When Chemish pressed on my stomach, I immediately doubled over and coughed—almost to the point of vomiting—just as he said. The crowd oohed and aahed in astonished delight. A few individuals even applauded. When I stopped retching, the nobleman was still scowling. He instructed one of his servants to repeat the test on me. Chemish handed the servant the strip of cloth, and the man hesitantly pressed it to my belly. I made sure the results were as spectacular as the first.

The nobleman groaned openly.

"*Must* this slave be put to death?" the auctioneer asked.

Chemish mused over the question and regarded me thoughtfully. "He might be cured . . . with the proper care, of course, in . . . a year. More likely two."

"Two years?" the auctioneer whined.

"I certainly will not wait two *years*," snapped the nobleman. "I withdraw my offer."

"Two years?" the auctioneer again whined.

The master healer nodded. "Until then, he'll be highly contagious to the other slaves. You really have no choice but to put him to death," he said, wiping his hands on his robe.

The auctioneer looked ready to collapse. Ten ezroms of gold was a massive fortune, and I was sure the man had thought he was set for life. Now, suddenly, his life of bliss had vanished.

Angrily, the nobleman left the square, with his servants in tow. The crowd was perfectly silent—as if collectively holding their breath. The auctioneer teetered drunkenly on tremulous legs.

Chemish continued to examine me. "Perhaps . . . perhaps *I* could use him," he said, as if thinking aloud.

"But—but you said he was sick," argued the auctioneer.

"Oh, he is. And he will undoubtedly die within a month. But he might prove useful to test my new medicines on, to see if they're safe. I have one I am developing right now, in fact. If it turns out to be a poison, it is no loss."

A murmur of approval rippled through the crowd. The auctioneer still swayed, silent and miserable. What the master healer said made sense—although I didn't like the idea of swallowing a potential poison.

"Tell me, my friend," Chemish said as he dug through a small purse. "How much did you pay for him?"

The auctioneer stared blankly at the master healer, as if he didn't understand him. His eyes were glassy, his mouth hung open, wanting to speak but not uttering a sound. I honestly believed he'd forgotten *how* to speak.

Chemish removed a handful of coins and placed them in the auctioneer's hand. "Regardless, this should cover your losses."

Before the auctioneer could respond, Chemish led me off the stage and into the crowd. The people scattered before us, clearly not wanting to contract my dread disease.

We walked silently through the large city and eventually entered an unassuming dwelling near the edge of town. It was modest in size; a stone and plaster exterior surrounded by a well-tended garden; a stable in the back with horses, goats, and fowl. I saw two men, possibly servants, tending to the livestock. We passed through a latticed gate and entered through a hinged door.

The interior of the dwelling surprised me. It was a mess. Littered with instruments, writing materials, scrolls and books, and all manner of crystals, powders, and plant matter, the main living area was in turmoil. There was no sense to it—no regularity or organization. And yet the room conveyed a feeling of usefulness and importance. At once, I recognized it as a room filled with knowledge. Off to one side was a cooking area that also held a table and benches.

Chemish led me up some narrow stairs along one wall to a loft. "You can sleep here," he said. "It is cool, dry, and quiet."

I wanted to thank him, but my throat was suddenly tight with emotion. This was perhaps the second or even third time he had saved my life. I owed this stranger so much, but then, he wasn't really a stranger. We had developed a friendship long ago, one I had chosen to break when I'd tried to escape. He owed me nothing, and yet he continued to show the greatest compassion toward me. In many respects, I saw a great deal of my father in him. It was easy to forget he was a Lamanite. And I willingly did just that.

Chemish regarded me as if trying to read my thoughts. Without hesitation, I stepped up and embraced him. "Thank you," I whispered.

Caught off guard, Chemish slowly brought his hands up and patted my back.

"Thanks are not required," he said, sounding as indifferent as possible. But I could hear a catch in his voice.

Swallowing the lump in my throat, I said, "Yes, they are. I had given up all hope until you came along. You saved my life *again*, and I swear by my name and my family's name, I will repay you."

He stepped back and shrugged. I sensed the emotions he fought to suppress. "Repayment is not important to me."

"But it *is* important to me. You just purchased me, so I will be your servant and will do as you wish. I give you my word I will never try to escape."

His smile was broad and genuine. "Then I accept." There was a shine in his eyes—one he did not try to hide. "If it's important to you, it's important to me. But of greater importance is getting you back to health." He pointed to a low platform lined with a thick length of fleece. "Rest now. You look exhausted. Don't worry about anything else. Just sleep and be assured you are safe."

I wanted to thank him again, but a wash of emotion made it impossible to speak. He gripped my shoulders warmly then climbed down from the loft.

CHAPTER TWENTY-SEVEN

"You know, I almost didn't recognize you," Chemish said that evening while pouring a thick brown liquid into a tiny cup for me. "You've grown considerably. You're no longer a little boy."

"I was never a *little* boy," I replied. "You said yourself that I was big for my age."

Chemish chuckled. "You're right. I did say that. You have an incredible memory, Jarem. How long ago was that?"

"Another life," I said softly.

With a look of apology, he handed me the small cup. "Here. Sip this slowly."

"Is it poison?"

"Almost," he said with a wink.

I took a sip. My eyes widened as the most delicious taste I had ever experienced filled my mouth. I drained the cup in a single swallow.

Chemish smiled and refilled the tiny cup. "I said slowly."

"What is this?"

"It's called cocoa. It's made from a bean that grows plentifully in the hills around here. Don't your people have it?"

"Oh, cocoa, yes. But only wealthy families drink it. My father said he tried it once, but it was too bitter for his taste."

"The cocoa bean *is* very bitter. I add sweet cane to hide the bitterness and longan fruit to thicken it. Most people use cocoa as a social drink, but I think it has medicinal value. I'm currently testing it on various illnesses. So far, I've found it has potent effects against depression, and it seems to increase endurance."

"Well, if this is the poison you spoke of at the auction, I will gladly test it for you," I said. The drink was absolute bliss.

Sitting in a nook created for cooking, I gazed into the adjoining main room. I marveled at the variety of plant materials: roots, bulbs, leaves and stems, seeds, fruits, and bark. I saw containers filled with minerals in differing coarseness and color. There were countless ceramic jars and bamboo cylinders and a large number of other things I didn't recognize. Along the far wall stood shelves filled with books, scrolls, parchments, and vellum. It was readily apparent that this man spent his life studying life.

"The first item of concern is to get you cleaned up and in some decent clothing," Chemish announced. "And from the looks of it, you probably haven't had a good meal in a long while."

"No, I haven't," I admitted. "But I'm not complaining."

Chemish grunted. "But then, you wouldn't, would you?" He went to a pantry and selected a bowl into which he broke a small loaf of bread and drenched it in milk. "You'll have to be satisfied with this for now. I doubt your system can handle anything too rich."

I thanked him and happily ate the food. It'd been so long since I'd tasted fresh bread I had forgotten how good it was. He then gave me a clean robe and took me to a public bath near his house. The hot water pouring over my worn-out body was so incredibly soothing it felt as if it cleansed my soul as well as my skin. Using a sponge and soap, I scrubbed away months of dirt, oil, and filth. After the bath, we went to a small market where Chemish bought me fresh clothing and a pair of sandals.

It was dark by the time we returned to his home. I had another bowl of bread and milk. I was so exhausted from walking I could barely make it up the stairs to the loft. A tiny window next to the cot allowed a view of the starry sky. The chirruping of hundreds of frogs and insects lulled me to sleep almost instantly. And for the first time in almost two years, I slept without dreaming.

*   *   *

I awoke to the aroma of something delicious. I rolled off my cot and stumbled down the stairs. Chemish was stirring a pot from which rose the rich smell.

He smiled. "I'm sorry it's just porridge, but I don't want you eating anything more substantial just yet."

"Porridge is more than I usually get, so I don't mind," I told him.

"Good. Now, what would you like to do today?"

I blinked and pretended to clear my ear with my little finger, as if I'd had trouble hearing him. "I'm sorry. What did you ask?"

"What would you like to do today? I have only four appointments, so my day is pretty much free."

"But . . . you're my owner. I do whatever *you* want me to do."

He chuckled warmly and favored me with a reproachful smile. "Jarem, I am no more your owner than you are my slave."

"But—"

"No, no. I won't have any argument about it. I stepped in yesterday because I couldn't stand the thought of you in the hands of that sodomite."

"What about the other man—the builder? I've done heavy labor before. Would you have stepped in if he'd won the bidding?"

Chemish's brow furrowed. "Absolutely. He kills more slaves than anyone I know. He literally works them to death. No, it's best you didn't end up with either man."

"So . . . what am I to do?" I was truly confused.

"That is for you to decide," he answered with a shrug. "For now, I think it'd be wise to stay inside and rest for a while. If you wandered through the city, it would look suspicious. Remember, you're supposed to have a terrible disease. We can't have you recover too quickly, now can we?"

"I understand," I said. But my voice was hesitant, unsure.

"If you feel the need to get out, you can stroll in my garden. Just don't leave my property." He paused and looked at my legs. "Speaking of which, how's that broken leg of yours?"

I smiled. "Your reputation is well deserved, Master Healer. I can't even tell it was ever broken."

He patted my shoulder. "I'm glad."

* * *

Throughout the next month, Chemish gave me free run of his house and garden. I tried to help by cleaning the cooking area, dusting the main room, and keeping the garden free from weeds. He said the work was not required, but I couldn't just sit around doing nothing. My life had become one of servitude, and I grew restless when there was nothing to do. Besides, constant work kept my mind off Zanesh and the hardships she must be experiencing.

One day Chemish spied me glancing through some pages of vellum.

"Can you read?"

"Yes. My mother taught me," I replied. "She said that knowledge is a gift from God and a pathway to the truth."

"Knowledge *is* a pathway to the truth," he agreed with a grin. "But be warned: seeking it will only give you a thirst for more."

"Fine. I love learning."

His grin widened. "Then you may read anything in this library you desire."

I was taken aback by his generosity. "Thank you. But won't that take time away from my chores?"

He closed his eyes as if exasperated. "Jarem. I have yet to assign you *any* chores. It is *you* who insist on being my servant."

Why he was so averse to me being his slave was a mystery. But since I loved to read and to learn, I took him up on his offer. From that moment on, whenever I was alone, I was constantly reading—sometimes all day long.

The master healer would treat whoever came to his house for help; but more often than not, he would travel to help those in need. His caring manner and open concern for others impressed me. If he couldn't heal them directly, he found another way to ease their troubles. Frequently, he would stay up very late at night studying his notes or concocting a specific remedy for someone. His was a selfless profession, one to which he devoted full vigor and purpose.

Quite often, Chemish would journey to distant cities to care for others or to purchase materials. I was always in fear for my safety when he was away. His neighbors knew of me, but we seldom interacted. I was a slave, and I acted the part when in the presence of others, whether Chemish liked it or not.

With good nourishment, adequate rest, daily exercise, and weekly trips to the bathhouse, my health returned quickly. The more often people saw me with the master healer, the more accustomed they grew to my presence. Some even exchanged salutations with me. Most people referred to me as "slave." I didn't like it, but I never said so. Besides, it made me smile inside. No slave ever had it as good as I did.

CHAPTER TWENTY-EIGHT

A FEW MONTHS LATER, A tearstained little girl showed up on the master healer's doorstep. Naturally, I thought she was sick, but after entering the house, she explained that her doll had a broken leg. I expected Chemish to toss her out, but he didn't. Instead, he treated the situation with surprising seriousness. After examining the doll, he carefully braced its leg with a small stick and wrapped it with some cloth. He then recommended plenty of fresh air, sunshine, and lots of embraces and kisses. The little girl left very happy.

"Was that part of your healer's training?" I asked in jest.

Not meeting my eyes, he said, "It is why I became a healer." The catch in his voice told me his explanation carried deeper meaning.

"What happened?" I asked, intrigued.

He sat and rested his elbows on his knees. "I was a seller of herbs and minerals in my former days," he explained. "I was young, modestly successful, and foolishly arrogant. My wife was about eight months pregnant with our firstborn, and—"

"You're married?" I interrupted, wondering why I hadn't met his wife.

"I'm a widower. My wife, Naomi, passed away during childbirth, as did my son." He paused, opened his palms, and stared at their emptiness. "I felt so helpless during the whole ordeal. There I was, a seller of herbs, and yet I could do nothing to help her in her delivery. I called for the midwife. She said the baby was positioned wrong. My wife had issued water and blood, but that's where everything stopped. There was nothing the midwife could do; it was all up to Naomi to deliver the baby. But she was in agony. So I called on the local healer—a shaman who was more soothsayer than physician. He chanted and danced and burned some incense. Not surprisingly, it didn't help. I pleaded with him to give her medicine."

An angry look crossed the healer's face. "The man insisted I sacrifice a goat and spread its entrails over my wife. That didn't make any sense to me.

I've always been the kind of man who has to understand something before I'll try it. When I refused to kill the goat, the shaman cried and wailed and rent his clothes. He claimed he'd foreseen this in the stars. He said he'd reveal his prophetic vision only if I paid him a large sum of money."

"Did you?"

"No. I called him a fraud and threw him out of my house."

Chemish continued to stare at his hands as if searching for an answer in the creases of his palms. He remained silent for a long time.

"So what happened?" I asked softly.

"Naomi's pain became unbearable—both for her and for me. I couldn't stand hearing her pleas for help knowing I couldn't answer them. Then I remembered hearing of the poppy resin from which a pain-relieving paste was made. I knew of a merchant a short distance away who had some. I ran to his house and bought it. When I returned, Naomi had issued more blood but still no baby. I panicked. I took the resin and gave her a measure. When her pain lessened, I gave her more. And more. I wanted her pain to end. I wanted—"

Chemish's voice choked off. He swallowed hard, shaking his head. Then he scoffed bitterly. "Her pain did end. She said she felt numb all over. She even smiled. I thought I had cured her. But her delivery had also stopped. The midwife and I tried everything we knew to encourage her, but . . . but she just laughed. She laughed! The medicine had not only stopped her pain, it had stopped her labor and put her in a stupor to the point of not caring. I tried to get her to swallow some mustard paste to make her vomit, but she refused. She got angry and called me all kinds of vile names."

The healer sat back and stared at the ceiling. He exhaled slowly, painfully. "She closed her eyes and went to sleep."

"I understand," I said, indicating that he need not go on.

He shook his head and continued in barely more than a whisper. "I'd lost both a wife and a son. For months I was filled with such sorrow that I rarely left my house. I blamed myself for her loss. And the more I thought about it, the worse I felt."

"I understand that, too," I said very softly, thinking of Zanesh.

"Then one day a little girl—much like the one who came here earlier—knocked on my door. She too handed me a doll and told me it had a terrible bellyache. I don't know why, but I pretended to give it something and told her to let the doll rest for a few days before playing with it again. Her eyes filled with tears of gratitude. She gave me a powerful embrace and said I was the wisest healer in the land."

He paused and again sighed deeply. "I know it sounds foolish, but that's what changed me. A 'wise' healer would've known what to do. I realized that, had I *known* more, I might have saved my wife and son. *Ignorance* killed them, Jarem, not the medicine. And ignorance was something I *could* change. I vowed at that moment that I would learn everything I could to relieve pain and suffering and, if possible, to prevent death."

"And I'm glad you did," I said, patting my formerly broken leg.

Chemish smiled and continued in a lighter tone. "It's a curious thing. I found that the more I helped others, the better I felt about myself. I call it selflessness—forgetting oneself in the service of others. Compassion is an emotion that feeds on itself. Being wholly devoted to the healing arts gave purpose to my life. It became my life."

He stood and began reorganizing items on a shelf as if the conversation had never occurred. I pondered what he'd just shared and marveled at how, through misery, he had found happiness. Suddenly, an idea flashed into my mind.

"Master Healer, I don't know if it's allowed in your land, but if I'm not to be your slave, may I be your apprentice?"

The man of medicine slowly turned to face me. He regarded me intently for several moments without speaking. I squirmed under his gaze but was resolute in my request.

"I learn very fast," I continued, "and my knowledge of the jungle will help with collecting plants or herbs or whatever else you need."

He continued to search me silently. I worried that he was seeking a way to gently deny my request. It made sense that he would. Why would a Lamanite master healer take on a Nephite apprentice? If it wasn't illegal, it was certainly foolhardy. Even so, Chemish had used the study of medicine and the love of helping others to give meaning to his life. Why couldn't I?

"I too need something to give purpose to my life," I said softly.

Chemish stepped to a bookshelf and removed a large bound stack of vellum. He placed it in front of me and opened to a specific page. "Read this to me."

I began to read aloud. It was a list of observations on water. *Water!* To me, water was something you drank, washed with, and gave to crops. What more was there to know? I kept reading. The master healer's attention to detail was amazing, and his explanations of why each detail existed were things I'd never considered. What's more, they all made perfect sense. I stumbled pronouncing a few strange words, but I continued to read until he stopped me.

He closed the stack and stared out a window. "You read very well, Jarem. Now let's see if you can reason well, too. Explain to me the different forms in which water is found in our world."

Different forms? I cleared my throat, pausing only slightly. "Snow, ice, water, and steam."

"No, don't list them, *explain* them."

I thought about what I'd just read. "Water becomes hard when it freezes into snow and ice, runny when it melts and becomes rivers and lakes or like the rain, and vaporous, as in the steam from cooking and the heavy air of summer."

"And where does water come from?"

I considered the question for a moment. I figured water had always just . . . *existed*. If he wanted to know who *created* it, the answer was simple. "From God," I said.

"No," he said curtly with a chop of his hand. "It's not some miracle to be reasoned away without proof or true explanation. It has to make sense. If there is a God, I'm sure He is one of order and rules; and if that is the case, then it should be possible for us to learn those rules. I refuse to accept anything as being a miracle from some god or Great Spirit, to be believed for belief's sake only, never to be questioned."

I sat speechless, not knowing what it was he wanted me to say.

He took a calming breath and stared out the window again. "I've had many others ask me to teach them what I know. Some have offered riches, others power. But I have refused them all because they could not reasonably answer the questions as I've asked you. I do not grant favoritism, Jarem. I do not care if you're Lamanite, Nephite, Zoramite, or any other '-ite.' I see in you the desire and ability to *understand*; not simply to accept. But you must give me an answer *I* can accept, or there will be no apprenticeship. Agreed?"

I nodded. "Agreed. How long do I have?"

Chemish smiled. "See? You're not giving up. I like that. I'll give you one hour."

Where does water come from? With a writing stick and parchment, I drew a lake with rivers running to it. Then I drew some big clouds over it. I knew that it only rained when clouds were present, so I drew rain coming down. I stared at the picture a long time. If rain came from clouds, then where did clouds come from? It made sense that if water came from clouds, then clouds must be made of water. That meant water had to get into the sky to form the clouds. But how?

My picture showed water moving in only one direction. If that were the *only* direction, then the world would soon be one vast sea. What happened to the water after it came to earth? It didn't just fall off some edge in the distance. My people had learned long ago that the world was like a ball. I then recalled seeing water dry up in a metal plate. The water didn't soak into the metal . . . so it must have gone into the air, back into the sky. Perhaps it was a very fine vapor—one we could not see. And then that vapor somehow gathered into a cloud . . . like the beads of water that formed on a pitcher of cold drink on a hot day . . . and when it became heavy enough . . . it fell to the ground. It was a great circle. We just couldn't *see* it happen. *Therefore* . . .

"It's always there," I said aloud.

Chemish lowered the scroll he was reading and raised an eyebrow. "Explain."

"We know that rain is water falling from clouds; therefore, clouds must *be* water. After it collects in lakes and seas, it travels back up into the sky, perhaps in a vapor of some kind—like when water dries up when left out in the sunlight. It's a circle—a great round. The water is always there, just in different forms."

The master healer put his fists on his hips and grinned. "Well, I am impressed. Not only are you quick, you're also correct. Even many of our so-called *wise* men cannot grasp that truth." He rubbed his chin as if deep in thought. "Very well. You are now my apprentice. But I warn you, you may not like what you've gotten yourself into."

I wanted to leap for joy. Finally, my life would have meaning again. It would have purpose. And hopefully, the pains of the past would vanish as I learned the healer's art—just as Chemish's had. I knew I could do it. I *knew* it!

CHAPTER TWENTY-NINE

MY TRAINING BEGAN IN EARNEST. Life with Chemish was so vastly different from the time I'd spent in slavery that it took a while to get used to it. He first insisted that I remove the blue stripe on my forehead.

"You are no longer a slave, Jarem. You are a healer in training."

I was flattered, but I'd been around Lamanites long enough now to know most were untrusting of Nephites.

"Thank you," I said. "But if you don't mind, until the people of Midian get used to me, I'd better wear it for my own safety."

He saw the reasoning in my argument and didn't say anymore on the subject.

We began every morning, just after sunrise, with a run to a lake just outside of the city and back. But we didn't stop for drinking or washing. We did it just to run. I'd never heard of anyone running without trying to get somewhere or without some purpose, some goal.

"There is a purpose, Jarem. It's health."

I remembered him saying something similar when we were taken from Oranihah so long ago. But those were memories I didn't like to dwell on.

After our run, we'd take a dip in a stream behind Chemish's house. The water came directly from the mountains around us and was always cool and clear. The master healer continually asked questions, encouraging me to ponder the life around us. And he questioned everything. His quest for knowledge was unquenchable, and I soon found myself with the same yearning.

"I wonder," I said one morning while bathing in the stream, "did this water come from clouds that formed over our mountains, or from clouds blown in from the western sea, or from clouds over the sea our forefathers sailed to this land? For all we know, this water could have originated from a spring in Old Jerusalem."

"Huh. That is curious." The gleam in Chemish's eyes told me I'd thought of something he'd never considered. I tried to create that look whenever possible.

My daily routine continued with breakfast and study. I was to read and copy the master healer's notes on the human body and how it worked, on herbs and medicines, nature and elements, and nutrition and numbers. His knowledge of the human body was understandable; he was a master healer. But his insights extended to areas beyond basic healing. And his reasoning was absolute. He believed veins fed every tissue in the body; carried blood, water, and nutrients; and that they possibly carried away toxins and waste. But some of those veins were so small they couldn't be seen.

"That's why you can bleed with even the smallest cut," he said.

That made sense.

His writings placed each animal into families according to attributes: where they lived, how they moved, different aspects of their bodies, means of procreation, and what they ate. He noted the one universal attribute was that all animals drank water; thus, he believed that much of their bodies contained that common element. He felt the same concept held true for man. He listed plants in the same way, each in a family having similar attributes of leaf, flower, seed, and structure.

The amount of information was overwhelming. I began to wonder if I'd ever learn all he knew.

Each afternoon, I'd pause for a meal, and Chemish would quiz me on the things I'd read. After that, we went on gathering explorations, worked in his garden, or ministered to the sick.

Initially, I did nothing more than carry his bag of medicines and tools. It seemed more fitting for a slave to do such work. We ran into few, if any, Lamanites from the auction who questioned my state of health. When we did, Chemish simply said the new medicine he gave me had worked—and that usually ended the subject.

"How much do you get paid?" I asked after one visit, noticing the man had handed Chemish a silver coin.

"It varies. Most people I treat are from lower classes; sometimes all they can give me is a small meal, a rabbit or chicken or iguana, or some vegetables."

"That must make it difficult to buy supplies when you need them."

He shrugged. "Sometimes I'll receive a coin or precious stone," he said, patting his small coin purse. "Occasionally I'll get a trinket or a bottle of wine. It doesn't matter. The upper classes often pledge elegant jewelry or vast sums of money for deliverance from their infirmities, but I typically get only a portion of the promised amount."

Chemish chuckled at the hypocrisy. I found it wretched.

"You mean those who can afford more give less?"

"Not always, but yes—especially among the nobles. They seem to believe they're entitled to it by birth."

I considered that for a moment. "I don't know that I'm entitled to anything. In fact, the things I value the most are the things I've worked hardest for."

The healer smiled. "Well said, my apprentice."

I truly enjoyed watching the master healer at work. From the serious to the imagined, he treated each patient as if they were his most important case by giving them his undivided attention. I began to think much of his success came from his approach rather than any medicine or treatment he gave. I mentioned this observation after spending most of one afternoon listening to a woman describe in great detail her husband's favoritism for her sister.

"I personalize each patient's care to convince them they'll heal. If they don't *believe* they'll get better, they won't, no matter what I give them. I'm convinced a goodly amount of all healing takes place in the mind." He shook his head and sighed. "If I could choose to fully understand the workings of any part of the body, it would be the mind."

"Why?"

"Because it's what governs the entire body, and yet it's the area I know the least about. I've had a few chances to examine the material inside the head, from both the dead and the living, and it appears to be nothing but folds of gray fat. There is no consistent organization to it on the surface, but I'm convinced that inside there is a maze of workings through which miraculous processes occur."

"Miraculous?" I chuckled. "I thought you didn't believe in miracles."

"True; however, there have been many times when I was certain a person would die, and yet they recovered. I know the mind has something to do with it. Even if it's something as simple as a bruise, I believe the mind is somehow involved. Sometimes, when I encounter an illness I cannot diagnose, I invoke this power by giving a false medicine."

"A false medicine?"

He nodded. "I have a few extremely bitter herbs that have never proven to do anything except taste bad—horrible herbs that make me cringe just thinking about them. Yet when I give them to a patient and tell them it is the strongest medicine I have, quite often they get better."

"How?"

"I haven't a clue. They just . . . do—when they *think* they will, that is."

This information was so mysterious and exciting I wanted to know more. "You mean you can *think* yourself well?"

He shrugged again. Staring off at some point in the distance, his brow furrowed in concentration. "Think about it. When you get cut, do you always bleed to death?"

"No. It depends on the size of the cut."

"True. But why do all cuts eventually stop bleeding?"

I hadn't ever considered that. I knew it happened, but *why* it happened was another matter. "I think the blood dries out."

"Yes, but what *causes* it to dry out? And why does only the outside dry while the blood underneath continues to flow? What makes the skin heal and form a scar? We don't *think* about performing these acts of healing, so why do they happen?" He began pacing about, waving his arms in frustration. "You have to breathe to live, but you only occasionally *think* about breathing. What happens when you're asleep? Why do you keep breathing? When your heart stops beating, you die. But have you ever *thought* about making your heart beat? No, it beats on its own. But why? And how? I suspect there are hundreds of processes that operate in our bodies without our direct knowledge. So what keeps them going?"

I shrugged.

"I believe it is some part of the mind I have yet to discover."

He rambled on, citing one bodily function after another—most I'd never heard of. I offered weak suggestions, but for every answer I gave, he had three more questions. My head was pounding, but he was unyielding in his barrage of questions. It was easy to see why this man had become so great. His mind was constantly questioning, constantly seeking, never idle.

After weeks of being under his instruction, I found myself doing the same thing. The more I studied, the more I understood. And the more I understood, the more I realized how little I knew. It was frustrating and thrilling at the same time. I looked forward to each day so much it was often difficult to sleep that night.

Time seemed to pass without my knowing. But I didn't mind.

CHAPTER THIRTY

I CONTINUED TO GROW IN strength and size but, more importantly, in knowledge and understanding. Each day also brought me greater insight into the man who was rapidly becoming a second father to me.

One day, while sitting by a stream, I watched Chemish spend several minutes jotting notes on a fold of vellum.

"What do you do with those once you write them?" I asked.

"I add them to my library."

"I see. And how often do you review them?"

"It depends. Sometimes an event can stick in my head so firmly I never have to review it. Other times I go back to my observations so frequently I eventually have to rewrite them because they wear out. What's important is knowing I have them if the need arises."

That made sense. "Should I start writing the things I find important in a record of my own?"

He pulled from his satchel a second fold of vellum and handed it to me. I dipped a sharpened twig of bamboo into a small jar of ink and wrote the names of the herbs I had learned that morning; what they looked like, where they grew, and how they were prepared and used. As I wrote, another question came to mind.

"Have you ever reviewed something so often that you know everything about it, but you still have no good answer?"

"Like the workings of the mind?"

"More than that," I said. "I mean something that has you completely perplexed? Something for which you knew you *should* have an answer, but one has never come?"

I half expected a laugh or a self-effacing comment on his intelligence. Instead, he put down his writing materials and began tugging at his ear. There was a frustrated, lost look in his eyes—as if my question had sparked a memory he'd rather not relive.

"Yes," he admitted. "I have."

Now I was really curious. I sat with my vellum and bamboo quill in hand, waiting patiently, hoping for a full recounting of the experience.

Chemish took his time before speaking. "I've been a master healer for many years. My skills are known throughout the land. As you well know, I'm often called to other cities—even other lands. I try never to turn down a single request because I want to help those in need, *and* because I may miss the chance to learn something new."

I nodded, encouraging him to continue.

"One evening, about ten years ago, a royal messenger knocked at my door. It was in the summer, miserably hot and vaporous. The young man was winded and drenched in sweat. When he could speak, he said, 'The king is dead.'"

Chemish's ear-tugging became more intense, as if he were trying to literally pull the memory from his mind.

"What king?" I asked.

"King Lamoni. He's the son of the high king of the land."

"I've heard his name," I said, trying to recall everything I knew about the man.

The healer nodded once. "King Lamoni lived some distance away, so the messenger and I left immediately. Along the way, he told me that a Nephite slave named Ammon had cast a spell on the king, killing him—but that many of the king's servants claimed he *wasn't* dead. He said the royal healers had examined him, but they couldn't decide either way. I found that strange. Determining if a person is dead or alive is rather straightforward.

"Anyway, when we got there the following dawn, the king and a few other people were lying on the floor of his court. I saw no knife wounds or spilt blood. There wasn't any purged vomit, which would suggest poisoning, or even any appearance of a struggle. I checked King Lamoni and found he was alive. His life signs were very weak, but I felt a slow heartbeat and confirmed he was still breathing. He seemed to be in a deep sleep—completely unresponsive. Nothing I tried would wake him. He bore no puncture wounds from a sharp weapon, no bruising on his neck from strangulation. In fact, all those who had collapsed were the exact same, including the Nephite slave. Some of the king's servants wanted to prepare Lamoni for burial. Many believed the Nephite had murdered him. I knew he wasn't dead, but I couldn't determine what *was* wrong with him."

Chemish scoffed harshly. "Admittedly, I was exhausted from riding all night. I had trouble focusing my vision and my thoughts. It was all I could do to stay awake."

The healer went from tugging on his ear to rubbing his eyes, as if the fatigue he felt back then was returning with the memory.

"His court asked me if Ammon was a god or a Great Spirit with mystic powers. Someone claimed he was a monster sent to punish them by killing their king. But I knew the king was *not* dead and Ammon was just a man, as far as I could tell. Many of them assumed Ammon had put Lamoni in a 'dead state,' which didn't make sense either because Ammon was in the same condition."

"Curious," I said, using Chemish's oft-used expression.

"Indeed. But then something even stranger happened. One of the king's guards stepped from the crowd, drew his sword, and said something about avenging his brother; but when he went to strike Ammon, he instantly collapsed to the ground. I immediately examined the guard and found him to be quite dead—no question about it—but I had no idea why he'd suddenly died. We all simply stood there, silently staring at the madness."

The healer was now forcefully wringing his hands. His eyes were knitted shut, as if the memory now caused a headache.

"Only a minute or two passed before a servant named Abish knelt beside the queen and touched her hand. When she did, the queen sat up, fully awake. I couldn't believe it. When I asked the queen how she felt, she got to her feet and began walking around the court praising the god of Ammon. She then took King Lamoni's hand and he too arose. After that, everyone that had been unconscious suddenly awoke, including Ammon. Just like that," he said, snapping his fingers.

"Did you question them?" I asked.

"Of course. I badgered them with a score of questions, but they didn't answer me. It was like they didn't even know I was in the room. They all sang praises to God and moved about as if nothing had happened. They were laughing and crying and embracing, all the while cheering about being purified and free."

Chemish paused and resumed his ear tugging.

"The rest is pretty unclear. Since King Lamoni was obviously well again, I left the court, found a cot, jotted down my impressions, and went to sleep. When I reviewed my record the next day, I was even more confused than before. I had written the events exactly as they had transpired, plus a few possible explanations. But none of them reasoned out. I conferred with the royal healers, but they were as confused as I was."

He glanced at me with what looked like shame in his eyes. "To this day, I still don't know what happened."

"I believe I do," I said, "but I'm sure you won't agree."

Chemish nodded. "I know what you're going to say, Jarem. But your explanation is one without any verifiable proof. You believe it was an act of God, correct?"

"Yes, I do."

"I thought as much. That's what Ammon claimed too. You see, he wasn't just a slave; he came to our land as a missionary. He maintained that King Lamoni's 'sleep' was a conversion experience." In a mocking voice, Chemish continued, "The Great Spirit had rendered the king lifeless and taught him in his sleep."

I should have been offended by his tone, but I wasn't. I'd spent enough time with the master healer to know how deeply rooted he was in his proof-oriented approach to everything.

Chemish frowned at me. "I'm sorry, Jarem, but that explanation is incomplete. What about the warrior who suddenly dropped dead? Why did God kill him instead of putting him in a trance and converting him too? Why were a handful of servants converted, but not all? And why did Ammon—a man who was *already a believer*—experience the same thing? It makes no sense. And how did Abish break the trance with a touch of her hand, and yet nothing happened when I touched the queen during my examination? None of it follows the laws of nature."

"I disagree," I stated boldly. "It makes perfect sense . . . if you will let it."

"What—*convince* myself that God did it? Talk myself into blindly accepting God's mysterious ways? Believe without questioning? You know me better than that, my young friend. I need *proof*—and there is none. My mind simply can't accept it."

"Perhaps that's the problem," I ventured.

His frown deepened—but more in confusion than anger. "Explain."

"You said yourself we know very little about the workings of the mind. You wrote that there are different divisions within the mind, both physical and mental. Perhaps the different divisions are for different commands. Perhaps there are earthly commands and spiritual commands. Perhaps the reason you can't figure out what happened is because you are using your earthly mind when you should be using your spiritual mind."

He began to laugh, softly at first, then much louder. I reddened, feeling rather foolish. I had to admit, a 'spiritual mind' did sound strange, but I knew I was right. I'd been taught that spiritual things were only truly understood by the spirit. And much of that understanding came through faith. Yet faith—and a spiritual mind—were clearly things the master healer found unacceptable.

Gathering my courage, I said firmly, "Someday you'll have faith enough to understand."

"That's what Ammon claimed," Chemish said, sobering. "A few days after the 'trance' experience, I found Lamoni and Ammon conversing in a meadow. I sat with them and discussed what had happened. It was a curious conversation."

"Why? What did they say?"

He smirked. "Lamoni was still in a state of euphoria. He claimed that, while in times past *I* had saved his earthly body from death, Ammon had saved his spiritual body from hell. He also said that Ammon could do the same for me."

"How did you respond?"

"I said I didn't believe in a spiritual body or in a hell. I told Ammon I was a healer, not a shaman; that I used the science of nature, not the empty promises of priestcraft."

I flinched. "You accused Ammon of priestcraft?"

"Not directly," Chemish said with a wry smile. "To his credit, he didn't take offense. Instead, he argued that my being a man of nature made me a man of God, too. When I asked how, he responded with a question: 'What governs the life of each plant and animal?' I said, 'The laws of nature.' I explained that everything behaved according to certain rules, that every action causes a reaction. If you pluck a blade of grass, it will die. If you pick up a stone and release it, it will fall to the ground. If you do not give water to a seed, it will not grow. Those are constant, verifiable facts. The same holds true with healing. There's no trick employed. It's the principle that *this* causes *that*. If you give a man too much wine, he'll get drunk. If you do not feed a child, it will die. If you eat a deadly mushroom, you will die. I told Ammon that everything on earth is governed by these laws of nature, and there is nothing we can do to change the consequences of those laws."

"Did he argue with that?" I asked.

"No. To my surprise, he said I was exactly right. But then he asked me who created the law. I said that no one *created* the law; it simply *existed*. He asked me whether a fig tree could instantly appear where nothing had stood the day before, whether stones and water came into existence of their own accord, or whether an infant child could suddenly, unexpectedly, appear at its mother's side. I remember laughing at him. I said that even a fool knows that everything on earth has a beginning. Nothing magically just *appears* on its own. He then posed a question that still plagues me. He asked if the same held true for the laws of nature."

The healer snorted. "I don't mind telling you I was stumped. I still am. Ammon was right: If the laws of nature held true for everything on earth, then that would *have to* include the laws themselves."

"That makes sense," I agreed.

"Yes. But for the life of me, I still can't decide where the laws came from. When I asked Ammon, you can guess what he said."

"From God?"

"Exactly. So I asked, 'Who is God?'—which was the wrong thing to ask a missionary! It gave him the opportunity to preach to me." He chuckled. "He told me all about God's great power and what He created. I asked for proof, something I could see and experiment with that proved it was of God, but he couldn't. He said exactly what you said: that someday I would understand, but I had to have faith to do so."

"And you never developed that faith," I said, more as a statement than a question.

"To me faith is a kind of blindness; it's the inability to explain things with a reasoning mind. It's asking someone to accept something that cannot be proved."

He stood and stretched. "Ammon and I argued long into the night, but neither of us convinced the other of anything. Lamoni was converted to your Nephite religion. And I have to say it made him a kinder man and a better king."

"But you still can't explain what happened that day, can you?"

Chemish shook his head. "Nor can I answer Ammon's question about the laws of nature. But that is not a surrender. There are many things I cannot explain. What happened to King Lamoni and his court is just one of them."

We returned to his house and prepared some materials for the following day. We were traveling to Giddoniha to see Magistrate Kumron. The journey was dangerous for me. Giddoniha bordered the land of Middoni, the Lamanite capital. Chemish said that many Lamanites were hostile toward Nephites— even personal slaves.

"It's a hotbed of political and racial unrest," he explained. "You are to stay close beside me and be on guard every moment."

"Can't I just stay here?"

"You can, but I feel you need this experience. As a healer you will often be called to go places you'd rather not—even to places that are potentially dangerous."

I nodded and smiled in spite of the nervous lump in my stomach.

CHAPTER THIRTY-ONE

THE JOURNEY TO GIDDONIHA REMINDED me of the times I'd spent hunting with my father, only there was no longer pain in those memories. Time had healed the sorrow of my loss so that all I felt was a strange mix of melancholy and joy.

Chemish and I filled the time with teaching each other. He'd point to a tree, a plant, or an animal, would ask its name, what use it had to man, and any unique attribute it might possess. In addition to my answers, I would identify animal trails, unique markings and signs, and explain how best to hunt the creature that made them. For both of us, the journey passed quickly.

Before long, villages grew into cities, each one bigger than the last. The closer we got to Middoni, the more hateful were the stares and glances I received. Despite my Lamanite clothing, the blue stripe on my forehead, and the company of the master healer, the fact that I was a Nephite seemed reason enough for the Lamanites to want to kill me.

"Middoni has had some bad experiences with Nephites," Chemish explained. "And these people know how to hold a grudge. Try not to make eye contact, and say nothing."

"What if I'm asked a direct question?"

"Pretend you're a mute."

He didn't elaborate on the "bad experiences," but he didn't have to. The glances I received were downright vengeful. So I spent most of my time reading—while remaining vigilant for any signs of trouble.

We tethered our horses in the magistrate's stables and entered his palace. I kept my head low and followed silently behind the master healer. We were led to a bench outside Kumron's chambers to await our chance to see him. A servant soon approached.

"Magistrate Kumron will see you now," he said with a bow. When we both stood, the servant glared at me. "Not you, slave. Only the master healer."

Chemish made a sharp motion for me to sit. I did so with my head lowered in chastisement. Only after they left did I glance around. I noticed all the servants were Lamanite. That didn't help to settle my nerves. I decided to make myself as inconspicuous as possible by engrossing myself in a book. From my pack I removed a volume bound in eel skin.

Just as I opened it, a loud crash sounded at the head of the hallway. A young man and woman—both only a few years older than I was—stumbled in, slipping and wobbling along the polished stone floors. It was easy to see they were both drunk. Trying my best to ignore them, I ducked my head and began reading. As they passed, their laughter abruptly stopped, and the book was ripped from my hands.

The man was dressed in an elegant but soiled silk tunic and feathered cape. His hair was tousled, his eyes puffy and red. The woman was dressed in similar finery. She seemed equally drunk. Sober, they would have been very comely people. In their present state, they were pitiful.

"Why isth thish Nephite . . . in *your* house?" the woman asked with a slur.

"And why isth he . . . reading?" the man said, barely forming an understandable sentence. "You should be . . . clean the sth—clean the sthab—clean where the horses are. Or digging a didcth . . . thomewhere."

Not meeting his eyes, I extended my hand toward the book. The tome was very old, and I didn't want any harm to come to it. The Lamanite frowned and held the book beyond my reach.

"Perhapth he can't speak," the woman suggested. "Can—you—talk?" she asked, emphasizing each word loudly.

"May I please have the book?" I said in a soft, even-tempered tone.

The two instantly burst into uncontrolled laughter, as if I'd said something incredibly humorous. Then, just as instantly, they sobered.

"You want thish?" the man taunted. "Jus you try and take it from me."

He held the book higher and stumbled back a step. The woman covered her mouth to hide her mirth. I couldn't believe this drunken fool was challenging me. All I had to do was stand and he'd probably cower into submission. I was a good deal taller than he was, and definitely in better physical condition. Yet I knew doing so would win me nothing but trouble.

"Please, sir. It's not my book," I tried to explain.

The man gasped. "You stole it!" he cried. "You . . . you! Our slaves cannot . . . cannot . . ."

"Read?" I finished for him.

"Yesth! Our slaves cannot read in my kingdom."

This winebibber assumed that because I was a Nephite, I was one of *his* slaves—even though he'd never seen me before. But the words "my kingdom" gave me an idea. Guessing he must be family of the magistrate, I reasoned that feeding his ego might gain me some advantage.

"You're the *master* of this grand house?" I asked in astonishment, knowing he wasn't. "My humble apologies, your nobleness." I bowed low and abjectly.

The woman's abrupt laughter caused her to lose her balance. She dropped to the floor with a shrill squeak.

"I'm not the . . . m-masther. But I *am* his sthon," he said, looking down his nose.

"My apologies. I should have known," I said, leaning back and crossing my arms. "A *true* master would understand the importance of increased wisdom."

The drunk scowled, clearly unsure what to say. He stood weaving slightly, the book still raised in one hand.

"I realize teaching a slave like me to read is nearly impossible," I continued, "but would the heir to a kingdom, such as you, want ignorant slaves? How would you like to be mocked because another nobleman's slaves are wiser than yours?"

His scowl deepened, and he cursed. "No one's slavesth are wisther than mine. I own the wisest in the kingdom."

"Exactly, your nobleness. Therefore, so that I might better serve you, please let me continue my studies. I promise to become your wisest servant, or my life is yours to take."

He staggered a bit but caught himself. The sheer quantity of my words was taking its toll on his ability to concentrate. He looked at the book then to the woman. She shrugged. He chuffed and tossed me the book. "You'd better learn well, Nephite. I'll be che—checking . . . on you."

"A prudent decision, oh, empty-minded one," I mumbled with a low bow.

The drunk chuffed again and helped the woman to her feet—which proved to be a challenge fraught with error. When they finally regained their footing, they weaved down the hall, giggling like fools.

I looked in the opposite direction and saw Chemish leaning against a wall a few paces away, watching the ordeal. He smiled broadly while slowly shaking his head.

"You are a flattering talker, Jarem," he said while walking toward me. "It's a pity I'm not teaching you law instead of medicine."

I chuckled, accepting his compliment with graciousness.

"What did the magistrate want?" I asked.

A shadow passed across Chemish's face. "He wanted me to concoct a fast-acting poison."

"For what purpose?"

"To kill masses of people. Nephites."

He put a finger to his lips for silence and motioned for me to follow him. We quickly refreshed our packs, saddled our horses, and left the palace. Once we were outside the city, Chemish shared the information he'd just heard.

"Bitterness and enmity has risen because so many Lamanites have converted to the Nephite religion. Magistrate Kumron told me that an anti-Nephite movement—of which he is a big part—is growing strong in Giddoniha and Middoni. He predicts the animosity will soon erupt in violence."

"Among the Lamanites?" I asked.

Chemish shook his head with a sigh. "The great king has sent a decree throughout his kingdom to purge the land of all Nephites. An army is being assembled solely for this purpose."

"Purge?" I asked.

"'Slaughter' is perhaps a better word. They expect the army to be ready within two or three months. Many citizens fear the Nephite slaves will try to fight back before then. Kumron thought he could gain the king's favor by poisoning the Nephite slaves before they learned of the slaughter. That way they wouldn't see it coming in time to fight back." He pinched between his eyes. "Such a waste of life."

"It sounds like being a Nephite is a risky thing right now," I said, trying to make light of a terrible situation.

But there was no humor on Chemish's face. "It's worse than you think, my young friend. Kumron told me that several other cities have already amassed weapons in preparation for the slaughter. Nephites are being put to the sword in the form of sport. He said rewards are being offered for any slave found without a master. From now on, do not trust anyone; go nowhere by yourself. You'll be risking your life."

"But I'm safe as long as I'm with you, right?" I asked without a smile.

He drew a deep breath and let it out slowly. "I fear being seen with me is only a temporary shield. We'd better begin thinking about getting you home."

I agreed. The citizens in Midian were used to my presence; I felt much safer there. When I said as much, the healer shook his head.

"No, Jarem. I mean getting you home—*your* home—across the border."

My heart tumbled at his words. As much as I missed my home and my people, I now felt there was nothing for me back there. My village had been destroyed, my family killed. My life at present was a wonderful existence. I had a caring, fatherly mentor teaching me a noble trade. My life had gone from a devastating low to an unbelievable high. I didn't *want* to leave. My home was now was in Midian, with Chemish. Why couldn't he see that?

We traveled in silence, my mind awhirl. If I left this land, I had to convince Chemish to come with me—not just to the border but to live among the Nephites as one of us. From what Chemish told me, the Nephite people had accepted many Lamanite converts in their lands. They would gladly receive a master healer, wouldn't they?

I frowned at the question. A single issue stood in the way of that dream: Chemish did not believe in our religion. He wasn't a convert. Would my people allow a nonbelieving Lamanite free passage in our lands? Would they allow him to practice healing as a nonbeliever? Would they trust him? Because I was his apprentice, would they even trust me? Even as I asked myself these questions, I felt I knew the answers.

Then another thought came to mind. I'd made a promise long ago that I would not go home without Zanesh. I'd sworn an oath to take her with me. I had no clue as to her whereabouts—or even if she was still alive—but I was determined to be true to my word.

I nodded to myself. Despite what Chemish had said, I couldn't go home just yet. There were too many reasons for me to stay.

CHAPTER THIRTY-TWO

EVEN AFTER CHEMISH'S WARNING, AFTER a week of confinement in his house, I grew restless and began to venture out on my own. Most everyone in our part of the city knew I was the healer's apprentice and accepted me as such. It gave me a sense of security when walking to and from the market. The people I saw daily smiled as I waved to them; some even waved back.

When no news of Nephite slaughter came to Midian, Chemish also grew less cautious. He began asking me to run errands for him—some even to small neighboring villages. I didn't mind helping in this way, but I had an unquenchable yearning to explore the jungle again. I missed our expeditions gathering raw materials. It took some convincing, but I finally got Chemish to let me roam the forested back hills by myself. Naturally, he urged me to be extra vigilant and wary. I promised to be as stealthy as a leopard.

I was up before sunrise the very next day. I packed a light satchel, making sure to include my letter of travel. I headed directly south, straight to a part of the jungle we had yet to explore. I followed light paths and vague animal trails, trying my best to stay off frequently traveled avenues. It wasn't long before I discovered a small clearing nestled high between two steep rises. A long, narrow field had been cleared amongst a dense stand of trees, secluded and well hidden. At one end stood a bamboo-and-lath hut surrounded by ferns and taro. Smoke rose lazily from a pot simmering over a cooking fire under a palm leaf awning and dissipated in the tree canopy above. Unless the fire got out of control, no one would ever see the smoke. A generous portion of the land had been tilled in preparation for planting. I slowly crept forward. The soil smelled freshly turned. I searched for a corral where the owner would keep a horse or an ox, but I saw none. Had the field been tilled by hand? Had they used slaves?

As I continued to scan the area, a young Lamanite man not much older than me, a very pregnant young woman, and a little boy of about eight years exited the hut. The boy and the father—as I assumed him to be—walked to a tiller made from lengths of wood, bamboo, leather straps, and a wedge of black rock. The father hitched himself to the plow; the son pushed from behind. They were both lean from hard work. But it also looked like they hadn't eaten a decent meal in a long while. I watched in fascination the determination of the father and son to tame the ground into soil suitable for planting. It was slow, painfully hard work, but neither of them complained. As they resolutely fought the stubborn field, the mother busied herself in the cooking area.

I couldn't deter my rapt fascination with the father and son duo. Perhaps I caught glimpses of memories with my father. Perhaps it was the tireless, non-complaining nature of the son. Whatever the reason, I sat there for hours, just watching.

After the sun had trekked halfway across the sky, the woman called to her husband. Although I couldn't hear the words, her tone was definitely cheerful. I eased my way through the jungle until I was close enough to hear them better. It was then I realized the woman was a Nephite! *That's why they don't live closer to the city*, I reasoned. Living in such isolation was dangerous; the jungle was filled with innumerable hazards, including predators and bandits. But they clearly wanted to avoid contact with anyone—undoubtedly because of the Lamanite attitude toward Nephites.

The little boy had a determined look on his face as he continued breaking up clods of earth while the man went to his wife. My heart softened as the husband knelt in front of his wife and placed an ear to her round belly. It was a touching scene, and I determined right then to help this young family any way I could.

When the sky grew dark, I secretly set some plantains and guava at the field's edge. I took a few bites from some of the plantains and smashed some of the guava to make it appear as if monkeys or sloths had left them. It was nighttime before I got home.

"What did you do today?" Chemish asked, looking over the materials I'd gathered.

My first impulse was to tell him about the young family, but I didn't. He might disapprove, claiming that interaction with them was too risky.

"Just some exploring. I found a nice growth of mushrooms up one of the hollows," I said, trying to sound indifferent.

"Excellent." He then helped me store the supplies but said no more on the subject.

* * *

The frequency of my excursions increased over the weeks. Each time I visited the young family, evidence of their industry was manifest: young plants poked through the furrowed field; animal skins were stretched and curing on racks. It must have been backbreaking work, but they persevered.

I learned that the little boy always followed a particular path to fetch water, to fish, or to gather handfuls of watercress. On my next visit, I left four fat fish at the trailhead by the river. I smiled as he gathered the fish and carried them home. I would have paid an ezrom of gold to hear him explain where they came from.

The following week, I snared a young pig in the jungle and tied it to a stump where the trail met the clearing. The boy quickly hauled that home also. Knowing such a find was too miraculous this far out in the jungle, I waited in the cavity of a large tree for the father to show up. It took only a few minutes. He had a dagger in one hand, poised as if ready for a fight. He searched for footprints and other clues but found none because I'd covered my tracks too well. He stood a long time in one spot, slowly looking around.

"Thank you," he finally said to the jungle. He then gave a curt bow and returned to his home.

I'm sure there was a royal feast that night. It made me feel good knowing they were eating well while their crops were growing. I wondered if Chemish would disapprove of my interactions. But then it occurred to me that by supplementing their food stores, I was actually preventing illness. Thus, I was fulfilling my apprenticeship.

The following week changed all that. I should have realized my secrecy would breed distrust—but it almost got me killed. As I approached the clearing, I nearly ran into the young Lamanite father. He was standing in the folds of a banyan tree with an arrow nocked in his bow, ready for shooting. Luckily, he was scanning the edge of the field instead of the trail I was on. I backed away softly and watched him for a very long time. Only his eyes moved as he surveyed the jungle surrounding the clearing. Obviously, he was looking for me. The food had become too common for coincidence, and he didn't trust the unknown source. I couldn't blame him.

I returned home knowing that if I wanted to continue helping, I'd have to reveal myself. But I feared he might not accept help from a Nephite slave.

I returned two days later. The father was out in the field planting sprigs of breadfruit with a bamboo spade. When his back was turned, I left a small pile of papaya and dried meat along with a note. It read: *You have a friend. Please let me continue to help.*

When I returned the next day, I found a small wreath of flowering vines where I'd left the food. Attached to the wreath was another note: *Strangers are friends only when they are no longer strangers.*

I smiled. He was wary, but not so much that he wouldn't take a chance.

The following day it began to rain—and it didn't let up for ten days. It gave me time to study, but I couldn't get my mind off the young family I'd befriended.

When the rain finally passed, I headed to the clearing. There, I watched father and son tackle the laborious task of weeding in the mud. As usual, the young one bore into the work without complaint, but I could tell something besides fatigue was sapping his energy. He frequently held his chest and coughed forcefully. By the time they reached the end of the field, the son was doubled over in a fit of deep coughing. He was sweating terribly and was wobbly on his feet.

As they worked their way back, the boy collapsed. I was instantly on my feet, my heart pounding in my chest. The father picked up his son and carried him into the shade. The boy gasped for breath. The father tried to give him water, but he couldn't hold it down. His coughing turned to retching, which turned to uncontrollable spasms.

I ran home, making it in half the time. Chemish wasn't there. In desperation, I quickly assembled a bag of medicines. I had a vague idea what I needed, but I wasn't sure. The boy was terribly sick. I'd seen his kind of cough and knew it could be serious—even life-threatening. I had to do something.

It was late in the day by the time I got back to the clearing. I thought of writing a note explaining the use of the medicines, but it was far too complex. I had to either abandon my secrecy or abandon the little boy. Would he, a Lamanite father, trust me, a Nephite slave, to help him?

The man was standing under their awning sweeping the surrounding jungle with his eyes, almost as if he was waiting for me. The woman sat in a hammock, looking in my direction. I couldn't see the boy. The man held the satchel I'd used on a previous delivery, which I took to be a sign of acceptance. But he also carried a long lance in the opposite hand. I had little doubt he knew how to use the weapon.

Taking a deep breath, I slung my bag over my shoulder and stepped into the clearing.

CHAPTER THIRTY-THREE

THE YOUNG MOTHER NOTICED ME instantly. Slouched in her hammock with her hands resting on her large belly, she regarded me with an approachable expression. I raised my hand in a friendly gesture, which she readily returned. She seemed wholly unafraid. Perhaps it was because I was a Nephite like her. She spoke to her husband, who was looking in the opposite direction.

The man sized me up in a glance. I was taller than he was, but not by much. The woman waved me forward. I advanced slowly but steadily, trying to show confidence but not aggression. The father met me halfway.

I extended my hand, showing an empty palm. "I am Jarem. I come as a friend."

"You're a Nephite," he said, pausing. "You wear the marking of a slave."

"Yes, I am a slave, though my master treats me as a freeman. I wear the slave stripe only as a precaution. I have brought medicines for your son—for his illness."

He looked me over again as if making up his mind whether to trust me or not. "It is dangerous for you to be here alone and yet you come anyway. Why?"

I shrugged. "Because I want to help."

His brow furrowed. "I don't understand."

"I am studying the healing arts with Chemish, Master Healer among your people," I explained. "I am his apprentice."

"Yes, I know of him," the man said. "But he is a Lamanite. And you—"

"I am very blessed," I said, interrupting him gently. "Chemish is a wise man and not a respecter of persons. He doesn't care about the color of a man's skin or whose family he is from; nor do I."

Slowly, his stance loosened and his frown turned into a smile. "Forgive my extreme caution, Jarem," he said, clasping my wrist. "I am Heth. You are welcome here."

We went to the hut where Heth introduced me to his wife, Leah. I wanted to ask how a Lamanite and a Nephite came to be husband and wife, but now was not the time. His son, Omni, lay trembling on a cot. The little boy greeted me with a half-smile, although the effort cost him greatly. He was very weak, sweating yet shaking with chills. I knelt beside the cot and held his clammy hand.

"Omni, my name is Jarem. I'm an apprentice healer from Midian. I want to examine you to determine why you are sick. Will you allow this?"

With watery eyes, the young boy looked to his father. Heth nodded his approval.

"Yes," the little fellow rasped.

I began to examine the boy the way Chemish had taught me: starting at the center of the chest and working outward. Placing my ear to his breastbone, I heard his heart beating very fast, too fast for a little boy at rest. I placed the tips of my fingers on the veins in his neck, under his arms, in his wrists, and inside his thighs, feeling for proper blood flow. All points confirmed a very rapid heartbeat. I put my ear to his back and listened to his breathing. It was shallow and raspy. Each time I had him try to draw a deep breath, he broke into a fit of coughing. His eyes were watery and distant, and thick drops of sticky tears dripped from his lashes. His breath smelled faintly of stale almonds, and his deep, barking cough produced thick spittle. Worse, he had a high fever. Omni's skin was hot to the touch, especially on his face and head. Chemish said a fever was the body's way of fighting disease, but if it got too high, it could hurt the mind. He said unless the patient was bleeding or wasn't breathing to always treat the fever first.

"High fever, raspy breathing, rapid heartbeat, pus in the eyes and throat," I said aloud to help me focus. "I believe there is disease in his lungs."

I mixed some willow-bark powder and ground parsley in hot water and sweetened it with honey. Omni drank it without pause and croaked out a raspy thank-you. I swabbed his face and body with a cloth dipped in cool water. Heth and I then moved his cot under the awning where a gentle breeze blew. Leah continued to swab as I encouraged him to sip small amounts of water. When their water bucket ran low, I sent Heth for more.

"We need to get him to the master healer as soon as possible," I told Leah.

"No, Jarem, we cannot," she said anxiously. "My husband is banished because he married a Nephtite. Even though he is from another city, his family has put a price on his head. It is better that we live in seclusion."

"I understand. But I am just an apprentice. I don't know how to cure your son; only how to ease his suffering."

She placed her hand on mine. "Do what you can, Jarem. I have faith in you."

Leah's words warmed me. I only hoped I could do some good before it was too late.

I mixed a paste of anise seed and elm leaves in some diced honeycomb and had Omni chew it gently. Mixed with his spittle, it would help to ease his cough. I next made a poultice of ephedra and eucalyptus, blended in some melted camphor crystals, and rubbed it on his chest. Breathing the strong vapors would help to loosen the thick mucus in his lungs. Lastly, I gave him a tea of coneflower and yellow root in orange juice for the infection.

I was using a lot of medicines, but Omni was very ill and didn't appear to have much strength left. I sat next to the little fellow, wiping his forehead, checking his fever and circulation signs, changing his sweat-soaked bedding, and encouraging sips of water when he was awake.

When the night air grew too cool, we moved Omni inside the hut. I knew I should return to Midian. Chemish had warned me not to be caught alone at night. But I didn't want to leave. I couldn't. I needed to be close by, just in case. Leah made us a small meal of taro porridge and palm hearts. Omni tossed all through the night, but his fever remained under control as long as he sipped the willow tea. Gradually, his strained breathing became more relaxed. I was tired but couldn't allow myself to sleep. My concern for this brave little boy helped keep me going. By dawn, however, I was completely exhausted. I leaned back and closed my eyes to rest them . . . just a little.

* * *

A soft hand touched my arm, making me jump.

Leah stood next to me. "Good morning, healer."

I sat up and rubbed my eyes. Daylight streamed into the hut, highlighting areas with harsh shafts of white. Embarrassed that I'd fallen asleep, I was more ashamed that I had taken Leah's cot. My gaze locked on little Omni. He was sitting up, eating some porridge. His eyes were clear, and his skin had regained most of its color. His breathing was still coarse but no longer labored. I rubbed my eyes again to make sure I wasn't dreaming.

"Good morning, healer," the boy croaked with a gravelly voice.

I got to my feet and paused for my head to clear.

"You slept fitfully," Leah said with concern. "I worried you might be sick too. How are you feeling?"

I ran my fingers through my tousled hair. "I'm fine, thank you. How is Omni?" I could tell he was still weak, but beyond that, he seemed remarkably well.

"He's much better, thanks to . . ." Her voice caught with emotion.

Kneeling, I gave Omni another examination. Some of the infection remained, but his body was doing a good job fighting it. Chemish said medicine was only to *help* the body do its own healing. I portioned out additional medicine and instructed Leah to continue Omni's treatment for another day.

With tear-filled eyes, she gave me a hug. "You've done so much for our family," she said. "May God always watch over you."

"And you," I said.

Heth was in the field, hoeing the soil. We clasped wrists warmly. "I don't know how to pay you for your services."

"Payment is not necessary," I said happily.

"Medicines cost money. I will not have a stranger pay for our needs."

"Then you have nothing to worry about, as I am no longer a stranger."

He laughed and clapped my shoulder. "I will repay you, Jarem. Count on that."

*   *   *

I made it home by midday. Chemish was in his garden tending to some herbs. He raised an eyebrow as I knelt beside him and began pulling weeds.

"And how was your night?" he asked in a hard tone.

His anger confused me. I certainly didn't want to compound that feeling by admitting what I had done.

"Not bad. I got lost in the jungle and spent the night in a tree."

His countenance changed dramatically. He tilted his head back and laughed.

"Jarem, stick with honesty. Your storytelling will deceive no one. First, having seen you navigate through the jungle, I doubt you could get lost even if you tried. Second, I noticed your medicine bag was missing—an odd cushion for a night in a tree, I must say." He stood and dusted off his leggings. "Come inside, and you can tell me all about your patient."

CHAPTER THIRTY-FOUR

"I'M IMPRESSED WITH HOW QUICKLY you learn, Jarem. Truly impressed. But at the same time, I would chasten you on your imprudence."

"How was I not prudent?" I asked.

"You know about the hatred rising in my people," the healer explained. "I've learned that the extermination army is assembled and preparing to sweep the land in search of Nephites. It's simply not safe to wander off alone. Not everyone knows you're in my service."

"But this family is hidden deep in the jungle. And Omni really needed my help. Isn't that what you said we do this for—to help others?"

His eyes narrowed. I sensed he wanted to chasten me for using his own words as an argument, but he knew I wasn't completely in the wrong. Something was troubling him, something beyond the latest Lamanite uprisings toward Nephites.

"Just be extra cautious, please. Now, what's to be done with the little boy?"

"Omni."

"Yes. From what you've described, I think he'll be fine. You did exactly what I would've done. Maybe not to the excess you did . . ."

"Can you see to him, please? Just to make sure?"

"Of course. Bring him here and—"

"I can't," I broke in. "They can't be seen. There is a price on Heth's head—"

"As there is on yours," he interrupted with a smile. "And yet you still chose to help them. It was foolhardy, but I admire you for it. Honestly, I don't think there is much more I can do for Omni. You are their healer, Jarem, not me. If his illness returns, then I will go to him. But I am confident you've done all that needs to be done."

* * *

A few days later I spied Chemish talking to a sandalmaker in the market near our home. Neither man saw me, so I slipped around a corner stall and approached stealthily from the side.

"Your ambitions are bold, Master Healer, but I know your real intent," the sandalmaker said in a teasing yet all-knowing tone.

"And what is that, oh, would-be prophet?" Chemish chuckled.

With a hand placed firmly on the healer's shoulder, the sandalmaker adopted a serious attitude. "We've been friends a long time, Chemish. I know the pain you still hold from the loss of your wife and son. Whether you admit it or not, this young Nephite apprentice is the son you never had. And understandably, you don't want to lose him."

Chemish sighed heavily. "You're right, my friend. He is a son any father would be proud to give his name to. But even as I fear for his life, I also fear losing him to his own people. I admit his loss would be a tremendous pain . . . one I don't think I could bear. And yet, if he is killed because I kept him here . . ."

What? Chemish and I were fast friends, true, and in many ways I looked up to him as a father as well as a mentor and master. But the notion that he felt the same way toward me was a shocking revelation.

Rehearsing his words, my heart swelled, and the corners of my eyes began to sting. Chemish spoke as if I'd already made the decision to go back to my people—which I hadn't. Midian was my home now. I was content here—even with the looming danger. I had to assure Chemish I had no intention of ever leaving.

As I slipped away toward home, my mind struggled to devise a plan that would satisfy both our desires; however, nothing seemed to work. If I left, it would devastate Chemish. The last thing I wanted was to bring him sorrow of any kind. But the healer seemed to think my life was in jeopardy—even in Midian.

A constrictive burning gripped my throat as I thought about returning to Oranihah. There was nothing there for me. There was no one there for me. And I didn't like the idea of being alone again—even among my own people. I envied Heth and Leah and their precious Omni. Even though they had few possessions and were forced into isolation because of their mixed marriage, at least they had each other. It opened my mind to the dreams I'd shared with Zanesh. Dreams I'd hidden away because I could not bear the thought of what might have happened to her. We'd talked about having a place of our own. Of starting a family. Seeing Heth and Leah was bittersweet. They faced their struggles as one, as a family. But like me, they also needed to be extra vigilant.

If my life was in danger, so was Leah's. If I had found their hidden clearing, so would others. It was only a matter of time.

To rid my soul of the painful conflict, I began to distill some alcohol from maize mash. Chemish returned a few hours later. He said nothing about his visit with the sandalmaker, nor did I. He watched me for a time, saying nothing. At first I thought he was analyzing my technique and progress. However, after a while, I saw he was watching *me* more than what I was doing. I could tell he wanted to say something but was stalling. I too wanted to express my concerns and feelings, but I was afraid of letting my emotions jumble my words.

I turned to him and opened my mouth then turned away.

"Is there something you wish to say?" he asked.

I nodded. There was so much I *wanted* to say—so much I *needed* to say— but in reality it all pointed to one thing. "Just . . . well, thank you. Don't ask for what; there are too many things to list."

He gave a quick nod and said, "You're welcome."

* * *

The following day Chemish packed two large satchels for an extended trip. He explained that he'd be gone roughly four weeks.

"Should I pack as well?" I asked, hoping to explore a new land.

"No. I'm going into one of the most hostile Lamanite territories. You wouldn't be safe—even at my side. Here's a list of assignments," he said, handing me a slip of parchment. "I've informed a number of my friends that you'll be alone and asked that they watch out for you. You'll be safe as long as you stay in this section of Midian."

"I will do as you ask," I said, both heartbroken and relieved.

The master healer left at noon, and the house was suddenly empty. I was on my own—free to do whatever I wanted. It felt very unfamiliar. Chemish had left me alone before, but never for this long. It was strange knowing I was a slave yet having no desire to escape. In Bashan all I could think of was escaping. But being an apprentice changed all that. Chemish had put his trust in me, and I wasn't going to betray that trust.

After finishing a few tasks, I packed a small satchel with food items and medicine and went to visit Heth's family. They were safely hidden in the jungle, so I had little worry of being caught so far from Midian. When I arrived, Heth and Omni were in the field. I said hello to Leah then helped the father and son work the crops the rest of the day. It felt good to do some hard labor again— only this time voluntarily. The work was fulfilling and refreshing. Omni had long ago recovered. He needed no more medicine. I couldn't help but feel a little proud of my accomplishment. At dusk, I returned home.

*   *   *

The morning of the third day dawned dark and gloomy. Thick clouds hung low, threatening rain. By midday the rain began, and by nightfall a deluge roared against the roof. Restless, I paced from the main room to the cooking nook and back. I didn't know why I felt so agitated, but I sensed something wasn't right.

As evening fell, a loud knock at the door made my heart skip a beat. I feared the Lamanite extermination army had found out I was alone. Then I heard a familiar voice calling my name. I opened the door and found Heth rain-soaked and gasping for breath.

"My friend, you're trembling. Come in and sit by the fire," I offered.

"No. Please, Jarem, it's Leah. She's trying to deliver. But the child won't come."

My knees went weak. I turned, looking for Chemish, knowing he wasn't there but seeking him nonetheless. He'd know exactly what to do. He'd been through this experience countless times. I'd read his notes on childbirth, but I'd never assisted with one—probably because the task was usually performed by a midwife. And reading about such a complicated process was vastly different from experiencing it. I felt horribly inadequate.

"There's a midwife not far from here," I offered. "We could go—"

"No," he snapped. "A midwife would tell others of our home. She may even try to kill the unborn child because it's part Nephite. No, Jarem, *you* must come."

I shook my head vigorously. "But I've never delivered a child before," I argued weakly. "I . . . I don't think I can."

His face showed confusion, then betrayal, then anger. "You are a healer! You healed my son!"

"Yes, but this is different," I pleaded. "You must understand; this is something I haven't learned yet."

I suddenly remembered that Chemish went through this exact experience with his wife and child—and had lost them both. Was I destined to endure the same tragedy?

Seeing my reticence, Heth grabbed my shoulders. "You have a gift from God, Jarem! Healing is in your soul. I do not understand why you hesitate. Why are you being so selfish?"

"But it's your child! What if I do something wrong and it . . . ?" I couldn't finish the thought.

"Listen to me," he said firmly. "If you do not come, the child *will* die—and perhaps Leah too. If you *do* come, then perhaps they both will live. You have only to gain. If you refuse, then you have already committed them to the grave."

The determined look in his eyes clashed against my feelings of utter incompetence. But he was right: I had to try. Ignoring the knot in my stomach, I gathered several materials and followed him into the rainy night.

CHAPTER THIRTY-FIVE

THE JUNGLE WAS DARK AND murky; the heavy downpour was disorienting. Mud sucked at my feet, making each step a battle. The darkness of the terrain had me stumbling over hidden roots and stones. As we neared the hut, blinding flashes of lightning split the sky, followed by peels of thunder that shook the ground.

I entered the hut and saw Leah curled on her cot. Omni was in tears but was still bravely trying to comfort his mother.

Heth knelt beside her. "Leah, Jarem is here. All is well now."

The knot in my stomach turned to acid. A single oil lamp offered enough light that I was certain they could see the fear in my eyes. I moved to Leah and felt her belly. It was extremely hard, quivering, but not going through rhythmic contractions. I used a roll of woven material to prop her into a sitting position. I then massaged her lower belly muscles, trying to get them to loosen.

"Just try and relax," I said softly.

"I can't," she hissed in pain.

"Breathe deep and slow."

She tried.

"How long have you been delivering?"

"Since this morning . . . just as the rain began," she said between gasps. "A crack of thunder . . . startled me . . . and my . . . birth sack rent."

"That's a long time. But rest assured: if this child wants to come, it will come."

I had Heth continue to gently massage Leah's lower belly as I prepared a tea of raspberry leaves, hops, and an extract of castor bean to stimulate her womb. I also added a portion of chamomile and kava to help relax her other muscles. At first I thought the child was stuck because the birth canal was too narrow, but then I remembered reading that that rarely happened after a previous childbirth. I believed Leah's extended labor had simply worn out her ability to push.

I massaged her neck and shoulders and whispered words of encouragement as we waited for the medicines to work. I wanted to give her something to lessen her pain, but Chemish's devastating experience loomed as a warning in the back of my mind.

Time seemed to stretch on forever. Leah was in terrible agony. I was at a loss, not knowing what else to do. The longer we waited, the less confident I became that the medicines would work. I instructed her to bear down every few minutes then to breathe deeply and slowly. She said she felt the child shift downward but only a bit. She was losing strength fast. She'd pass out before long. Tears streamed down her cheeks. Her breathing sounded coarse and raw.

I was near panic when Omni said something I couldn't hear above the storm. I told him to speak up—a bit more harshly than I intended to. The little boy cowered as tears welled in his eyes.

Heth placed a gentle hand on his shoulder and smiled encouragingly. "Go ahead, son. Tell us what you want to say."

His voice was small but confident. "Perhaps we should ask God to help."

Humbled by the simplicity and awesome power of the request, I nodded. "That is a wonderful suggestion."

Kneeling beside his wife, Heth offered a sincere prayer asking God to help their child enter this world. He then asked me to pray. I pleaded with God to allow the medicines He had placed on earth to do their intended good. Then Omni offered a prayer: "Father in Heaven, please help my mother to have a good baby. Amen."

Almost instantly Leah's contractions stabilized into a strong, steady pattern. She was able to bear down with each pulse. On the fourth effort, the child's head showed. On the fifth, Leah bore down, screaming through gritted teeth, and the child slid into my hands. It was a stout, healthy boy. Leah's sigh of relief was drowned out by the child's wail. I brought the infant up and into her arms, then tended to the afterbirth according to Chemish's notes.

Everyone in the small hut was crying along with their new son, including me.

*   *   *

I stayed until the following afternoon. As Leah, Omni, and the infant slept, Heth and I cleaned up the damage from the storm. We talked about farming and hunting, about life and relationships and the miracle of birth, and about the gathering of the extermination army. Because of their isolation, they hadn't heard the latest news.

Fresh anxiety creased Heth's brow. "You should be extra careful, Jarem."

"As should you. In fact, you should probably head toward Nephite lands as soon as possible."

"We are protected in this valley," he said with an unconvincing shrug. "Very few even know of our existence, and I feel we will be passed by should an outbreak occur. But living in Midian, *you* are very exposed. I fear for your safety more than ours."

I looked skyward and sighed. "I doubt I'll leave—mostly because I don't want to. Midian is on a major roadway, but it's a fairly unremarkable city; there's nothing it's really noted for."

"Nothing except its master healer and his Nephite apprentice," he said with a raised eyebrow.

I had no reply. We were in similar straits—neither of us wanted to leave, Heth because of his family, me because of my new life. We promised to watch out for each other and prayed we'd be overlooked by vengeful Lamanites.

* * *

I returned to the clearing each day to check on the small family. They named their son Lachonius. Omni loved having a little brother, and Heth was the picture of a proud father. I was happy for them . . . and truly envious. I prayed that someday I might be equally blessed. But who knew if that day would ever come?

CHAPTER THIRTY-SIX

IT WAS JUST AFTER MIDDAY when a well-dressed servant knocked on Chemish's door. He came from a lowland province to the east called Shilom. He was on an urgent errand. The king's daughter was deathly sick. The servant was already very nervous; when he found out the master healer was away, he began to panic.

"If I return without the master healer, my family will be put to death—as will I."

"Perhaps I can help?" I asked, hoping to calm him. "Can you describe to me what is wrong with her?"

"The princess is very sick with fever."

"Fever accompanies almost every illness. The difficulty is determining the cause of the fever. How old is she?"

"She's in her fourteenth year."

I began packing my satchel. "Please continue," I prompted. "Tell me all you know."

He swallowed hard and nodded. "She's been ill for nearly two weeks. She started with mild headaches, but they suddenly got much worse. Her sight is blurry, she's extremely weak, and now she's afflicted with muscle stiffness and chills."

Severe headache, muscle soreness, blurry vision, weakness, fever, and chills. Something was coming to mind . . . but slowly. I knew it was no simple ailment, but . . . I couldn't put my finger on it.

"Is anyone else in the palace sick?" I asked.

"A few, but none as severely. Many of our citizens are ill with fever. It is the season for the blood fever, and this year has been exceptionally bad."

"Blood fever?" I remembered hearing the term, but I wasn't sure what caused it. I began rifling through Chemish's notes to find anything on the topic. The messenger paced anxiously at the doorstep.

After a moment, I paused and looked up. "If this is a common ailment in your land, why can't your healers attend to it?"

"They have tried. The princess has an exceptionally bad case. Many of her healers are dead because of their inability."

"Dead?"

"Put to death." The servant shifted from one foot to the other. "When will the master healer return?"

"I'm not sure. I expect him back any day now."

The man groaned as if tormented by a demon. Tears pooled in his eyes as he fell heavily into a chair. I felt sorry for him. His fate rested on the competence of someone else's guesswork. It wasn't his fault the palace healers had guessed wrong. Still, the princess wasn't dead yet, which meant there was still hope.

"Just relax," I said. "Let me think for a moment."

Chemish's library held several scrolls and books from other healers, which I had yet to read. I scanned through a bound stack of vellum on blood diseases. The writing was old and faded, but I was able to discern most of what was compiled. I found a list of symptoms that matched those the servant mentioned. Regrettably, few of them had any known remedy.

"You say this fever is common at this time of year?" I asked without looking up.

He squeaked out something that sounded close to "Yes."

"Can the fever be passed from one person to another? Do you know how it's spread?"

He wiped his eyes with his dirty sleeve. "We really don't know. Either you get it or you don't. Our healers don't know how or why. Some say it's from bad water; some from the vapors in the swamps. The royal shaman claims it is a punishment."

Remembering Chemish's warning about straying too far from Midian, I asked, "Can the king's daughter be brought here?"

"No. She is too weak. She'd never survive the journey."

I nodded, thinking. "Will your king allow *me* to help?"

The man's eyes widened with fright. "We've never had a Nephite slave in the palace. It's a standing law to allow no Nephites into our lands. There is no way the king would ask you to come."

"But if I came anyway? Would he let me help?"

"I . . . cannot guarantee your safety."

I knew that each time I left Midian without Chemish at my side I took my life into my own hands. But a young girl was terribly sick. I made an instant decision to help. It was a prompting really, something telling me that this would result in a good thing. I copied a few pages of text and gathered some additional medicines.

After a full day of nonstop riding, we reached Shilom. The city sat on the edge of a vast marshland. Numerous sections of ultrarich farmland bordered marshy areas, and some of the wetland had been sectioned off for growing rice. The crops there were thick and lush. The road on which we traveled took a winding route to avoid the deeper waters, but we were still forced to wade through a number of boggy areas. The bad roads, however, were a minor annoyance compared to the swarms of insects which arose from the marshes. I wore a hooded shawl to hide my nationality, but it barely helped to thwart the plague of biting flies and mosquitos.

The palace was a modest one in relation to others I'd seen with Chemish. Still, it was well-built and formidable, and the people within appeared to follow strict rules of conduct. I kept my head hooded while the messenger led me directly to the room where the king's daughter lay.

The princess was a beautiful girl with thick dark hair and high, full cheekbones. Her name was Olgath—a decidedly unattractive name for one so pretty. She was dangerously feverish; her skin felt tacky and hard. Her clothes and bedding reeked of stale sweat. Her labored breathing rasped and gurgled, and her eyes were sunken and vacant.

I knelt beside her and removed my hood. Her two maidservants drew a sharp breath when they saw I was a Nephite.

"Princess Olgath, my name is Jarem. I am apprentice to the master healer of Midian. He was not able to come, and the nature of your fever demands immediate attention. Will you permit me to help you?"

"Yes," she said in a sticky whisper.

Her eyes were crusted shut. I wiped them with a moist cloth, which allowed them to peel open. She blinked a few times but didn't appear alarmed that I was a Nephite. Perhaps she was simply too sick to care.

"You have very green eyes," she said with a faint smile breaking through her parched, cracked lips.

"And you have beautiful brown eyes the color of cocoa."

"I love cocoa," she said with forced happiness.

"As do I, but you cannot have any until I get you well again. Will you let me try?"

"Yes." Her dry, hoarse voice was painful to listen to.

"Shh. No more talking. I'll do my best to heal you, I promise."

I gave her some fever drink made from willow bark and golden seal and instructed the maidservants to bathe her with fresh water and to change her bedding to sheets of linen. I moved to a corner of the room to organize my satchel and to give her some privacy. Once she was toweled dry, she fell asleep again. I told the servants to repeat the procedure every evening so bedsores wouldn't form on her delicate skin. I then sat under a window to read what I had copied earlier.

I concentrated so hard that I lost track of time. The answer was there . . . but I was missing something. I moved to the princess's bed and wiped her arms with a cloth moistened with aloe. It was then that I got a closer look at the numerous blisters on her arms, legs, and neck. What at first looked like fever sores now resembled insect bites.

"You there! Stop!" an angry voice shouted behind me. "Get away from her, you cursed Nephite."

I turned to see an elaborately dressed man marching toward me. His eyes seethed with hatred. Two huge men followed close behind with swords drawn. I knew right away it was Olgath's father, the king of Shilom. He grabbed me by my tunic and threw me to the floor. The maidservants fled from the room.

"Touch her again and I'll personally remove your head!" he roared, placing a hand on the hilt of his sword.

I slowly rose to one knee and bowed abjectly. "Great King, I mean no harm to the princess—"

"Silence, Nephite slave!" He drew his sword and shoved the point under my chin. "Guards. Take this son of vermin to the prison."

The guards grabbed my arms and yanked me to my feet. I offered no resistance as they led me out of the room, down a labyrinth of dark corridors, and threw me into a small stone chamber. The prison master whipped me several times with a cane before slamming the cell door shut. The room was cold, dank, and dark.

I believed if I could just explain things, the misunderstanding would be corrected. But the king was in such a state of angst over his daughter that I decided to keep silent until his temper subsided. How long that would take was the pivotal question. Would it be in time to save Olgath? Or would he execute me before I even got the chance?

CHAPTER THIRTY-SEVEN

I HAD NO WINDOW BY which to reckon time. I don't know how long I was in that black, moldering chamber. Two days at least, I guessed from the emptiness gnawing in my stomach. The guards gave me a little water but no food. The constant flicker of a torch glowing under the base of the door was the only light I had.

Whenever I heard footsteps, I'd yell through the door, explaining who I was, but I never received a response. My only visitors were the prison master placing a cup of water through a slot at the base of the door and an occasional fly or mosquito. Once I saw a spider as big as my hand scurry out under the door. Luckily, it never returned.

I wondered what Chemish was going to say when he learned of my situation—*if* he learned of it. With sinking acknowledgment, I realized that I hadn't left a note explaining where I'd gone. He might only learn what had happened *after* my death. I should've stayed at home and waited for him. It was foolish to venture off to an unfamiliar city, and I deserved what was coming to me. I was miserable, but I refused to give up hope.

To cope with my wretched surroundings, I concentrated on the princess and her illness. I was certain the fever mix I'd given her had worn off by then. I wondered if she'd already died. She was certainly a beautiful girl—surely the pride of her father's heart. But she was also very sick. I had to help her . . . somehow.

I was certain the bumps on her neck and arms were insect bites. I'd seen some vicious insect bites in Midian. They mostly caused local pain and swelling; other times they made a person sick with prolonged fever; occasionally the person died. Chemish reasoned that many insect bites instilled some kind of poison. Wasps, bees, and scorpions had the same effect when they stung. He also assumed most spiders carried venom in their bite. But not everyone who was stung or bitten died. Evidently, the poison was not as potent from one insect to the next.

Just then, a mosquito landed on my arm. I swatted it, creating a smear of blood on my skin before it had a chance to bite me. Staring at the blood, my jumbled thoughts focused into perfectly clarity.

I know what's making the princess sick!

The common factor was that everyone with fever had presumably been bitten by mosquitos. They were everywhere. I was certain the disease came from a poison in their bite! And the princess was covered with mosquito bites! Their poison must have gotten into her blood.

I again rehearsed the information I'd read. One of the pages mentioned treating lowland blood fever with a tea made from the bark of the cinchona tree. It didn't mention mosquito bites or where the disease came from, but I felt certain the cinchona tea would help her fever. And I'd seen a few cinchona trees just outside the city.

"The princess has mosquito poison in her blood!" I yelled, pounding on the door. "I know how to help her!"

I repeated the words until my throat burned with rawness. I could taste blood. Although no one seemed to hear, I continued pounding on the door. The ignorance of these Lamanites infuriated me. The bitter blindness of Olgath's people would be the cause of her death.

My strength gone, I sat with my back against the door. I wanted to wail in frustration, but I didn't have the energy for that either. Just then, the door flew open and I fell on my back into the hallway. The king stood over me looking worse than I felt. His face was clouded with unfathomable anguish.

In a hushed tone I asked, "Is the princess dead?"

He dropped to his knee and interlaced his fingers beseechingly. "She's at—at death's door," he sobbed. "My healers are preparing her sepulchre as we speak." He took my hand and helped me sit up. "I've learned you are a healer, trained by the master healer from Midian. That is why you came. But I have treated you as an enemy."

"I am his apprentice. And I believe I know how to help your daughter."

He brought my hand to his forehead. "I pray my misjudgment of you has not turned you against me! Please forgive my shortsightedness. You are my daughter's last hope. Please—help her. I will give you anything you ask. Anything!"

I found myself surprisingly calm even though I was weak for lack of nourishment. "Please bring me some bread and meat, and I promise to do what I can."

The king got to his feet and helped me to mine. I instructed a runner to gather some cinchona bark and another to boil some water. The king led me to his dining hall.

As I was eating, a servant washed me, and another one then fitted me with fresh clothing. The runner soon returned with the tree bark, and I dumped half of it into the boiling water. The proper tea concentration was not recorded—the notes merely said that the tea was useful for lowland fever. But it also said that pure cinchona bark was deadly. So if the mosquito poison didn't kill the princess, perhaps my tea would. I pushed that thought aside and dumped the rest of the bark into the basin.

While the tea steeped, I went to the princess and found her wrapped in burial cloth. She was deathly still; her face was ashen and waxy. I rinsed the crusted tears from her eyes and opened them. Her gaze was vacant, unfocused. I leaned close and positioned my eye under her nostrils and felt a tiny movement of air. I removed the burial linen and swabbed her face and neck with cool water and aloe. I had a maidservant massage her arms and legs, her feet and hands, to encourage the circulation of her blood. I parted her lips and tipped a trickle of water into her mouth. She coughed and gasped. That was a good sign. She still fought for life.

Putting my lips to her ear, I said, "Princess, it's Jarem. I need you to drink what I give you. Even if you can only sip it, swallow as much as you can."

She moaned softly. Her lips moved slightly but she said nothing.

Her bed was soaked with sweat and smelled rancid. I instructed her servants to change her bedding as I returned to the cooking room to check on the tea. The liquid was dark and smelled horribly bitter. I strained it twice and cooled it with some fresh water. I considered adding some honey but figured Olgath was too sick to care about taste.

Back in her chamber, I tipped her head and poured some tea into her mouth. I wasn't sure how much got in her because she gagged, causing much of it to spill down her chin. But I dosed her again and watched her neck muscles move to swallow. A few minutes later, I gave her some more. I repeated the dose every few minutes, and each time she was able to swallow more of the foul liquid. On the last dose, I added some fever mixture. When the cup was empty, I again put my lips to her ear.

"Rest now, Princess. Let the medicine work as you sleep."

Within three hours, she was breathing slowly and steadily, indicating a calmer slumber. I continued to wipe her face and arms with a damp cloth. As night fell, a servant brought me bread, meat, and drink. The drink was the king's best wine, but I politely refused. "I need to keep a clear mind until the princess is out of danger. If you could bring me a container of cool water instead, I'd be grateful."

I stayed by her bedside all night, wiping the sweat from her skin, keeping her cool and dry. She awoke sporadically, and each time I gave her more cinchona tea.

By morning I was totally spent. I staggered to a bath and refreshed myself. The servant brought me a wonderful porridge and some herbal tea. I walked to a balcony and looked out over the vast flatland. It had an undeniable beauty of its own, but I preferred the forested mountains of Midian.

When I returned, Olgath was awake and propped up in her bed. "Good morning, Healer," she croaked pleasantly. She was still very weak, but color had returned to her skin and radiance showed in her eyes.

I sat beside her and felt her neck and face. The stickiness was gone, as was her fever. "Good morning, Princess. I'm glad you're awake and looking as beautiful as ever."

She lowered her eyes, her cheeks reddened, and all my cares vanished. She was healing. I ordered her servants to administer the half-strength cinchona tea morning and evening for seven more days.

"Do I have to drink that?" she whimpered. "Your tea tastes like ditch water."

I chuckled. "It's medicine, Princess. It's not supposed to taste good."

"You do everything the healer asks," the king said from behind me.

I turned and bowed. He shook his head and took my hand. "Do not bow to me, healer. I should bow to you and beg your forgiveness. My messenger has told me how your master forbade you to leave his house because of the dangers a Nephite faces in these lands. Yet you came anyway—to help a total stranger. And because of your bravery, my daughter is alive. I was a fool for thinking you were here to hurt her. Can you forgive me?"

I took his hand in both of mine. "You had no idea who I was. You were expecting the master healer and instead got his Nephite apprentice. I hold no grudge."

"Apprentice?" the king laughed. "What you have done is worthy of a *master healer*, and I shall think of you as no less."

I stayed another day, recovering from my own weariness and seeing to the princess's needs. By the time I left, Olgath was able to walk a little and was brimming with the impatience of youth. She hugged me and kissed my cheek.

The king offered me a huge reward, but I declined it. Quite honestly, I didn't know what to expect as payment, and I didn't feel any was necessary. My reward was seeing Olgath healthy and smiling. The kiss on the cheek wasn't bad either.

* * *

I arrived in Midian late in the evening. The king provided an armed escort to ensure my safety. I expected to find Chemish at home, but he had yet to return. Not long after my return, a messenger came to the house.

"Are you Jarem, the master healer's apprentice?"

"I am."

"The master healer says you are to pack everything in the house and ready yourself for a journey."

"Everything? What do you mean?" I asked.

The messenger shrugged. "The master healer says he will be returning very soon. He wants everything in as few packs as possible. You're going away."

"Away to where?"

"I do not know."

The messenger left, and I stood staring at a room full of books, scrolls, plant material, powders, and hundreds of other items—and wondered how I was to store it all in "as few packs as possible."

CHAPTER THIRTY-EIGHT

EARLY THE NEXT MORNING I made a quick visit to Heth and Leah. The reunion was bittersweet. The moment I got there, I knew something was wrong. The family was quiet and withdrawn. I shared my experiences in the lowland provinces with them as we harvested a crop of maize and saw to a few other needs.

Without warning, Omni threw down his tool and blurted, "Why must we leave? I like it here. Jarem is here."

My surprise must have shown plainly. Both parents lowered their eyes as if in shame.

"You're leaving? Why didn't you tell me sooner?" I asked.

"I'm sorry, Jarem," said Heth. "We should have, but . . . well, I don't need to tell you how dangerous it is for Nephites in these lands. Now there are even hostilities between my people and the Anti-Nephi-Lehis."

"Who are the Anti-Nephi-Lehis?"

"They are Lamanites who have converted to the Nephite religion," Leah explained. "There are over a thousand of them now, perhaps more. Many have left to go to Zarahemla."

"We have friends among those still remaining," Heth explained. "I met some six days ago when I was trading in Middoni. They . . . they have asked us to go with them."

"What?" I couldn't believe I hadn't heard any of this. But then, I *had* been in Shilom a long while.

"I fear for my family, Jarem," Heth confessed. "I must take them from this land *now*, before it's too late."

For the hundredth time since arriving in Lamanite territory, my spirits sank. I felt frustrated and deceived. I'd grown so close to this family, and I knew they felt the same affection for me. Still, their fears were founded in truth. I couldn't fault them for their decision.

"You can come with us," Omni said eagerly. "You can have half of my food."

"I'm sure the Anti-Nephi-Lehis could use a good healer," Leah added.

With a heavy heart, I shook my head. "I cannot leave Chemish now. He's counting on me to help him in his work, and I am far from being a true healer. I still have so much to learn."

"But is it safe for you?" argued Heth. "They say *all* Nephites are being killed by the extermination army, regardless of who they belong to."

Their argument was valid. The smart thing to do was to go with them. But if I left before Chemish returned, I'd betray the trust he'd shown me. I was committed to staying with him as long as I could. I trusted in the master healer and my God. I knew my Heavenly Father was with me as long as I had faith in Him. And yet there was no denying that Heth was right. He knew Leah's life was in peril simply because of the color of her skin—as was mine. Once again, my thoughts turned to Zanesh. Had the army found and killed her?

My head pounded and my heart ached as I wrestled with the decision to stay or go. With tears burning my eyes, I bid farewell to Heth, Leah, Omni, and Lachonius. On the trek home, I pleaded with God for a clear answer. I tried to have the faith and patience to await an answer—but it was an answer that could not wait.

At home, I sat pondering my tenuous situation. I was despondent and unsure. Depression soon overwhelmed me. I wanted to crawl onto my cot with the hope that everything would be right in the morning. I found myself growing bitter too easily, too quickly. Negative emotions filled my heart as I sat idly, sulking through the night. Why was this happening all over again? First, I'd lost my family in the raid at Oranihah. Then I'd found happiness with Zanesh—until she was taken from me. Now my love for Heth and Leah and their children was being mocked. Was I destined to lose everyone I loved?

Finally, I found myself on my knees. I begged my Father in Heaven to calm my troubled heart and to help me find the answers I so desperately sought. I promised to do all I could to serve God and my fellowmen if He would prepare the way for me. Then, as I lifted my head, a calmness flowed through me, leaving in its wake clarity and assurance. The master healer had asked me to pack everything for a reason.

With renewed vigor, I packed what I considered necessary for a long journey. A few close friends helped. I finished just before dawn and fell asleep on the floor of the main room.

* * *

Chemish burst through the door, spilling sunlight across my face. "We have to go," he snapped. "Did you pack everything?"

I sat up with a groan. "Welcome back," I said through a yawn while pointing to five large packs.

He pulled a large satchel from a shelf and began cramming it with notebooks, medicines, and other items I had not packed. When it was full, he grabbed two large baskets, tossing one to me.

"Is there something in particular I should have packed?"

"Everything," was his curt answer.

Together we stored nearly half the room in whatever bag, basket, sack, or satchel we could find. Chemish had a man who tended his horses bring four of them from the stables. We loaded two with our packs and saddled the other two.

Watching Chemish tether a goat to one packhorse, my curiosity became overwhelming. "Is there something I should know about all this?" I asked, gesturing to the horses.

He nodded and paused to drink from a flask. "The extermination army is headed this way. They're killing all Nephites, regardless of their standing."

"What about the Anti-Nephi-Lehis?"

His eyebrows lifted, a surprised look crossing his face.

"I know all about the Lamanite converts and the extermination army. But you are an influential man in this land. Couldn't you simply explain that—"

"No," he said, cutting me off. "This army has sworn a blood oath not to let anyone escape. I've already tried reasoning with them. It did no good."

"And you're sure they're coming directly here?"

He nodded slowly, ominously. "They know about you, Jarem."

I frowned. "They know about me? How?"

"It doesn't matter. We must leave today. Immediately."

A deep voice sounded from behind us. "Then the young healer will be needing food and drink for the journey."

We turned to see the king of Shilom coming toward us with a number of servants in tow. It looked as if he was headed to the market with a caravan of trade goods. Two servants unloaded hefty sacks of food while another handed us several skins of drink.

Speechless, Chemish gawked at the king, then at me. The confusion on his face was priceless. I smiled as I accepted the offerings from the king.

"Thank you, Great King," I said.

The king nodded then extended his hand to Chemish. "You must be the master healer. I am Abnonjihaz, King of Shilom. We have not met, but I owe you a great debt for training your apprentice so thoroughly. Please accept these few provisions with my sincere gratitude."

Without waiting for a reply, he turned and made his way toward the center of the city.

With both eyebrows still raised, Chemish turned to me and waited.

"It's a long story," I said.

"One I'd love to hear someday," he finally said. He quickly mounted his horse and turned to the stable keeper. "You have your instructions. Keep the house and livestock in order. If I do not return within a year, all that is left is yours."

The man stared, slack-jawed, as did I. But the man quickly came to his senses and bowed. "As you wish, Master Healer."

I couldn't believe my ears. *Did I hear him right? A year?* I'd assumed we'd simply disappear somewhere until the extermination army had passed. Did he really expect we'd be in hiding that long?

CHAPTER THIRTY-NINE

WE TRAVELED ON MAJOR ROADS all day. With the extermination army hunting down all Nephites, I thought we would follow back roads and trails to stay hidden.

"Such trails take more time. We need to get away from Midian as quickly as possible," Chemish explained.

Outside Midian, I received hateful glares from nearly every Lamanite we passed, but no one ever threatened me. Chemish and I spoke little as we continued south. I sensed extreme tension in his demeanor—an angst not due solely to the extermination army.

Toward dusk, we took a small trail that led west into the mountains. When the moon was about one-quarter of its way across the eastern sky, we made camp in a small clearing. We ate a cold meal. No campfire, little conversation. The night passed without incident.

We were back on the trail before sunrise the next morning. We rode hard, heading up the heavily forested mountainside for many hours. We finally rested at the base of a slender waterfall. We unloaded the horses and led them to a small pool to drink. I stood at the base of the falls and delighted in the mist it created. My sweaty body and parched lungs absorbed the moisture like a dry cloth. Chemish wanted to continue right away, but we both knew the horses would drop dead if we kept up the fast pace.

"Don't worry, Master Healer. I've been reading the trail signs. No one has used this path in months. Trust me. I don't believe anyone is following us."

"I concur. I've been watching and listening, just like you've taught me," he said with a smile. "I feel we can afford a slightly longer rest."

"Thank you," I said, dropping from my saddle.

We made sure the horses were safe then moved a few paces downstream to hear ourselves over the roar of the falls. I sat on a flat rock, removed my sandals, and plunged my feet into the cool water.

"When do I get to learn where we're headed?" I asked, stretching.

He jabbed a thumb toward the mountain. "Up to Helam. We'll exchange the horses there. There's also something I want to check on. It's going to be a long journey from there."

"We sure packed a lot of reading material," I said with raised eyebrows. "Are we setting up a library somewhere beyond Helam?"

"Hopefully," he said with a derisive snort.

"Where?"

He looked at me as if I'd asked a totally nonsensical question. "We're heading to the Nephite border, Jarem."

I flinched. I'd assumed we were simply hiding or going to a friendly Lamanite city he knew of. But we were heading home—to *my* home. And Chemish was leading the way. I was happy and confused at the same time.

"I . . . I don't understand."

"It's my responsibility to get you to safety," he said softly, almost as if he didn't want to believe his own words. "I'd never forgive myself if something happened—" His voice cut short, and he looked away.

"I'm a grown man, Master Healer," I huffed, trying to mask the emotion constricting my own voice. "I take responsibility for my own actions."

He turned back, but he wasn't smiling. "Jarem, you're in grave danger. I haven't said as much so as not to worry you, but you *personally* are being hunted."

What? Who would be hunting me? I couldn't remember having offended anyone in a long time—intentionally or otherwise.

"By whom?"

Chemish shook his head. "That's not important. What *is* important is getting you across the border."

"What will *you* do when we get there?"

He shrugged. "I'm not sure. I haven't thought that far in advance. I'm not sure I could cross over as easily as you."

"So you don't consider yourself . . . well, one of the Anti-Nephi-Lehites, then?"

The healer kicked at the water. His face plainly showed his inner frustration he was battling. Weariness plagued his voice. "The Nephites are a good people. I truly admire their industrious nature and devotion to each other. But the whole idea of God and commandments and creation and . . . Well, there simply isn't any proof."

"Does there always have to be?" I asked tentatively.

"Yes! Believing something simply because some soothsayer says to is just . . . it's something I cannot do."

I wanted to explain the beauty and power of faith to him, to have it all make sense to him, but I couldn't find the words. It really *was* that simple. This generous man with his amazing wealth of knowledge had so much to offer and yet so much still to learn. His wisdom had brought him far; I had no doubt he understood many things even our prophets found confusing. The difference was that our prophets didn't *need* to understand everything. They relied on faith and let that guide their actions.

I silently prayed for a way to teach this powerful principle to this learned man. I wasn't very good with words, but if Heavenly Father would help me, I knew I could help Chemish understand. If the healer could merely accept the *idea* of faith, everything else would fall into place. A wise prophet had said to be learned was good, *if* one also listened to the counsel of God. But Chemish didn't believe in God.

"It's curious, isn't it?" he stated, pulling me from my thoughts.

"What is?" I asked, watching him look up and down the height of the waterfall.

"How such an awesome amount of power can be contained in so simple an element."

I waited for more, knowing it would come as he organized his thoughts.

A moment later, he continued. "A single drop of water alone can do very little to the landscape, but when added upon itself tens of thousands of times, it can uproot trees and carve out soil and rock. It can even move mountains."

I looked up to the sky and smiled. *Thank you, Father.*

"That's exactly how my parents used to talk about faith," I said.

He kicked at the water again. "Faith. I've had many discussions about faith with your people, but I just can't see how something so unquantifiable can have such all-encompassing power."

There was mockery in his tone—but it came more from exasperation than insult.

"Perhaps it's because you're looking at it too broadly," I suggested. "At first, faith is not so vast, so all-encompassing. At first, it's really very . . . small. And simple. But even in its smallest form, it contains the *potential* for great power."

Chemish raised an eyebrow. "Explain."

"It's like this waterfall. You just said one drop of water could do nothing until added upon itself. Well, faith begins small, like a single drop of water, but when multiplied many times, it expands and develops into a very powerful thing. The prophets say it can even move mountains."

He thought for a moment then nodded. "I saw it change the life of a man I thought would never change. King Lamoni was a man who loved to rule with the sword. He thought nothing of killing a servant for the slightest infraction. To see him change into a kind, compassionate person was truly astonishing." He looked at the waterfall again. "But . . . if it was done by faith . . . then whose was being used? Lamoni certainly didn't have any faith before he met Ammon."

"Faith can be exercised by all or by a few, or by one for the benefit of another."

"But there again is the dilemma. You claim Ammon used faith to convince Lamoni, and yet he couldn't convince me. Did his faith suddenly run out? If faith is an all-powerful force, then why didn't I succumb to it? The whole concept of something like that—"

"There's your mistake again," I interrupted. "At first, no one can comprehend *everything* completely. Don't try to understand the 'whole concept.' Instead, think of it as a single drop of water. What can it do by itself? Not much. But even a single drop can stir life in a seed. So start with just one drop. After a while, add another drop, then another. Before long you'll have a stream; later, perhaps a river or a waterfall. Can a single drop of water cut through a jungle? No. But this waterfall has," I said, pointing, "and it began with a single drop somewhere high up this mountain, didn't it? In much the same way, we can only understand faith drop by drop."

He stared at me for a full minute but said nothing. I could almost see his mind working. I'd seen that look in his eyes before. He was beginning to understand. Maybe not *accepting* it, but allowing the idea to take shape. It was a start, and my heart leapt with joy thinking he was acknowledging the reality of faith for the very first time. He again stared at the waterfall for a long time.

"A single drop," he said softly. "A single, simple element would suffice. And from there it grows, one drop at a time."

I was nodding, thanking the Lord for this small blessing, praying it would continue. "Sometimes just the *desire* to believe is enough."

His eyes snapped to mine. "Like when I give a medicine that I know will do nothing, and it still cures the patient."

"Yes. Because they had *faith* in you."

He stood and moved toward the waterfall. I heard him mumbling, "A single drop . . . the *desire* to understand . . . one drop at a time . . ."

I wanted to teach him so much more, but I knew we shouldn't linger any longer. I harnessed the horses and began settling their packs by myself, letting Chemish ponder my small lesson. After a moment, he quietly pitched in, all the while smiling like a child. Clearly, he was still working the lesson in his mind. And that alone made me very happy.

* * *

It took us two additional days to reach the outskirts of Helam. That evening, Chemish led us directly to a very nice house on the edge of town. I expected we'd buy new horses and continue riding through the night. But I was wrong. We tethered our horses and stretched our legs. Almost instantly, a weathered old man appeared and showed us through a gated door.

"Whose house is this?" I asked softly.

"A merchant named Kish."

The entry foyer was worthy of a king—excessive and ornate, flaunting the prosperity of the owner. Adorned with colorful rugs and tapestries, the expansive room fairly dripped with wealth. The hallways had low, multicushioned couches on which guests could relax while awaiting an audience with the merchant. The ceiling boasted silvery mosaics depicting known constellations along its length, and every oil lamp gleamed with the luster of fine, polished brass.

Soon, a robust Lamanite in a shimmering purple robe approached. He wore a wide smile through a dense growth of beard, and his dark eyes were filled with mirth. I found myself returning his smile without effort.

"Good evening, my friend! What can I offer the great master healer of Midian this night?" he sang in a resonant voice. Then, eyeing me with surprising approval, he added, "Perhaps you have come to sell me this impressive slave for my pressing needs?"

"Actually, he's my apprentice, and no, I couldn't sell him," Chemish said lightly. "I've devoted too much energy to his training to sell him. I'm merely passing through your fair city and need a place to rest for the night. Being the man of great importance that you are, perhaps you could suggest an inn, as the hour is late."

The merchant held his enormous girth and laughed boisterously. "A man of great importance, you say? Not so, Master Healer, not so. The only one in this room that holds that station is you, my friend." He extended a meaty, lavishly bejeweled hand. "And I wouldn't think of condemning you to one of the inns in this city when I have room to spare—assuming, of course, you and your assistant wouldn't be offended by these pitiful accommodations."

Chemish smiled and shook the merchant's hand. Much to my surprise, the merchant turned and offered his hand to me.

I took it with a humble bow. "I am honored," I said.

Kish roared again and slapped our backs. "It is done."

He then barked orders to a servant and led us down the luxuriant hall. He talked constantly, although I'm not sure he ever said much. I think he liked to hear his own voice. Chemish smiled and occasionally smirked at me, rolling his eyes. Kish stopped at a large door, which opened as if by magic, and led us into a magnificent room.

"I again apologize for such humble accommodations," Kish said with a flourish of his hand.

I noticed our packs and gear piled neatly in one corner, as if Kish had anticipated our stay. Fresh flowers and incense filled the room with a heady perfume. The room was as spectacular as the rest of the house.

"This is truly more than we require," Chemish said, playing up to the merchant.

Kish waved off his comment. "It is not worthy of *you*, Master Healer. But I wouldn't dream of offering you any less. Please, I'd be honored if you would accept it."

Chemish smiled and gave a bow.

Kish instructed his servants to provide anything we requested. Then, placing his hands on our shoulders, he said, "Now, refresh yourselves; rest, bathe, whatever you like. Then we eat!"

CHAPTER FORTY

AFTER SUCH A LONG, HARD ride, it felt good to relax on the piles of overstuffed cushions. Even so, I felt nervous about staying.

"Shouldn't we keep moving?" I asked, knowing a city the size of Helam would be frequented by countless Lamanites. "I thought the army was right behind us."

"Perhaps, but I'm confident they have little idea where we are. We'll be safe for one night."

"Even though I'm being hunted?" It came out more forcefully than I wanted.

His expression was a mix of earnestness and sorrow. "Jarem, I worry about that more than you know. But several people saw us heading south on the main roads, so that's where they'll think we are. No one followed us on the trails in the mountains. You made sure of that yourself. So we're safe . . . for now."

As usual, his reasoning was solid, and I allowed myself to relax a bit. "Do you think Kish knows about the extermination army?"

"Undoubtedly. His connections reach far and wide."

"Do you think he'll sell us horses?"

"I have no doubt of that either. It's a chance to profit from our urgency," he said with chuckle.

A knock sounded at our door, and an elegantly dressed servant entered. This was the probably the tenth servant I'd seen—though none were Nephite. I suspected Kish was much wealthier than he appeared. "My master bids you come feast," the man said with a low bow.

"Thank you," I said.

The servant looked up at me sharply, shocked that I had spoken. He then flashed Chemish a questioning glance, but seeing no reaction from him, bowed again and left.

"You probably shouldn't speak unless asked a specific question," the healer suggested. "Remember, everyone thinks you're my slave." He tapped his forehead, indicating the blue mark on mine.

"But Kish referred to me as your 'assistant,'" I argued. "He even shook my hand."

"A formality. Those riding with dignitaries are given an elevated status themselves, but they're still expected to act in their true stations."

"You mean act as a slave would act," I stated.

He nodded and winked. In reality, I *was* the healer's slave. It'd just been so long since I performed slave-like labor, the thought irked me.

The dining hall was as opulent as the rest of the house. Kish was sitting at the end of a long table set with gold utensils and broad silver plates. The table was laden with so much fruit, meat, breads, and drink it overwhelmed the mind. I couldn't help but stand and gawk. Chemish did the same.

Several servants lined one wall, awaiting command.

"Come, come, my friends!" Kish encouraged us. "Come and share what meager food and drink I have to offer. I pray to the gods of the harvest it is to your liking."

"I'm sure it will be more than satisfactory," Chemish replied.

As I reached for a chair, Chemish quickly cleared his throat, stopping me. The number of place settings led me to assume one was for me. Chemish saw my confusion and nodded toward a low table in a corner. I walked to it and waited for Chemish to sit before I did. Kish seemed delighted at my training and manners.

He clapped his thick hands. "Fresh meat for my honored guest!" he bellowed as if there wasn't enough on the table already. He gestured toward Chemish. "Please, eat. I shall have more presently."

An old woman entered from an adjoining room and placed a steaming haunch of tapir in front of the merchant. He cut a generous slice and had the woman deliver it to Chemish.

"So, my friend, what brings the great master healer to my humble home?"

"As I said before, we are simply traveling through and are in need of rest and fresh horses. You are heralded as a merchant of uncompromised reputation; that is why I expressly sought you out."

I was impressed with Chemish's fawning delivery. He was downplaying our being here while feeding Kish's pride. If the merchant knew we were on the run, he didn't show it.

"I will have someone see to your needs immediately," he said, snapping his fingers. A servant bowed and left the room. "You shall have the finest horses by morning."

"Thank you," Chemish said with a quick tilt of his head.

As Kish picked up his goblet, a servant sprang to refill it. He took a sip then said, "As you know, Helam is central to many provinces. That is why I live here; it is a good vantage point, yes? But a healer of your skill and renown is surely needed in the palaces of the highest nobles—all of which are some distance to the north. Tell me, my friend, what brings you *here*?"

"You speak the truth, my wise host," Chemish said after swallowing a mouthful of yam. "Helam *is* remote. But a healer's skills are needed wherever there is sickness, is this not so?"

Kish's shoulders dropped a fraction, but he continued smiling. He took a large mouthful of meat and began chewing noisily. "I'm curious," he mumbled through his food. "Is it true that your slave—oh, forgive me—that your *assistant* has healed many Lamanites?"

Chemish chuckled briefly. "Yes, it's true. He may be a Nephite, but he is quickly becoming a fine healer in his own right."

"And you . . . *trust* him?"

"With my life," he said without hesitation. "In fact, he has already—" Chemish stopped abruptly and stared at the doorway to the kitchen. "Now, there's a lovely sight."

"Ah yes," Kish said, enjoying the fact that the healer was so distracted.

I leaned forward to see what had captivated his attention. A fair-skinned woman, probably a Nephite, entered the hall carrying a tray. She was tall and slender and wore a simple yet elegant gown that emphasized her femininity. Her lustrous black hair was pulled back and secured by a golden brooch accented with pearls. She paused and bowed to her master and to Chemish.

"Good evening, young lady," Chemish said formally.

"Good evening, Master Healer," she softly replied, focusing on her tray rather than meeting his eyes.

She then noticed me and turned to bow. I smiled—then gasped. My heartfelt as if it had leapt into my throat. All the air was sucked from my lungs.

It was Zanesh!

CHAPTER FORTY-ONE

ZANESH WAS MORE BEAUTIFUL THAN I remembered. And despite a large bruise on her arm and a faint one on her cheek, she still carried herself with a dignity and self-confidence. She looked freshly bathed and combed and seemed to be in good health. The blue stripe had been washed from her forehead—but I had little doubt she was still a slave. A flash of anger scorched through me as I realized she was being used as a showpiece, as an object for Kish's guests to lust after. But that anger quickly vanished at my joy in seeing her. I wanted to cry out, to leap up and take her in my arms and tell her how desperately I'd missed her.

She gave me a confused stare then shook her head as if trying to clear a clouded mind. I smiled and gave a long wink. Recognition finally spread across her face. She brought her hands to her mouth, dropping the tray of freshwater clams.

"You clumsy wench!" Kish shouted.

Zanesh continued to stare at me, ignoring her master's outburst. Faster than I thought he could move, Kish leapt up and delivered a harsh slap across her face, sending her to the floor. I was on my feet, my fists clenched. Chemish jumped up and gave me a sharp look. It took every measure of restraint I had to remain still.

Kish thrust a thick finger at Zanesh. "You clean up this mess immediately, you good-for-nothing harlot. How dare you embarrass me in front of my guests!"

Zanesh rolled to her knees and kept her head bowed.

"I should beat you until you beg for mercy, you worthless slave. I don't know why I bought you in the first place. You bring more trouble than the plagues of Egypt!"

I saw Chemish take advantage of the distraction to stealthily sprinkle some powder in the merchant's drink. If the other servants saw his trickery, they didn't react. Everyone was focused on Zanesh.

"It's quite all right," the master healer said, calmly stepping to Kish's side. "I wasn't in the mood for clams anyway. Come, sit down and have some more drink. It'll calm your nerves."

Kish sat and gulped down his goblet of wine in three loud swallows. He wiped his beard with the back of his hand and favored Chemish with a forlorn expression. I yearned to help Zanesh clean up the mess, but I knew better.

"My apologies, Master Healer. The carelessness of this impudent servant proves how hard it is to find good slaves these days." He shook his head. "And with all this religion spreading through the land like a vile plague, slaves are as temperamental as my wives—and cost me twice as much."

Chemish patted the merchant's shoulder then returned to his chair. "I'm not offended, my good friend. No harm is done."

Kish gulped another goblet of wine. "I pray your slav—your *assistant*—doesn't give you one-tenth of the trouble this Nephite gives me."

As Zanesh cleaned up the mess, she kept glancing my way. I tried to assure her with my expression that all would be well. Her eyes brimmed with tears, but I couldn't tell if they were from joy or sorrow or pain.

Chemish acted astonished. "I can't imagine what trouble such a lovely young woman could ever bring."

Kish laughed scornfully. "Ah, Master Healer, you of all men should know that not everything is as it seems. Are not the wonderfully colored dart frogs also the most deadly? Will not the prettiest of the forest mushrooms poison your blood? This slave is no different. On the outside she is more beautiful than a quetzal in flight, but on the inside she is more venomous than the green Naja snake. I too was at first beguiled by her beauty."

Zanesh took the ruined shellfish back to the cooking room and returned with a plate of cheese. She offered it to Kish, who angrily waved her toward Chemish.

"Thank you," the master healer said, selecting a few portions.

When she offered me the plate, I started to whisper something, but she shook her head, forbidding the act. I took some cheese, and she left.

I ate in silence as Chemish and Kish shared conversation on various subjects throughout the meal. Zanesh never returned. I prayed she was all right.

Toward the end of the meal, Chemish began to stare strangely at our host, as if concerned about something he saw. It made Kish squirm, but he said nothing. Finally, Chemish pointed a skewer at the merchant.

"Kindly tilt your face toward the ceiling for me, please," Chemish instructed.

Kish frowned but slowly obeyed. The healer leaned forward, narrowed his eyes, and after a long pause, grunted softly. "Ah. Thank you."

Kish shifted in his seat. "What is it, Master Healer?"

"Oh, nothing. I thought I saw something on your neck, but it must be the soft light in this chamber."

The room seemed bright enough to me.

"Saw what?" Kish asked, groping at his neck.

Chemish picked up his goblet and swirled the drink inside. "Let me ask you a few questions first. Being a merchant—and a very successful one at that—you must certainly come in contact with all sorts of people, correct?"

"Countless. Countless! Sometimes I meet the most delightsome people, charming and full of life." His voice turned to gravel. "Other times I am forced to cater to the vilest souls humanity offers." He tried to take a sip of wine, but the trembling of his hand made it impossible. "Why do you ask?"

"Oh, no reason," Chemish said as if unsure of his own words. "It's just that . . ." His words trailed off into silence. He continued to swirl his goblet, apparently deep in thought.

Tiny beads of sweat formed on Kish's forehead. He wiped his face and neck with a napkin. A look of panic filled his eyes; his breathing became a labored task. I assumed the sudden onset of symptoms came from the powder Chemish had put in his drink. I had no idea what the substance was, but I trusted the healer knew what he was doing.

"What is wrong, Master Healer?" Kish demanded feebly, unable to remain cordial. "What did you see on my neck?"

Chemish shook his head. "It's probably nothing. Forget about it."

"No. You must tell me. What do your trained eyes see?" Kish cried in panic.

The master healer stared at him a moment before asking, "Have you had any recent encounters with Amalekites?"

"Of course," said Kish. "I deal with them on a regular basis."

"Curious," Chemish said, standing and moving to the merchant. He reached for the back of his robe. "May I?"

His face awash with horror, Kish nodded. Chemish loosened his robe and poked the nape of his neck several times, grunting knowledgeably to himself. He then felt around Kish's neck and head, looked at his eyes and tongue, and grunted some more.

"Tell me if you feel this," Chemish said, jamming his thumb into a pressure point just below the merchant's ear. Kish screamed from the intense pain and fell to the floor.

"Oh, did that hurt?" Chemish asked innocently.

"By the gods, I should say it did!" Kish said, gingerly rubbing the spot.

Chemish waved me over. "Jarem, take a look behind the merchant's ear."

"Don't touch it again," Kish cried. "Just look."

I bent toward him, looked, saw nothing—and instantly knew what Chemish was up to. "Uh-oh," I said softly and made a long, low whistle.

"You see it too?" the healer asked.

"That looks bad," I replied. "Amalekite?"

"Yes. Amalekite rot."

With wide eyes, I grabbed a napkin to cover my mouth and nose and stepped back a couple of paces.

"Amalekite rot?" Kish whimpered.

"It's a dreadful disease," Chemish explained. "Worst case I've ever seen. It causes severe sweating and trembling."

"I've got that! You can see for yourself," Kish whimpered again. He then tipped his head back and wailed. "Those cursed Amalekites and their devil diseases! I knew their wretched ills would ruin me someday. A pack of cur dogs, that's what they are. Untrustworthy, lice-infested, swineherds—the lot of them. They should rid the land of all Amalekites, not just Nephites; that's what I say."

So he is aware of the extermination order, I thought. Chemish flashed me a quick glance as he helped Kish back to his chair. He'd caught the same message.

"I beg of you, Master Healer. You've got to help me. I'll pay anything. Anything . . ." His words trailed off in a warble of sobs.

Chemish instructed Kish's servants to bring a litter onto which we rolled the sniveling merchant. It took six slaves to carry the large man. We followed them to his room and laid him on his bed. Chemish had me fetch his medicine bag, from which he gave Kish a large dose of kava, valerian, and hops—enough sedative to knock out a horse.

With scholarly seriousness, Chemish told Kish, "The only cure for Amalekite Rot is continuous bed rest. If this disease is exposed to fresh air and sunlight, it will spread into the mind and will turn you into a muttering imbecile."

I turned away to hide my smile.

"No, anything but that! I'm a respected merchant," Kish sobbed.

"I mean it," Chemish warned. "No activity, no business, no visitors—not even interaction with your servants—for at least two weeks. Do you understand?"

Kish nodded fervently as he wiped the tears from his reddened eyes. "Thank you, Master Healer. It was a blessing from the gods that you came. A blessing, I tell you. Thank you. Thank you!"

"Yes, you're welcome. Now be silent," Chemish said. "You need to rest. I'll prepare a mixture to rub on the infected spot on your neck in the morning."

"Thank you. Thank you. I owe you my—"

"Shh. No more talk."

The pitiful man nodded again.

Chemish conferred with Kish's servants, giving instructions on feeding and caring for the merchant with minimal contact. We then left him to his nightmares—I was certain he'd have plenty.

Back in our room, I quietly asked, "Are we leaving now?"

"Soon. Kish is so scared he'll probably not leave his bed for a month. But I fear he's already sent word of our arrival."

"And Zanesh? I can't leave without her."

"I suspected as much. I'd heard rumors of Kish's beautiful Nephite slave. I wasn't sure it was her, but I thought it'd be worth a look."

"I am very glad you did."

"I'll go make up a story so she can come with us. They'll think she's running an errand with us to save her master's life. By the time they figure it out, we'll be far away. Get some rest, Jarem. We'll be leaving before sunrise."

I fell back on a huge overstuffed cushion and breathed a sigh of relief. Images of Zanesh filled my head—how she looked now compared to a few years back. I couldn't believe she was alive and in this house! And soon we'd be together again. It was an answer to a prayer I'd held in my heart ever since they'd taken her away.

I wondered what she'd experienced in that time. Had she been through the physical and emotional torment I had? I sensed that she had; perhaps even humiliations more terrible than I dared imagine. But whatever she'd endured, I vowed to do everything I could to fill her new days with happiness. I'd take her away from this terrible place—this cursed land—and never let her go.

I tried to sleep, but I couldn't stop thinking about her—until another realization crept into my mind. We were still deep within Lamanite territory, and an extermination army was after us. The longer we delayed, the closer we both were to death.

CHAPTER FORTY-TWO

CHEMISH WOKE ME WELL BEFORE dawn. He whispered to ready everything for a quick departure then left the room. Within a few minutes, he returned with Zanesh. She was bleary-eyed and confused, but when she saw me, excitement brightened her entire frame. She bounded into my arms. I held her tightly. She fit perfectly in my embrace. I didn't want to move. Zanesh felt so good next to me, so right. Her touch, her fragrance, her warmth filled me with a joy I had not felt for a long, long time. I wished for the world to vanish around us, but I knew that would not happen while we were still being pursued.

"We must go," Chemish whispered. "I've learned the army is camped in Kadesh, only a day's journey from here."

I took Zanesh's hands in mine and kissed them. "Are you ready?"

She gently pushed away. "I've been ready since Bashan."

* * *

The sun crested the horizon long after we'd left Kish's house. Chemish rode one horse and led another carrying our goods. Zanesh and I rode a third horse.

When I asked what happened to our fourth horse, Chemish explained, "I went through our belongings last night. We simply had too much. I packed only what I felt was absolutely necessary."

I didn't question his decision; in fact, I was grateful for the lighter load. It meant we could travel faster.

From our position on the mountaintop, we had a clear view of the wilderness below. It was a glorious dawn, but none of us took time to enjoy it. We couldn't. We rode steadily all morning, talking little, on full alert to anything warning of danger. By late midday, exhaustion compelled us to rest.

"We'll stop at the crest of the next ridge," Chemish stated. "It's the highest point around, and we'll be able to spot anyone behind us."

At the next peak, we dismounted and stretched. I couldn't see any signs that we were being followed, which made us all breathe a bit easier. Chemish suggested we extend our rest and have a small meal while he scouted the trail ahead.

Zanesh and I sat in the shade of a large gum tree and held hands. For a while, we just sat without speaking. She leaned against my shoulder and put her arm in mine.

"Are you all right?" I asked gently.

"Yes. I'm fine." Her voice seemed unsure.

I waited for more, but nothing came. Even though she was right next to me, holding my arm, she seemed so far away.

"I am so very happy we found you," I continued softly. "I can't begin to describe how much I missed you."

She gripped my arm tighter. "Tell me I'm not dreaming, Jarem. Tell me I won't wake up and still be in Helam."

The tone of her request confused me. Did it mean she still cared for me . . . or was it more that she feared going back into slavery?

"You're not dreaming, Zanesh. I'm really here, and we're really heading for home. With God's help, I'm sure we'll make it."

She drew a shuddering breath. "I'm not sure God knows who I am anymore."

"Of course He knows who you are," I said, lightly caressing her arm. "He's always with us, even when we think He isn't. In fact, I remember you once saying, 'If God wasn't with us, we'd be dead right now.'"

She nodded. "And you? Do *you* know who I am anymore?"

I wanted to answer that of course I did, but I sensed she meant something more profound. I pulled her hand to my lips and kissed it. "I know how my heart nearly leapt out of my chest when I saw you again. I also know that I still have deep feelings for you. Is there something more I should know?"

"Yes," she said in a tight whisper. "But . . . now is not the time. I'm just so happy right now, and I want it to last—even if it *is* just a dream."

Her meaning suddenly became clear. Her life as a slave had been miserable—probably even humiliating, demoralizing. If her sorrow matched the depths I'd reached before Chemish had saved me, then I understood why she was so afraid to trust in any happiness.

I wrapped my arms around her. "Fair enough. Let's just talk about pleasant things."

She nodded again and leaned into me. We chatted continually but reservedly, careful not to tread on any past sorrows. The trouble was, as slaves, sorrow filled the majority of our memories. Still, I endeavored to be uplifting.

Zanesh mostly wanted to know about my apprenticeship with Chemish. She was amazed and, at times, disbelieving. Like me, she considered the master healer's intervention in my life a miracle. When she asked about the time between Bashan and Midian, I shared only the happy memories. But there was still one burden that continued to harrow my soul—and now was as good a time as any to unload it.

"I am so sorry I gave you that bracelet," I said softly, feeling my throat constrict. "I hope you can forgive me."

She pulled away and frowned at me. The pure, crystalline blue of her eyes held tenderness and reproach at the same time.

"Don't you ever say that again," she insisted. "I loved that bracelet. I know you probably think it's the reason we were torn apart, but you're wrong. It was *my* carelessness that did that. I've been wondering all this time if *you* could ever forgive *me*."

I was stunned. Did she really think I felt that way? "Zanesh, you're not guilty of anything. I . . . we . . . we are slaves—*were* slaves. Anything could've happened for any reason. I know we're still in God's hands because we're together again. But until we are safe in our own land, let's not dwell on regrets. I am overwhelmed with happiness at seeing you again. That's all that matters."

She looked hard into my eyes and searched my face, but soon her expression softened and she again leaned into my arms.

"I must say, all you've experienced has shaped you into a handsome, noble, and very wise man, Jarem. I like that. Very much."

And I liked hearing her say as much.

Zanesh then relayed more of her experiences. As I suspected, few were pleasant; most were horrible. She said she often cursed her beauty; it seemed only to inspire the lusts of her masters. I suspected she left out the more ignominious experiences to hide her shame.

"I honestly don't know how many masters I've had," she said. "Each time I was sold I hoped for one who had converted to the Nephite religion, or even just one who was kind and principled. But it never happened. When each new master proved to be just as vile as the last, I created as much trouble as I could. Sometimes it only brought greater punishments. Other times . . ." She lowered her eyes and curtly shook her head as if to remove distasteful memories.

I stroked her hand; her skin was rough and calloused. The few years of constant toil had hardened her, yet she still possessed a femininity that kept her features soft.

"Kish bought me a year ago. He seemed kind at first; he gave me good food, clean clothes. But then he started using me as a showpiece to his clients. I really didn't mind being a house servant. All I did was help serve meals and such. But then he began forcing me to dance for his guests dressed in . . . well, let's just say my attire wasn't very modest. When they expected more, I'd refuse, and he'd beat me." She paused to collect her thoughts and emotions. Her voice was tinged with pain but was steady and firm. "Kish was a contemptable master, full of charm and personality on the outside; but inside, he was a monster. They were all vile. I hate Lamanites."

"Not all of them are monsters," Chemish said, walking up to us.

Zanesh looked up, embarrassed. "I apologize, Master Healer. Jarem says you're an honorable man, and I believe him. But . . ."

"No need to explain, Zanesh. I know many men just like the ones you described."

She wiped her eyes. I hadn't realized she'd been crying. "Kish's temper came in cycles . . . and he was close to another outburst when you came. I . . . I doubt I can ever repay you."

Chemish smiled tenderly. "Seeing how happy you've made Jarem is payment enough."

When an awkward silence filled the air, I stood and helped Zanesh to her feet.

"So where do we go from here?" she asked.

"To Zarahemla, of course," Chemish said without pause.

Zanesh blinked; I flinched. I knew we were heading to the Nephite border, but his comment implied that *he* was crossing the border with us—all the way to the capital city of his enemies. Chemish grinned, openly enjoying our astonishment—almost as if he'd expected our looks of bewilderment.

"Kish's servants told me of a large group of your converts heading there now. I'm hoping to join them before they cross over."

"And when you say you're crossing the border *with* us . . . ?" I asked, leading.

"It means I'm coming with you," he stated.

"But—"

My words were cut off by Zanesh's cry. "Look!"

She pointed at a mass of riders who had just crested a ridge north of us. They were clearly warriors—and they appeared to be in a hurry.

"Let's go," Chemish said, heading to the horses.

"Can't you talk to them?" Zanesh asked, thinking the same things I had earlier. "You are an honored man. I've heard your name mentioned many times and with great respect."

"Trying to reason with them would do no good," he said flatly.

"Why not?" she asked.

"To do that, I'd have to convince their leader that your lives are worth sparing, and *that* would be impossible."

"You know who is leading them?" I asked.

"Yes, and so do you."

"I do?"

The master healer nodded gravely. "It's Shem."

CHAPTER FORTY-THREE

WITH ZANESH'S ARMS CLINGING AROUND my waist, I heeled our horse into a full run. *Shem* was a name I hoped never to hear again, and he was definitely a man I hoped never to meet again. I was certain Zanesh felt the same. She kept urging me to go faster.

We rode until our horses were frothing. Pausing at a small stream to rest, Chemish scanned the path ahead while I surveyed the trail behind. I couldn't see the army, but that didn't mean they weren't there. We made our way along the rocky slope to hide our tracks. The going was difficult, but Kish's horses were mountain bred, and they took to the unsteady ground without pause. Leading the way, I tried to recall the many trails I'd learned from Abinikek so long ago. That knowledge might just save our lives.

We continued to travel on bare rock and through water as much as possible. By nightfall we were near total exhaustion. We headed into the forest and found a large cavity of rock concealed in a thicket of tree ferns. We tethered the horses in the hollows between the plank roots of a huge kapok tree and draped a cloth over each to keep them dry. Using the skills I'd learned in my youth, I hid all evidence of our passing up to a mile behind us. When I was done, I doubted even the best trackers could find us.

Now that we had a moment to breathe, I decided to ask Chemish about his shocking declaration to go to Zarahemla. "Forgive my boldness, but are you sure about leaving your homeland? You'll be giving up so much."

He shrugged. "It's nothing I can't rebuild in another land . . . if permitted. My Lamanite brothers have never understood my hatred for killing, and I'm tired of justifying my actions. From what I know of your people, I'd be better off with them. I have no family close to me, few true friends, and no compelling reason to stay. Besides, you haven't finished your training." He picked up a stick and tossed it to me. "What is the medicinal property of that wood?"

"It's from the Amargo tree—probably the one right behind you. It's used for worms in the gut."

"And?"

I frowned. My mind was more focused on escaping than on being an apprentice. "I don't know," I admitted.

"I've used it for several disorders of the gut. The reports from other healers claim many curative properties I have yet to prove. That's why it is so important to keep studying it out on your own. To experiment with it, a portion at a time, bit by bit."

"Kind of like faith," I said with a knowing smile.

I expected Chemish to reply negatively. Instead, he thought for a moment then said, "Yes. Exactly."

*   *   *

Chemish and I took turns staying awake that night, listening for any untoward sound. In the end, neither of us got much sleep. Hours before sunrise, we headed down a faint trail at a brisk pace. My head pounded from a lack of sleep and the constant jarring of the horse. Zanesh looked as weary as I felt. At our next rest, I made a quick dilution from willow bark mixed with feverfew and ginseng leaves. Chemish watched the preparation with open admiration. We all partook of the bitter drink, and within minutes felt much better.

Before we continued, I climbed a tall fig tree to look for the extermination army. The sun was fully up and the sky nearly cloudless. At first I saw nothing—then a flash caught my eye; probably a piece of armor or a saddle buckle glinting in the sun. Then other signs began to show: a small flock of birds startled from their roost, the screeching of monkeys, the faint *clink* of metal. By these signs I was able to follow the army's march without actually seeing them. They were heading toward the valley instead of following our mountain trail. In the distance, a wide river wound to the horizon. I recognized it as the river Sidon, the river that marked the boundary between Nephite and Lamanite territory.

The Sidon had few bridges in this part of the land; it was either too fast or too wide—crossing it would require materials we didn't have. Abinikek had said that he knew of only two places where the river narrowed sufficiently for a bridge crossing. I guessed the warriors were heading to the closest bridge. If we were to reach it before they did we'd have to double our speed. We could search for the other crossing, but Abinikek hadn't had much information on it. I had no idea how far away it was.

I climbed down so fast it was more like a barely controlled fall.

"The river Sidon is up ahead," I said, settling in front of Zanesh on our horse. "Shem is trying to cut us off at the bridge crossing. We may reach it first, but it's going to be close."

"Why is the bridge so vital? Won't they simply follow us across?" she asked.

"Possibly. But we'll be in Nephite lands. Our chances of finding help are much better there."

Riding at breakneck speed, we headed down the mountain and made it to the river just before nightfall. The large waterway had carved a gorge of varying depths through the forest. Following sheer embankments, we soon found the bridge. It was a massive, solid structure, spanning the length of nearly four hundred cubits across the water. The drop from the bridge to the water was about forty cubits. Several torches illuminated the bridge, eliminating almost all shadow. I was certain this was not the same bridge we'd crossed long ago when entering this land.

The extermination army wasn't there, but four Lamanite soldiers guarded each side of the structure.

"They look like regular army, not Shem's butchers," Chemish said quietly.

"Do you recognize any of them?"

"No. But it wouldn't matter if I did. Word of the Nephite extermination has spread across the land. We'd better keep hidden until it gets darker."

We backed away and found a reasonably clear trail on which to release our horses. We couldn't use them anymore, and they were too easy to see in the jungle. We quietly stripped them of all harnesses and shooed them back toward the mountains. A few minutes later we heard the commotion of the extermination army.

Riding at the head of the column, Shem reined up, dismounted, and drew his sword in a single smooth motion. His rage was visible even from a distance in the dark. His eyes glowed fiery in the stripe of black war paint across his face.

He spent a long time questioning the guards at the bridge as his army set up camp. It didn't look like they were going to make an outright search for us that night, so we settled farther back to discuss our options for crossing the river.

Freedom was so close I could feel it. Yet it seemed like a dream—one in which, no matter what we tried, we couldn't reach the one and only thing that would save our lives.

CHAPTER FORTY-FOUR

FEELING CONFIDENT WE WERE WELL hidden, I allowed myself a brief sleep. Waking two hours later, I decided to spend the night scouting along the river. My hunting skills were in full play as I slithered between the plants and leaf litter without a sound. A few minutes later it began to rain. I was grateful for that. It meant I could move faster.

Stealthily making my way toward the bridge, I wasn't sure exactly what I was looking for, but I hoped I would find something useful. I crawled along a shallow wash covered with broadleaf plants and dense ferns. It made a perfect byway. It took a long time, but I finally reached the edge of the clearing at the bridgehead where the army was camped. Only a few warriors ventured out into the night rain. The ones who did were probably under orders.

The unexpected snapping of a branch made my breath catch. A Lamanite warrior I hadn't noticed was making his way around the camp perimeter. He paused less than an arm's length from me and scanned the jungle. Fortunately he never looked down.

A second warrior approached the first one. I lowered my head and concentrated on slowing my breathing and listening over the rain.

"Shem wants to send a few men to the next bridge," the second one said.

"That's two days' journey upriver—three in this rain," grumbled the first warrior.

"If Shem says go, you ask which direction," the second replied without humor.

"Exactly," the first one said, moving on.

I eased back up the wash to a thicker part of the jungle then carefully worked my way to where Chemish and Zanesh waited in a ditch that emptied into the river. By the time I got there, the sky was brassy with early morning light.

"We thought they'd captured you," Zanesh whispered, hugging me tightly. "You were gone so long."

"What happened?" Chemish asked.

"There's a bridge two or three days upriver. Some of Shem's men are going there soon, so heading there is out of the question."

"And crossing this one isn't going to happen," Chemish grumbled.

"What do we do?" Zanesh asked, her voice laced with anxiety.

Just then a warrior yelled a few paces away. "Here! I found tracks over here!"

We cowered deeper into the ditch.

"Jarem," Zanesh whined, clutching me forcefully.

"Perhaps I *should* try to talk to them" Chemish whispered frantically. "Perhaps I can lead them away."

"Not with Shem here. He hates you, remember?"

The healer sighed. I'd never seen him look so despondent.

Edging to the rim of the embankment, I looked down to the river. The drop wasn't as high as it was near the bridge, but still a good thirty cubits above the water.

"Over here! I found a pack!" a warrior yelled. "It looks like medicine and writings."

Only then did I notice Chemish didn't have his satchel. Luckily, I still had mine. The healer stared in the direction of the voices, his expression strained. Complete terror filled Zanesh's eyes.

"It's medical writings. Go get Shem! The master healer is here," a third Lamanite yelled. "Continue to search the area!"

Chemish edged next to me. "Any ideas?"

"Yes. We swim."

He peered over the edge. "It's a long drop."

Zanesh grabbed my arm and shook her head.

"We can make it. The river looks deep enough," I urged.

"It'll take us right under the bridge," Chemish pointed out.

"Yes, but the river is narrowest there, so the current is faster. And the sun hasn't fully risen, so we'll be harder to spot."

Zanesh tugged at my hand. Tears streamed down her face; she trembled uncontrollably. "Jarem, no."

"I found some more tracks!" a warrior hollered.

Chemish nodded firmly. "Let's do it."

"Jarem!" Zanesh hissed.

"What?"

Her lips moved but little sound came out. It didn't matter. Her mouth had formed the words, *I can't swim.*

"Tighten your search," a man shouted just paces away. "They're around here somewhere."

I put my lips to Zanesh's ear. "I will not let you be captured again."

"But Jarem—"

"I'm a strong swimmer. You put on my pack. I'll cinch it tight, and it'll help you float."

"No."

"It'll be fine. We'll jump together. Then you cling to my back."

"I can't," she cried hoarsely.

"Yes, you can."

"Over here!" a warrior shouted directly behind us. "I heard something over here!"

"I love you, Zanesh. Trust me," I whispered as I secured the satchel to her back.

I held her hand and crouched on the cliff's edge. Chemish took her other hand. Zanesh's face had blanched. Her eyes were scrunched shut.

"I'll go first and wait," Chemish said.

"There they are!" a warrior yelled. "Don't move, Nephites!"

Chemish winked. "I'm not a Nephite," he said before pushing off. A splash sounded many moments later.

"I said don't move!"

"On three," I said. "One, two—"

An arrow zinged past my ear, causing it to ring.

"Three."

We seemed to fall forever. All sounds blended into the rushing of wind. Then we were underwater. Again, it seemed forever before we stopped sinking. I pushed Zanesh to the surface and came up beside her. Zanesh's eyes were wide with panic. She thrashed about, gasping for breath before finally latching onto my back. Chemish was too far away to help. I swallowed several gulps of water as she continued to flail, making it difficult to remain above the surface.

"We've got trouble," Chemish shouted above the roar of the water. He pointed toward the bridge.

A group of warriors had assembled there, bows drawn and nocked with arrows. There was no way to avoid passing directly below them. Even in the subdued morning light, it was unlikely they would miss.

We were carried toward the bridge at a tremendous pace by the speed of the current. Then I saw Shem join the warriors. He drew his bow and took aim.

Chemish yelled, "Go under the surface!"

"No," Zanesh cried.

"Just hold your breath and close your eyes. I'll do the rest," I said.

Chemish swam farther away from us—I assumed so we wouldn't tangle under the water. The deafening rumble of the river amplified as the gorge narrowed.

"On three again. One—"

Two arrows pierced the water beside Chemish. Another plunged just behind Zanesh. A third landed right in front of me.

"Two—"

I heard Zanesh take a deep, terrified breath.

"Three!"

The roar of the water muffled into a loud thrum as we sank. Zanesh tightened her grip around my neck. The noise, the cold, the violent currents—all seemed to close in on me, but I had to keep swimming. A spear passed close to my face. I pushed it aside and kept heading downward. I heard Zanesh groan sharply and knew she was out of air. I felt her grip loosen. I grabbed her hands with one of mine and began to swim toward the surface. I didn't know how far we were from the bridge, but I had no choice—we had to come up.

Our ascent was painfully slow. Every stroke I took felt futile; the current seemed to drag us down. Zanesh jerked from my grip and clawed for the surface. Then we broke through.

Zanesh latched onto my back and gagged and coughed water from her chest. I sucked in huge gulps of air. Panting heavily, I fought to stay above water. Thankfully, the bridge was farther away than I'd guessed it would be. Angry Lamanites launched arrows and spears to no avail. Every stroke took us farther out of range.

I glanced over at Chemish. He was struggling to stay afloat but still managed to flash me a wonderfully foolish grin.

"That was exciting. Are you two all right?"

"Yes, but I can't go much farther."

"Just a bit more," he urged with a pain-filled grimace.

The current slowed as the river widened, and swimming became a little easier. Craning my neck, I saw a place downstream where the walls of the gorge lowered enough to crawl out.

"There's an outlet up ahead," I said, pointing with my chin.

"Good," Chemish said while coughing. "When we get out, you can remove the arrows from my back."

CHAPTER FORTY-FIVE

WE CRAWLED OUT OF THE water and collapsed on the riverbank. Seeing the full extent of Chemish's wounds, I wondered one thing: how had the warriors missed Zanesh and me? There was an arrow in his right shoulder, one in his upper back, and one in his right leg. Then it came to me.

"You didn't go underwater, did you? You knew if you were the only target, they'd aim at you instead of us."

He smiled as if he'd been caught in a prank—and I had my answer.

I immediately began tending his wounds. I easily removed the arrow in his leg. It had entered just under the skin along the side of his thigh and didn't damage much muscle. The one in his back had hit his shoulder blade. The arrowhead had torn up the tissue around the wound but had only stuck in the bone by the tip. I dislodged it with very little effort. Zanesh bravely helped with both extractions. She proved a valuable assistant, not at all fainthearted or squeamish. From my pack, I mixed tea-tree paste and hyssops extract on a broad leaf and applied it to both wounds. The containers in which I stored the medicines had mostly stayed dry. Zanesh then bandaged the leg and wrapped a compress around his back. I had every confidence both wounds would heal rapidly.

The arrow in Chemish's shoulder was a different matter. It had lodged between the bones of the joint. The skin and muscle around the wound were shredded and bleeding steadily. The sharp edges of the stone arrowhead had ravaged the skin with each movement of Chemish's arm. The fact that he'd made it at all astounded me.

"It's in pretty deep," I told him. "I can't pull it out."

Chemish was sweating now, his breathing ragged and heavy. I knew he was in extreme pain, and it angered me that there was little I could do to lessen it. Ever since I'd met this man, he had seemed to be an invincible force, both mentally and physically. He'd helped me more times than I could count. He had healed me physically and emotionally. Now he was *my* patient . . . and I felt incapable of helping him.

"I think I need to separate the bones to remove the arrow, but I don't have the proper tools."

Chemish nodded and issued a shuddering, heavy sigh.

"If I can keep your shoulder from moving, it may help until we get to Zarahemla," I said.

"Zarahemla?" Zanesh gasped excitedly. "How far away is it?"

"I'm not sure. Perhaps a week's travel. Maybe more. Can you make it until then?" I asked Chemish.

He coughed and grimaced. "I don't have much choice."

After carefully breaking the arrow's shaft at the tip, I applied the tea-tree-hyssop mixture to Chemish's shoulder wound and padded the area with moss, packing it tightly. I tried to be gentle, but Chemish winced and hissed several times as I worked. Zanesh helped me tie his arm to his chest with strips of cloth and vine. It held reasonably well. I gave him the remainder of the fever medicine, hoping it would also help with pain.

"We'd better get moving. Shem won't let us get away this easily. Can you walk?" I asked, pointing to his wounded leg.

Chemish slowly got to his feet in answer to my question. I grabbed a stout, dead branch for him to use as a staff, and with it, he took a few halting steps. He then turned to me and grinned. "This is a curious twist on history, isn't it?"

"What is?"

Holding up the staff, he said, "Didn't I make *you* one of these once?"

Zanesh held up the arrows I'd removed. "Why are there multicolored feathers on this one, while these others have only single-colored feathers?"

"It's an identifier; a signature," Chemish said, taking the arrows from Zanesh. "Three different patterns means three different warriors hit me. I don't recognize the arrows from my leg or shoulder, but the one from my back is definitely Shem's." He scoffed in mock amusement. "Right in the back, directly over my heart. I had no idea my brother was such a good shot."

My mouth dropped open in shock. Zanesh's face bore a similar look of disbelief. We stared, slack-jawed, at the healer as he continued to examine the arrows.

"Shem is your brother?" I finally asked in astonishment.

"Yes," he said, tossing the arrows aside. "I'm afraid so."

Without further word, Chemish headed up a trail, away from the riverbank.

My mind whirled as we walked. How could Shem be Chemish's brother? It didn't make sense; they were such complete opposites. But the more I pondered, the more connections began to form.

We walked for nearly an hour before Chemish leaned against a tree to catch his breath. He was pale and drawn. At my insistence, he agreed to rest for a while.

I sat beside him and offered him some water. "I should have known you and Shem were related," I confessed. "You're the same size, you have similar bone structure, your mannerisms are alike, and you have the same level of intelligence."

Chemish gagged and coughed. "The same level of intelligence?"

"Well . . . yes. Not the same *amount*, just the same *level*. You know medicine to an extreme; he knows warfare."

"He knows how to cause misery and to kill."

"I'm still surprised he tried to kill *you*," Zanesh said. "You're his brother."

Chemish closed his eyes and leaned his head back. "You don't understand Lamanite ways," he said with great effort. "A Lamanite warrior prides himself on conquest; in hunting, business, sport—it doesn't matter. But the pinnacle of conquest is warfare. It's in the blood, so to speak. I never saw the need for it, myself. I detest the wanton killing of man or animal, and I'm not afraid to be vocal about it either. To Shem, I am a disgrace to the family, an embarrassment. To him, a passive Lamanite is worse than a cowardly one. So the only surprise to me is that he didn't launch that arrow years ago."

* * *

We walked about two more hours before Chemish gave out again. It surprised me how easily he fatigued. Even with his wounds, I was certain he could go longer distances between rests. He hadn't really lost that much blood. Yet each time we stopped, the healer found it harder to get back on his feet. Plus, he continually stumbled on roots and stones a healthy person would easily avoid. That meant his vision was fading, too.

As the afternoon wore on, we found ourselves approaching a divide in the trail.

"Which way now?" Zanesh asked.

I suggested she take one trail and I take the other to scout ahead for any signs. Chemish was content to wait in the shade and rest. He looked worse with each passing hour. He seemed to be suffering from more than just pain, but I didn't know what.

Heading up the trail, it wasn't long before I found numerous footprints from converging trails. A large mass of people had come this way fairly recently. I hoped it might be the converts Heth had mentioned. I ran back to tell Chemish of my discovery and found Zanesh kneeling beside him, softly crying.

"He's dying, Jarem. Look."

Chemish was ghostly pale and sickly. His heartbeat was weak, and he struggled for each breath. His back was hot to the touch and soaked with sweat. I helped him drink some water, but he got little down.

"We're very close," I explained. "There are fresh tracks ahead—hundreds of people, maybe more. We should keep moving."

"I'm sorry, Jarem. I can't make it," the healer wheezed. "Please. Just move me somewhere safe."

Zanesh and I dragged him to a shady patch of spongy moss to one side of the trail. I swabbed his forehead with a wet cloth and tried to diagnose his rapid turn for the worse. His symptoms didn't make sense. He might have caught an illness from the river, but it wouldn't come on this fast. Something else was wrong.

"I know you're in pain," I said to him. "But I can't determine why you suddenly have no strength."

Chemish swallowed hard and asked, "Was there anything on the arrowhead in my back?"

I couldn't remember anything specific, but Zanesh did. "There was some kind of black pitch coating the arrowhead."

"She's right," I confirmed, recalling the substance. "There was a pitch or resin of some kind, but I thought it was slime from the river."

Chemish released a shuddering breath and closed his eyes. I could see his muscles twitching uncontrollably just under his skin. Zanesh continued to wipe his face with the wet cloth.

"What was it?" I asked.

"Poison," Chemish croaked through puffy lips. "Shem always tips his arrows with poison. I didn't mention it before because . . . I didn't want you to worry."

"But if it was poison, shouldn't you be dead already?"

He licked his lips. "The river may have . . . diluted it somewhat; but . . . enough got into my blood to . . . do its work."

I wanted to scream. My mind raced with questions. Did Chemish absorb enough poison to kill him or just make him sick? Would an antidote work? If so, which one? What should I do?

As if reading my mind, Chemish said, "There is no . . . antidote."

I could barely hear him—his voice was terribly weak. He touched my arm; his hand was shockingly cold. His skin felt . . . dead. "Go find . . . the converts. Bring back strong men. There may be . . . one chance."

"But how?" I cried.

He shook his head and passed out. Zanesh continued to wipe his face and neck. "Go. I'll stay with him," she offered.

Springing to my feet, I raced up the trail as fast as my legs would carry me.

CHAPTER FORTY-SIX

I RAN IN A NEARLY blind panic. I didn't know when or even *if* I would find the converts, but I had to try. Chemish's life depended on it, and I owed him several of those. The trail was steep and winding, making me feel as if I hadn't gone anywhere. My lungs burned and my eyes watered, but I never slowed my pace.

As I rounded a stone outcropping, I almost ran over a young Lamanite woman. She was carrying a basket filled with berries and roots. I stopped and rested my hands on my knees to catch my breath. She stared at me with a hint of amusement in her eyes. Curiously, she didn't seem afraid, even though I was a Nephite.

Swallowing, and forcing words between gasps, I asked, "Are you . . . one of the . . . converts?"

"Yes. We call ourselves 'Ammonites'—after the missionary. We're gathered in a valley beyond the next rise." She paused placed a hand on my shoulder. "Are you all right? You seem to be in terrible haste."

"I am. I need help," I panted. "I have friends back down the trail—a great distance. One is hurt very badly."

She closed her basket and secured it to her back. "Follow me."

We jogged to the next valley and came upon a huge gathering of Lamanites. There had to be well over a thousand, perhaps two thousand. Some sat about, some slept, others performed light tasks. The young woman led me to a group of men in the center of the multitude. She introduced me as an escaped slave, probably because of the stripe on my forehead.

"You are welcome to stay with us until the Nephite army arrives," said an elderly man I assumed was their leader.

My heart was pounding. The thought of being reunited with Nephites— free Nephites from *my* own land—was overwhelming. I was home. I was safe. And free!

"Do you travel alone?" another man asked.

My joy plummeted with the recollection that my friend was at death's door. "No, sir. I'm in desperate need of help," I said urgently. "I have a companion back on the trail—a Lamanite who is very sick and cannot walk."

"Is he a convert?" the man asked.

"No. But he is a good man, one with many skills. In fact, he's a mast—"

"We cannot go back," another man cut into the conversation. "We are too near the border to risk betraying our location."

"Zaakib is right," a third man joined in. "King Lamoni will be back soon with the Nephite army. We should wait."

"King Lamoni?" I gasped. I had no idea he'd be with this group, but it made sense. A significant portion of these people were probably his. "When will he arrive?"

"We do not know," the first man said. "He has been gone a few days already, and we are praying for his speedy return."

"But my friend will die if he doesn't get help soon! Can't anyone help me?" I cried, looking around in a frenzy. All those present lowered their eyes to avoid mine.

"Please. I beg you!"

A moment of silence passed before a familiar voice said, "I will help you, Jarem."

I searched the crowd for the person who spoke my name. How did he know it? A young man quickly pushed his way forward. It was Heth! Speechless, I embraced him warmly. My heart nearly burst at the blessing of seeing my dear friend again.

"It's good to see you, my friend," he said with a tight voice. "Perhaps I can now repay the life I owe you."

"No! You cannot go," the one called Zaakib snapped. "We cannot risk it."

Heth spoke without hesitation. "I am going to help this man, Zaakib. We won't give away our position, I can promise you. Jarem travels through the jungle like a shadow and is only seen when he wants to be seen. Besides," he added in a hardened voice, "King Lamoni will not like hearing his council was responsible for the death of the master healer."

"The *master* healer? The one called Chemish?" the second man asked.

"The same," Heth said. "Jarem is his apprentice." He then pointed to two stout young men. "You two, come with us."

"Why didn't you say so—that he was the master healer?" Zaakib asked, stumbling on his words.

"Because you didn't let him," Heth said, grabbing my arm and leading me back through the crowd.

We ran at a steady pace all the way back. The young men brought with them a folded litter on which to carry the healer. We reached my friends in half the time it took to find the converts.

Chemish was unconscious. He looked worse than when I'd left him—ghostly white, lifeless. I could barely feel his heartbeat. I was afraid he wouldn't make the journey back to the Ammonites, but I knew we had to try. Zanesh was still daubing his face and neck with a moistened cloth. Her face was stained with tears.

The young men lifted Chemish onto the litter, and we headed back up the trail. Time seemed to slow as we climbed the mountainside trails. My sense of urgency threatened to erupt from within me. The healer's life was in my hands—assuming it could still be saved.

CHAPTER FORTY-SEVEN

WHEN WE ENTERED THE CAMP, only a few people seemed to notice. Most were focused on some commotion toward the center of the valley. We learned that King Lamoni had just returned with a number of Nephite soldiers. They were organizing the camp for an exodus. Everyone had an assignment. We sat Chemish in a shaded area to one side of the crowd. Barely a breath from dying, he mumbled for water. I helped him drink while Heth pushed his way to the center of the crowd.

I was gently wiping Chemish's clammy skin when a strong voice spoke in astonishment. "I don't believe it."

I looked up into the face of a regal-looking, powerfully built Lamanite. He radiated an unspoken majesty that commanded respect. He extended his hand to me. "I am King Lamoni, my young friend. You are the master healer's servant?"

I swallowed hard. "His apprentice."

"Apprentice?" he said, openly surprised. "A Lamanite healer with a Nephite apprentice . . . Now that's a story I'd like to hear some day. For now, tell me what we can do to help."

Chemish groaned and opened an eye. The beginning of a smile pulled at the corners of his mouth, but that's as far as it got. He closed his eye and sighed heavily.

"He was hit with a poisoned arrow, Great King. The poison—there is no antidote and—" Overcome with emotion, I choked on the words.

"So the master healer is in need of healing," he said. The king knelt beside Chemish and put his mouth to his ear. "Chemish, my old friend. What can I do to help?"

Chemish coughed and wheezed. Thick spittle foamed on his lips. King Lamoni tenderly wiped it away with his robe. When Chemish did not reply, the king ordered water, never taking his eyes off the healer. Chemish coughed again but managed to swallow a few small sips. His body trembled and convulsed; his face paled even more; his shallow breathing sounded like shifting sand.

"You're going to be all right, my friend," the king said, daubing Chemish's forehead and stroking his hair.

The healer slowly opened his eyes. He tried to whisper through his swollen lips but couldn't do much more than wheeze. King Lamoni gave him more water and waited patiently.

Finally, Chemish managed some faint words. "Nothing . . . you can do . . . you old fool. I am . . . dying." He gave a partial grin, with taxing effort. "But I will . . . finally know all the answers . . . to all questions."

My eyes stung. Burning tears ran down my cheeks. Zanesh held my arm with one hand and slid her arm around the small of my back. I was shaking my head in denial, wanting to do something but knowing there was nothing I *could* do. My dear friend—the man who had become a second father to me— was dying right in front of my eyes. I wanted to scream at the injustice of it. I wept openly. The anguish in my soul was unbearable.

Chemish gazed vacantly at me, his eyes struggling to focus. "Don't weep, Jarem. You must be strong . . . your people, to . . . to be their healer." He closed his eyes and exhaled heavily.

King Lamoni placed a hand on the healer's chest. "You will walk with angels, Master Healer. You've always had a good heart. Our Lord knows that."

Chemish coughed again, and a thin trickle of blood seeped from the corner of his mouth. "Take care of . . . of this young man," he wheezed softly. "He has been the son . . . I never had. You . . . you will grow to love him . . . as I have." He drew a raspy breath and let it out very, very slowly. His chest didn't rise again.

I fell to my knees and grasped Chemish's hand. Bowing my head, I cried, "No, please. Please, God, don't take him. Please, not now."

King Lamoni gripped my shoulder and softly said, "I am very sorry."

Zanesh slipped her arm around me again. It felt so very distant. I was lost in a thick mist of strangling sorrow.

Then a soothing, resonant voice pierced the haze. "Can I help?"

I couldn't answer. Words caught in my throat.

King Lamoni rose, and another man knelt in his place. He took Chemish's other hand. "You love him very much, as Christ taught us to love one another," he said to me.

The deep timbre of his voice filled me with comfort. He was an old man with flowing white hair and piercing green eyes. As he smiled, I felt a great weight lifted from my heart. I nodded and whispered, "Yes."

He leaned close to Chemish's ear. "Master Healer. I know you are not a convert, but I have learned you are a good and honorable man. I am Alma. I would like to place my hands on your head and bless you through the power of the high priesthood, which is after the Holy Order of God. Do you have enough faith to allow me to do this?"

Chemish didn't move.

"He has faith," I managed to say. "Not a lot, but he was beginning to understand."

Alma gave me a questioning glance.

I wiped my eyes. "I am teaching him about faith. I feel he knows it's true in his heart."

Alma nodded and asked another man to join him. The two anointed Chemish with oil and commanded him not to die in the wilderness. The moment the words were said, Chemish suddenly drew in a long, deep gasp. Alma paused, and I felt a strange warmth coursing through my body. When Chemish released his gasp and began breathing normally, my tears came again, but this time they were not shed in sadness.

Alma continued. "I bless your body to recover fully and you to have the courage to believe in something you cannot prove." He then closed the blessing in the name of Jesus the Christ and rose to his feet.

"He is a good man, as are you," Alma said to me. "Look after him, for he will need a good deal of care during his recovery."

"Thank you," was all I could manage to say. But it felt like enough.

CHAPTER FORTY-EIGHT

THE FOLLOWING FOUR OR FIVE days were a mass of confusion. I slept little. Chemish was in and out of consciousness. His muscle spasms came and went. At times I thought he'd left this life—he slept so peacefully. Other times he twisted and moaned through the night. But I never left his side.

Zanesh and Leah became close friends—almost like sisters. They helped me care for the healer while he fought off the poison, although there wasn't much we could do. While waiting, Zanesh tried to scrub the blue stripe from my forehead, but the dye had stained the skin deeply. It would be some time before I was rid of that mark.

"Mine took about three months to fade," she explained. "Kish had it scrubbed every day."

"Why did he want your slave mark removed?" I wondered.

"I think he wanted his friends to believe I was living with him of my own choice. As if *that* was ever a possibility," she said with a roll of her eyes.

A large contingent of the Nephite army had come to escort the Ammonites to their new home. The Nephite people had given the Ammonites Jershon, a small city that lay on the edge of the sea, well beyond the Lamanite border. Not surprisingly, the Ammonites were very grateful.

Heth and Leah decided to go to Jershon instead of Zarahemla, as was originally planned. They begged me to go with them, but I graciously declined. Young Omni was the most disappointed.

"You will visit, though," Leah entreated. "Promise you will."

"I promise, but I can't say when. Chemish is still very weak, and when he recovers, we'll be very busy with my training."

Leah hugged me. "And you'll be the best healer in Zarahemla, I'm sure. We will miss you terribly."

"You are always welcome in our home," Heth said.

"Yes, you *must* come," Omni said, holding Lachonius in his small arms.

"And when you do, you must bring Zanesh," Leah added.

I turned to Zanesh, who was standing behind me. Her cheeks colored slightly. "That's another promise," I said.

*   *   *

I stayed beside Chemish's litter as we made our way toward Zarahemla. Walking with me, Zanesh seemed strangely withdrawn. The past few days I'd been so focused on Chemish that Zanesh and I hadn't had much time to reacquaint ourselves. We'd been running for our lives ever since we'd reunited. When we got the chance, our conversations lasted only a few minutes—either because of pressing matters or because the mood wasn't right. She seemed distracted, reserved, almost as if she was unsure about opening up to me. And the closer we got to Zarahemla, the more withdrawn she became.

"Please tell me what's the matter," I asked once again, fearing my persistence might be pushing her away rather than drawing her nearer.

"Nothing," was all she said, staring at the ground with an unfocused gaze.

She walked without vigor, matching my pace but doing so as if putting one foot in front of the other brought her closer to something she dreaded.

With mounting frustration, I continued. "If I've done something wrong, please tell me what so I won't repeat it."

"It's nothing you've done," she said softly.

"Is it something I *haven't* done?"

Her response was prevented when a large man on horseback reined up beside us. The pleasantness of the man's features and the confidence he bore filled me with instant trust. He smiled and asked, "How is the master healer today?"

"He seems to be much better," I reported. "His heartbeat is strong, and his muscles are loosening."

"That is good news," he said with a nod. "Chemish is a great man. Let me know when he is awake. I would like to speak with him again. Maybe this time I'll have more success."

"I will. But whom shall I tell him to ask for?"

He laughed. "I thought everyone knew me by now. You must be new to this people. I am Ammon. The master healer and I have spent many hours together as good friends. Please let me know if I can help in any way."

I thanked him before he rode on.

"He's the one who converted King Lamoni," I told Zanesh.

"I know," she replied.

We stopped at a small lake where the people watered their horses, ate, and rested. The men assisting us moved Chemish under a stand of palms and gave us some loaves of unleavened bread and dried meat. The company's spirits were high, and many individuals splashed playfully in the lake. Children chased each other while mothers shared stories. Many others joined together in singing hymns of praise. Beyond the next rise, our road intersected with the highway to Zarahemla. We were all but home.

The sights filled me with indescribable joy, but that joy was tempered because of Zanesh's solemnness. She seemed oblivious to the happiness surrounding us.

Sitting next to her, I tenderly took her hands in mine. "Zanesh, I'm worried about you. When we saw each other in Helam, your joy was unmatched. Now, nothing seems to bring you happiness. If you tell me why, perhaps I can help."

Tears welled in her eyes as she looked at me, but she said nothing.

"You have nothing to fear anymore. Everything will be just like it was before; you'll see," I offered as encouragement.

"Will it?" she replied harshly.

The bitterness with which she answered shocked me. I didn't know what to say.

She yanked her hands from mine and angrily wiped at her eyes. "I'm sorry, Jarem. I didn't mean to snap at you. I'm just being selfish."

I sat in silence for a moment, my mind spinning to come up with the right thing to say. "Listen, everyone here is nervous about the future, because it's so uncertain. But Chemish is doing much better now, and we're too far into Nephite territory to be in any true danger." I reached out and wiped a tear that hung from her chin. "So there's really nothing to worry about."

"Isn't there?" Her response confused me, and the look she gave me filled me with frustration and angst.

"Tell me what, then. What's worrying you?"

She drew a breath. "How can everything be the same, Jarem? It can't. It's impossible. You don't have a clue what I went through the past few years. I wasn't just a slave, I was . . . my sins are too . . . I'm just so afraid." She looked down at her hands, open and empty in her lap. Her voice was shallow. "You've got such a promising life ahead. You came out of this experience a better person. I'm—I'm afraid once you find out what I went through, you won't want me anymore."

I scooted close and gathered her in my arms. "Zanesh, we've both experienced things we'd rather forget. You committed no sin."

"But I—"

"No—listen to me. Let me say what I need to before I lose my courage. Whatever has happened, it won't change how I feel about you. The mere fact that you're alive proves the mettle of your will and your resolve to keep fighting. Those are just a few of the traits that made me fall in love with you on the way to Bashan. Since then you've shown nothing but faith and courage, which only deepens my feelings for you. No one needs to know what you've gone through—not even me. If you feel the need to talk about it—to me or the high priest or whomever—then do so. Nothing will change the fact that I love you."

"How can you say that? How can you be so sure about me or about any future we might have together?"

I held her at arm's length and looked steadily into her eyes. "I can't. But I have faith that if we try, if we work together to forget the past and start fresh, with a new life in a new city, we will succeed."

Her eyes flicked back and forth, searching mine. "Please, tell me again I'm not dreaming, Jarem."

I cupped her face in my hands and drew her lips to mine. The kiss was magical for me. I hoped it was for her.

"I love you, Zanesh. That's all that matters."

"I love you, Jarem—more than you can ever know."

CHAPTER FORTY-NINE

WE REACHED ZARAHEMLA TWO DAYS later. The trek was uneventful except for the last evening when I went to clean Chemish's wounds. As I unwrapped the dressing on his shoulder, the arrowhead dropped free. I picked it up, dumbfounded.

"What happened?" Chemish asked, craning his head.

"It fell out."

"What did?"

"The arrowhead. It was deep in your shoulder. How did it work its way out by itself?"

"Let me see it."

He examined the obsidian head then threw it into the jungle with a hiss.

"Don't you want to keep it as a trophy?" I chuckled.

"Oh, so every time I look at it I can be reminded of a brother's hatred and that he almost killed me?"

I was going to point out that the arrowhead he'd tossed wasn't Shem's, but I wisely held my tongue. I cleaned the flesh around the wound and was surprised to see that much of it had healed. It was still red, but the torn tissue had knitted nicely.

"This is incredible," I said. "I can hardly believe it."

Chemish began laughing and couldn't seem to stop. Dressing the wound, I asked what was so humorous, but he wouldn't say.

We reached Zarahemla and were instantly and unconditionally welcomed into the house of Zoram, the general of the Nephite army. Alma had forwarded word of our coming, and the general was more than pleased to have friends of Lamoni and Ammon in his home.

Zoram's household treated Zanesh like a princess. She resisted the attention at first but soon accepted the fact that they truly wanted her to be happy. So did I. That's why I made a trip to the city market the first chance I got.

A few days later, we went for a walk in Zoram's vineyard. Many of the women in Zarahemla painted subtle colors around their eyes, and the servants had done so with Zanesh. The light hues brought out the prominence of her cheekbones and highlighted the almond shape of her eyes. They had also applied a red hue to her lips. She was dressed in a blue silk tunic that shimmered as she walked. It was simple yet elegant. My knees weakened at the sight of her.

"You are the most beautiful woman I've ever seen," I gasped.

She took my arm. "Thank you," she said, unable to hide a wide smile.

We walked in silence for a few paces before I stopped and said, "And yet something just doesn't look right."

Her brow furrowed. "What do you mean?"

I studied her, cocking my head from one side to the other. "Something's missing."

She looked at her apparel, confused. "What?"

I snapped my fingers. "Ah—that's it. Because your slave mark is gone, all the unmarried men in Zarahemla will think you're eligible. You won't last a day outside of Zoram's house. And I can't allow that."

Her eyebrows lifted in challenge. "What are you saying—I can't leave this house?"

"Not without this," I said, handing her a small pouch.

"What's this?" she asked, the smile creeping back.

"A memory. And a promise."

She opened the pouch and drew a sharp breath. Inside was a bracelet of braided ziff woven gracefully around five evenly placed, clear-green stones. It looked almost exactly like the one Abinikek had given me.

"I've thought a lot about this and decided that the bracelet was a key element in our lives. I used to think it was what had caused our separation in Bashan. For the longest time I hated myself for ever having given it to you. But then I remembered how much you loved it, how your face always lit up when you wore it. In reality, the bracelet is what got us both out of Bashan. Ever wonder what would've happened if we weren't torn apart and Shem had returned to his city? I believe neither of us would be alive right now—which means we wouldn't be together, safe in Zarahemla. So I offer it to you again. Only this time I pray it will be a reminder—not of a sorrowful time but of an awkward young man who gave it to you as symbol of his affection. And as a token to remind you of the undying love this hopeful young man has for you now."

"Hopeful?" she said in a tight whisper.

I tenderly slid the bracelet onto her wrist. "Hopeful you will spend the rest of your life with me."

Speechless, with tears shimmering in her eyes, Zanesh threw her arms around me and kissed me firmly.

"That's what I wanted," she said, breaking from the kiss. "You had all these wonderful plans, but I wasn't sure they included me."

"They will always include you," I said before kissing her again.

* * *

The following week, Chemish asked me to accompany him to the marketplace, claiming he wanted to locate a seller of herbs. Zanesh sent us on our way, saying she was much too busy preparing for our marriage to tag along.

Chemish was silent for some time. The sights of Zarahemla fascinated me, but I wasn't distracted by them. Chemish had something on his mind, and he was searching for a way to express it. I recognized his mood and knew that patience would eventually reveal his concern.

We sat on the rim of a fountain in a public bazaar and watched the people mill about. The day was warm and pleasant.

"Jarem, I'd like to strike a bargain with you," he finally said.

"A bargain?"

He nodded. "I will finish teaching you all I know about healing . . . if that is what you still want."

"Of course it is," I said. "But in return for what? I have nothing to offer."

"Yes, you do." He paused and watched the waters of the fountain dance about. "I can teach you much about healing from a natural point of view, but that is all. I would like you to teach me about the kind of healing Alma performed."

I scratched my head, flattered by his proposal but unsure of my ability to do what he asked. "Wouldn't Alma himself be a better choice to teach you that?"

He shook his head. "I've spent countless hours talking with Ammon and others about your religion but never got anywhere. I simply couldn't understand it—let alone accept it. Then you explained faith to me and . . . well, it made sense. You likened faith to water, remember? I'd never understood faith until then; however, the more I've thought about it, the more I think I can accept it."

"Yes, but—"

"No, let me finish. I think—no, I *feel* there is something to your beliefs. I can't prove it yet, but I know there's something there—something wholly apart from the laws of nature yet in perfect harmony with them. It's an entire world of other knowledge to which your people have access. It'll take time to understand and accept your ways, but if you're patient with me, I will do my best to learn."

I was astounded. This all-knowing man of science was asking me to teach him about our religion! "You really believe *I* can teach you this?"

He shrugged. "I'd like you to try. Jarem, you know as well as I do that Shem's poison should have killed me. He uses curare, a poison that paralyzes the muscles in the chest, stopping the ability to breathe, suffocating the victim. There was absolutely nothing you could have done to save me. Yet here I am, quite alive and quite well. My life *was* saved . . . somehow. And *you* did it."

"I did nothing. It was Alma—"

"No, my friend, it was you. Alma asked if I had faith. I didn't, but I knew you did. It was *your* faith that healed me. And that's what I want you to teach me."

I didn't know what to say. My faith may have helped, but it *was* Chemish's faith in *my* belief that had saved his life. How could I explain that to him? How could I help him trust his own feelings and develop his own faith?

As the fountain gurgled, a few spits of water landed on the back of my hand. The tiny drops shimmered in the sunlight, quivering on my skin. I smiled.

Adopting a serious tone, I said, "Fair enough, Lamanite, you have a bargain. Are you ready for your first lesson?"

Chemish grinned broadly. "I am."

I pointed to the water on my hand. "Think of this single drop of water as faith."

TO THE READER

THE MEDICINES, PLANTS, HERBS, AND procedures in this novel are not intended to diagnose, treat, cure, or prevent any disease, and are not to be construed as medical advice. In other words, don't try these at home! That being said, all the therapies in this novel are authentic and have been used for hundreds (if not thousands) of years.

The research I did to make sure the therapies in this story were accurate was exhaustive. But that was nothing compared to the challenge of keeping the language accurate. There are many common words and phrases that simply should not be in a Book of Mormon novel because they were not used in those times. A short, non-exhaustive list of words I needed to use but couldn't include are: *okay, fun, feet* (as a unit of length) and *inches, funny, brain, stupid, humid, supervisor,* as well as many medical terms. Do a search of the Bible and Book of Mormon for these words. You won't find them. Some readers might not care if such words are used, but I always try to be as accurate as possible when writing a period piece, because I think it makes for a more authentic read.

A special thanks goes to Bible and Book of Mormon historical fiction author extraordinaire Heather B. Moore. She pointed out many instances when I used idioms too modern for the period. Trust me—there were a lot!

The modern words I *did* include were the names of the herbs and medicines. This is because I know of no references that translate common plant names into a Toltec-based language. I'm sure they are out there, but I decided to use the modern names so the reader would be able to identify with what I was talking about.

The plant-based medicines I used were all referenced through http://naturaldatabaseconsumer.therapeuticresearch.com. I trust this site because its conclusions are based on thorough research and not anecdotal evidence.

ΛBOUT THE ΛUTHOR

Gregg R. Luke, RPh, was born in Bakersfield, California, but spent the majority of his childhood and young-adult life in Santa Barbara, California. He served a mission for The Church of Jesus Christ of Latter-day Saints in Wisconsin then pursued his education in natural sciences at SBCC, UCSB, and BYU. He completed his schooling at the University of Utah, College of Pharmacy.

Gregg currently practices pharmacy in Logan, Utah. He is a voracious reader and has been writing stories since childhood. He has been published in *Skin Diver* magazine, *The Oceanographic Letter*, *Destiny* magazine, and the *New Era* magazine. His fiction includes *The Survivors*, *Do No Harm*, *Altered State*, *Blink of an Eye*, *Bloodborne*, *Deadly Undertakings*, *Twisted Fate*, and *The Healer*, six of which were Whitney Award finalists.

Find out more about Gregg's novels at www.greggluke.com.